"Just relax and float…"

Trey closed his eyes, allowing his body to become one with the water. Regaining this small bit of movement was a defining moment for him—he felt a sense of freedom he'd thought was long gone.

"You're doing fantastic," Gia murmured.

Trey's heart turned over in response. There was no fighting it any longer. He wanted something more than friendship. He was crushing on her like before—what he felt now defied words. However, reality sank in. What could he offer Gia? Yet the way she looked at him motivated him to take a chance.

At the end of the session, Gia assisted him back into his wheelchair.

He decided to take the leap. "Will you have dinner with me? As in a date."

"I'd love it." Gia handed him a towel. "But I can't unless you fire me, or I quit. It's not ethical for me to date my patients."

"Then…you're fired," Trey said.

Dear Reader,

This is the second book in the Polk Island series. Trey was introduced in *A Family for the Firefighter* and had just been deployed to Afghanistan. In this story, Trey comes home a wounded veteran and with survivor's guilt and PTSD. He reconnects with Gia Harris, whom he refers to as "the one who got away." Her efforts to help him are at times thwarted by Trey's refusal to ask for or seek help.

This story was inspired by my father, a proud marine. I loved seeing my father in his uniform, and I remember the fear of never seeing him again during his tour in Vietnam. He did return home and without physical scars, but it was the ones unseen that haunted him. I am thankful that he did not let the invisible wounds of war go unnoticed and was able to live a happy, fulfilling life.

I hope you will enjoy Trey and Gia's journey to everlasting love. Thank you for your never-ending support. I appreciate each and every one of you.

Best,

Jacquelin Thomas

HEARTWARMING

Her Hometown Hero

—

Jacquelin Thomas

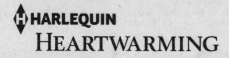

(H) HARLEQUIN®
HEARTWARMING™

Recycling programs for this product may not exist in your area.

ISBN-13: 978-1-335-42658-1

Her Hometown Hero

Copyright © 2022 by Jacquelin Thomas

This edition published by arrangement with Harlequin Books S.A.

For questions and comments about the quality of this book, please contact us at CustomerService@Harlequin.com.

Harlequin Enterprises ULC
22 Adelaide St. West, 41st Floor
Toronto, Ontario M5H 4E3, Canada
www.Harlequin.com

Printed in U.S.A.

Jacquelin Thomas is an award-winning, bestselling author with more than fifty-five books in print. When not writing, she is busy catching up on her reading, attending sporting events and spoiling her grandchildren. Jacquelin and her family live in North Carolina.

Books by Jacquelin Thomas

Harlequin Heartwarming

A Family for the Firefighter

Harlequin Kimani Romance

Five Star Attraction
Five Star Temptation
Legal Attraction
Five Star Romance
Five Star Seduction
Styles of Seduction
Wrangling Wes
Five Star Desire
Forever My Baby
Only for You
Return to Me
Another Chance with You

Visit the Author Profile page
at Harlequin.com for more titles.

Dedicated to my father and all our veterans, service members and families.

I thank you for your service and your sacrifice to keep America safe.

"The soldier above all others prays for peace, for it is the soldier who must suffer and bear the deepest wounds and scars of war."

—Douglas MacArthur

CHAPTER ONE

TREY ROTHCHILD STARED out the window at the sea of people lined along the sidewalk waving flags and holding up signs and posters. Friends and neighbors standing around chatting, some sitting in lawn chairs, waved as the vehicle passed them. He dreaded the moment when he would have to exit the SUV.

When people look at me, they're only going to see half a man in this wheelchair. A burden to my family and a failure to my team. Trey's heart was filled with the shadows of guilt, incredible loss and shame, and he wasn't at all sure he would ever be able to leave that darkness behind.

"Looks like everyone on the island came out for you," his brother, Leon, said, "and they don't seem to mind standing out there in the sun on a hot June day."

"Yeah," Trey muttered. For the first time in his twenty-nine years, he hated being the center of attention. *The life I wanted is over, so it would've been better if I'd just died along with my team.*

Almost as if Leon knew what he was thinking, he said, "I'm so glad to have you back home safe. I was afraid I'd lose you, too."

"I made it," Trey said, but he wasn't grateful or thrilled about being a so-called miracle, as the doctors had exclaimed. They hadn't expected him to survive his injuries, but he'd surprised them all—including himself. He didn't feel worthy of being alive when his team members hadn't survived. Although he'd been told over and over he'd done nothing wrong, Trey felt differently. He failed his team and their deaths weighed heavily on him.

"Aunt Eleanor never gave up hope," Leon was saying. "From the moment we got to Walter Reed Hospital, she wouldn't leave your bedside. She just sat there praying for you."

Trey continued to stare out the window, blocking out the sound of his brother's voice.

Leon parked the SUV, then looked over at Trey, smiling. "We're here. Welcome home, little bro."

A wave of apprehension swept through Trey as he scanned the crowd outside a second time. The faces and the wording on the signs suddenly began to blur. He felt dizzy as beads of perspiration broke out above his lips.

"I—I need a minute," Trey stammered.

Leon looked instantly concerned. "Are you okay? You in pain?"

"No…" It wasn't exactly true, but Trey wasn't one to complain. "I just feel overwhelmed and need a moment. I didn't expect to see *everybody* on the island."

"You're still Mr. Popular around here," Leon said.

Not after they see me in this wheelchair. I can no longer take care of myself or anybody else. I'm no hero.

GIA HARRIS STOOD alongside other residents of the Polk Island community to welcome Trey home. All around her, people held up signs and colorful banners to celebrate his return. She hadn't seen Trey since she left for college, except on those few occasions when she came home on a school break.

Leon's vehicle slowed to a complete stop just yards away from where she stood. Gia watched him retrieve the wheelchair from the back, then bring it around to the passenger-side door. Her heart pulsed in a sharp rhythm and minuscule pains shot through her ribs as she witnessed Leon's efforts to place his brother in the chair. She noted that Trey's legs had been amputated just below the knees.

She hadn't seen him in years. A memory of him when they were in school pranced across her mind. Images of Trey in a football uniform, dancing at the homecoming celebration, and of their first and only kiss.

Trey glanced up and met her gaze. He seemed surprised but happy to see her. "Gia…"

She stuck her hand in his, their fingers intertwined, sending tiny tremors up her arm and down her spine, all the way to her toes. She reluctantly eased her hand away. "I'm very happy to see you, Trey. Thank you for your service."

He almost seemed to wince at her words. After a moment, he asked, "Are you home for good?"

Gia smiled. "I am."

Before Trey could say another word, Leon interjected, "Hey, Gia…it's good to see you. I'd better get him inside. Maybe we can catch up later."

"Of course."

A young woman standing near Gia uttered, "He's still fine, but I can't deal with a man in a wheelchair like that. He can't do nothing for me."

"That man is a *hero*," an older lady responded before Gia could say anything. "The poor dear lost his legs protecting this country, but it doesn't make him less than a man. *Just you remember that.*" Sneering at the insolent young woman, the lady stated, "He's much too good for the likes of you anyway."

The girl looked appalled, then strutted off with her friends.

Gia bit back a smile. She couldn't agree more. In her eyes, despite what some may think, Trey was still very much a man. He was handsome and had a whole lot of living left to do.

She'd recognized that vacant expression on Trey's face. Her father had had that same look when he'd returned home from the Gulf War. His right arm had been maimed, rendering it useless for the rest of his life. Although he'd hated being away from his family, he had always talked about feeling honored to serve in the military. When he couldn't do it anymore, Eugene Harris had sunk into a depression while also suffering from PTSD. Alcohol became his coping mechanism. Her father never fully recovered from his injuries physically and emotionally, but he had eventually learned a better way to cope.

He was a hero, and to honor him, Gia had become a physical therapist to help others regain mobility and a sense of freedom. Her motto had always been to let go and enjoy the ride, despite what life threw at you.

SOFT BUT LIVELY music served as a backdrop to the laughter and the various conversations going

on around Trey. Lost napkins fluttered from tables and booths as customers sat around talking and enjoying their meals. The sizzle of food
cooking, silverware clinking, dishes breaking,
servers taking orders—all familiar sounds that
evoked memories of his youth. Trey had spent a
lot of time in the café growing up. His mother
had worked there until his parents' death. He
would come after school and do his homework
in the last booth near the kitchen so his aunt Eleanor could keep an eye on him.

Eleanor and her first husband, Walter, had
opened the doors of the Polk Island Bakery almost thirty years ago. Five years later, they'd
purchased the building next door and renovated it to include the café. In recent years, the
kitchen had been remodeled after a fire, with
all-new appliances. His aunt and her current
husband, Rusty, had decided to paint the café in
honeyed hues, which Trey thought was a good
choice. The color seemed to add a sweetness
and warmth within. The tables were a rich, dark
brown—the color of coffee. On the other side,
the bakery was painted a soft green color, and
behind the counter were rows of muffins, cakes
and other delicious treats.

Whenever Trey talked about the Polk Island
Café & Bakery, he told folk it was the best
doctor and medicine combined. The coffee,

the music and smiling employees, a chance to enjoy company—he considered it a fragment of heaven. Trey was appreciative of the warm welcome home, but he would've preferred to have just gone straight to the house without all the fanfare. The flight from Washington, DC, to Charleston, then the thirty-minute drive to the island, had taken a toll on him, and the throbbing ache in his knees was not easy to ignore. He'd already taken his pain medication, but it hadn't kicked in yet. He struggled to keep his expression unreadable, but the exhaustion and the pain were becoming increasingly unbearable.

Trey fought against his personal agony to make small talk with old friends and neighbors who stopped by the table to personally welcome him home. Every time he heard the words *Thank you for your service*, he felt nauseous.

"Son, you look tired," Aunt Eleanor observed aloud. "And you hurting. I can tell."

"I am," he responded. "I don't want to be rude. It was nice of these folks to come out to see me, but I just want to go home."

"'Scuse me, everyone," Eleanor shouted. "We wanna thank y'all for the warm welcome back to Polk Island but Trey needs his rest. We gwine get him home now."

"Thanks, Auntie," Trey said in a low voice.

"Don't you worry 'bout a thing, suga. We gwine take you to the house and put you to bed. Did you take your medicine?"

He nodded. "I think I waited too long to take it, but it should kick in soon."

A few minutes later, Trey was back in the SUV with Leon, driving to Eleanor's former house, their childhood home after their parents died. When Eleanor married Rusty, she'd moved into his house and deeded her place to Trey, since Leon had his own home with wife, Misty.

Eleanor sat in the back seat. She insisted on seeing that Trey was settled and comfortable. She leaned forward to pat him gently on the shoulder. "I'm sho' glad to have you back home so we can take care of you."

That's just it. I don't want anyone feeling like they have to be my caregiver. His aunt and Rusty had only been married for a few years. Trey didn't want them focusing on him—they were in their prime and deserved to just enjoy their time together. The same went for Leon and Misty, who were raising two children.

"We changed some stuff and renovated the place," Eleanor said as they turned on Forest Avenue, where the house was located.

Leon pulled into the driveway and parked.

Trey gazed at his childhood home in amazement. There was now a wheelchair ramp made of wood leading up to the porch, painted and styled to match seamlessly with the exterior design of the Victorian house.

Inside, his cousin Renee was waiting with balloons, some of which floated all over the living room. "Welcome home," she exclaimed before rushing over to give him a hug.

"I'm happy to see you, too, roomie," Trey said. Renee had left New York a couple years ago and opened a high-end boutique on the island. It was his idea that she live in the house instead of leaving it empty. He glanced around at his surroundings. He'd always thought he would come back here to raise his family once he retired from the marines.

"When did y'all do all this?" Trey asked, thoroughly surprised to find that the interior of the house had been completely renovated to make it accessible for his comfort. "Auntie, I thought you meant y'all had it painted. I figured you moved some things around, but not all this."

"We got started on the renovations as soon as we heard you were coming home," Leon replied. "We had a lot of help from the community. Boyd Davis…you remember him from the football team? He's an architect. He offered to make the house more functional for you. The sunroom is more of a living room now. We made the first-floor bedroom bigger and added a full bath and roll-in closet for you."

"Suga, we installed an intercom by your bed in the event you need Renee for anything," Eleanor said.

He gave a defiant tilt of his chin as his body tensed. "I don't need anyone to babysit me, Auntie. I can take care of myself. I didn't come home to disrupt anybody's life."

"Trey, I'm here if you want to watch a movie together, take a beating in Scrabble or whatever. That's why we installed the intercom," Renee interjected. "It was my idea."

He chuckled. "Beating me at Scrabble…that's not the way I remember it."

"Y'all always been competitive," Eleanor said, shaking her head at them.

Trey cleared his throat, then uttered, "I want to thank y'all for everything. I appreciate everything y'all done for me." He found himself getting choked up as he considered the many gestures of love behind all the renovations. The Rothchild family was close-knit, and Trey knew the sacrifices they'd made on his behalf. He was grateful but decided they'd done enough for him. Others like him had found a way to live independently, and so would he.

For now, however, he was happy to be reunited with his family. Trey had missed his aunt and brother more than anyone could imagine. In truth, he'd missed everyone on the island. He was truly thrilled to be home.

"We just wanted to make you as comfortable as possible," Leon said. "I put your music collection and your books in your room. Your friend Greg shipped them to me."

Trey smiled. "Sounds like you thought of everything."

"We tried," Leon replied. "You ready to see your room?"

Trey gave a slight nod.

On the main floor, the renovated bedroom was now fitted with a barn door wide enough to maneuver his wheelchair through. One wall featured shelving from floor to ceiling. "We put your music collection at the top. We figured you wouldn't be playing the records…"

"No, I just want to keep them," Trey said. "I like that all my books are on the shelves low enough for me to reach—I won't have to constantly yell for Renee to come downstairs just to get me something to read."

"That was my idea, too." Renee chuckled. *"I know you."*

He was happy with having his cousin as a roommate. When she moved in, Trey liked the idea of family living in the house while he was away. He didn't want to leave it sitting empty or to rent it out to strangers.

"Your bed has an adjustable frame, which should help you get comfortable," Leon stated. "I know you're more a fan of the minimalist style, so we tried to open up as much space in here as possible. Misty and Renee did all of the decorating."

"I know *you* didn't do it. Everything's not one color," Trey said with a short laugh. Behind the gray wooden shelves, the wall was painted a dark navy blue. The other walls in the room were more of a light blue. There were bright yellow accent pieces placed around the room to match the throw pillows on the navy blue sofa positioned in a corner near the door.

Leon grinned. "They redecorated the whole house. There's lots of color everywhere."

Trey rolled his wheelchair over to the closet, noting the lower rods and accessible shelving.

"We can put up a door there if you'd like," Eleanor said. "Renee didn't feel that it needed one."

He glanced back at them, saying, "It's fine, y'all. I like it just the way it is. I'm really glad there's no carpet on the floor."

"Leon told me you would prefer hardwood floors, so Rusty updated the ones that were in here before."

Trey planted a genuine smile on his face. "Auntie, y'all really did a great job."

"Check out your bathroom," Renee suggested.

The roll-in frameless shower could fit at least four people. Trey appreciated the built-in seat and storage for the shower items, and the metal rails. He especially liked the double shower-heads.

"Rusty came up with the design for it," she said.

They knew how much he valued his independence and had clearly kept that in mind during the remodeling. "I can see that a lot of thought and love went into this project," he responded. "I don't know if saying thank-you is enough."

"We're so glad you're home, son." Eleanor bent down to embrace him. "I'm happy to have my boy back here with me. I'm gwine stay here a few days to make sure you're eating and taking your medicine the way you should."

"You don't have to do that, Auntie. You should be home with Rusty," Trey said.

"He and I both will be here," Eleanor announced. "Just for two or three days."

"You might as well give up," Leon stated, so Trey let the subject lie, and ten minutes later, Leon had him situated in his bed.

"Are you hungry?" Eleanor asked. "I noticed you didn't eat anything at the café."

"No, ma'am. Just tired."

She nodded in understanding. "I'll leave you be. C'mon y'all. He needs to rest."

When Trey was alone in his room, he closed his eyes, hoping to escape the rest of the day by sleeping. He was tired from the traveling and his wounds were burning in agony. He massaged his left thigh, then did the same with the right. Trey hated taking pills of any kind, but he reached for the prescription bottle to take another one to fight the pain.

The attack had happened four and a half weeks ago. The reality that he was back at home began to sink in deeper. Trey knew it in his head, but it was taking his body longer to process that he was no longer in danger. He was safe. He could sleep without worry of being attacked by insurgents. Trey relaxed his body and mind.

An image of Gia Harris danced across it. She was the last person he'd expected to run into—the last he'd heard was that she lived in North Carolina. He was glad to see her, but he wished Gia hadn't had to see him like this—in a wheelchair. He wondered why he hadn't seen her father. He knew without a doubt that at some point, Master Gunnery Sergeant Eugene Harris would pay him a visit soon.

The years had been kind to Gia—she hadn't changed much from the way she looked back in high school. She'd been in Leon's class—two years older than Trey. She was still absolutely beautiful, with her short hair in honey-tinted curls and her dark hazel eyes.

The one kiss they'd shared in high school was still imprinted on his heart. Trey forced the thoughts of Gia out of his mind. There was no point in venturing down a road he could never travel.

CHAPTER TWO

SAND STUCK TO Gia's flip-flops as she strolled down the grassy knoll toward the ocean, the tiny granules massaging her ankles. South Beach was littered with giant umbrellas, colorful towels and beach chairs. There was a group of teens playing volleyball while couples, groups of friends and families enjoyed sunbathing or splashing around in the frothy water.

When Gia left Polk Island after graduating high school, she never thought to return except to visit her parents. Now that she was home, she realized just how much she'd missed it. She'd moved back from Charlotte a month ago, after her last patient's wife had launched a smear campaign to ruin her professional reputation.

I never should've taken the job with Chris Latham. I knew what people said about him. I never should've trusted him.

Gia dropped down onto a large boulder; her chest palpitated as she fought off a display of emotions. "Stupid. Stupid. Stupid," she whispered.

Chris, a professional athlete with the NFL,

had spent most of his time in physical therapy flirting and making sexual advances toward her. However, when his wife caught him in the act Chris had accused Gia of being the seducer. Unfortunately, his wife, Cindy, believed him.

Chris had no idea that Gia had recorded his many attempts to seduce her. The only reason she hadn't come forward with the recordings was because of his children. She didn't want them to get caught up in the fallout. Cindy had no problem trying to humiliate her, but Gia had decided she would take the high road regardless of the personal cost.

Gia had lost her elite clientele and had been left with no other choice than to leave Charlotte, North Carolina, regroup and start over. Despite her initial mixed feelings about moving back home, she now considered it a blessing. At thirty-one, Gia thought she'd be well on her way to owning her own physical therapy clinic, a longtime dream of hers. After coming home, she'd decided that Polk Island was the perfect place for the facility. Her mother had also approached her with the idea of turning the house left for Gia by her grandmother into a bed-and-breakfast. She'd jumped at the opportunity of partnering with her mother and never once regretted it. They had always been close and it delighted Gia to work with Patricia. They were in the midst of renovations on the house. Gia felt optimistic about the venture, which would also help her with opening her own PT facility—something extremely important to her.

She spotted Leon Rothchild and his wife strolling along the water's edge. Gia sat back and watched as they ran into the ocean and swam around. She was happy that Leon had found love with Misty. They seemed perfect for one another.

There were times when she wondered if she'd missed her chance to marry and have a family. Gia had pretty much given up on the idea. Not because of a bad breakup, but because she was focused on making her dreams a reality.

Cindy Latham's smear campaign had cost her clients and threatened to derail her goals, but Gia was determined not to let that happen. She was infuriated with Chris for allowing things to progress this far. He'd reached out to her a few times via phone and email, but she refused to answer his calls or respond to his written pleas to see her.

Angry tears rolled down her cheeks. Gia prayed she never had to lay eyes on Chris or Cindy Latham again. She couldn't understand how people like them—deemed as positive role models to the community—could behave so badly.

She was so caught up in her thoughts, she never saw Leon and his wife get out of the water.

"Gia…"

She glanced up to see Leon and his wife walking toward her.

Gia swiped her cheeks, hoping the telltale trail of tears didn't show. "Hey, again…"

"I don't think you've had a chance to meet my wife," Leon said.

"I haven't, but I heard that you're the new owner of the bakery and café. I've also heard all about your delicious baked goods." Gia grinned at Misty. "I plan on coming by the bakery at some point this week to sample them for myself. I've been avoiding sweets for the last couple of months. But to be honest with you, I'm so ready for a cheat weekend."

"It's a pleasure to meet you and I hope you will," Misty responded with a sincere smile. "You'll have to tell me what my husband was like when he was a kid. I want to hear all about his exploits."

"We may have to make a lunch date for that intel," Gia chuckled. "I can tell you about the summer we worked as lifeguards."

Leon raised his hands in mock resignation. "Be kind."

"I promise to only tell Misty the truth." Gia paused a moment, then asked, "How's the water?"

"Nice," he replied. "You should go in."

"I wish I could," Gia said. "I'm supposed to

meet my friend at my mom's house, but I couldn't resist coming to the beach for a little while. I love the sound of the ocean and that salty smell that lingers in the air when the waves come roaring through."

Misty nodded in agreement. "It helps me clear the clutter from my mind."

"Thanks for being there to welcome Trey home," Leon said.

"It was my pleasure. I was sorry to hear what happened to him, but I'm so thankful that he's alive." Gia could hardly contain her joy when she heard that Trey was coming home. She needed to see him for herself that he was alive and well… He was alive, but haunted. After some time at home surrounded by family, Gia believed Trey would be more himself.

"We feel the same way," Misty said.

Gia stood up, then brushed sand off herself. "I'd better get going, but I hope you two enjoy more of this wonderful weather."

"I'll probably take another dip before we head home," Leon remarked. "Tell your mom I said hello."

"I will." To Misty, Gia said, "I'll stop by soon so we can sit down and talk about the good ol' days with Leon."

"I'm looking forward to that conversation,"

Gia heard Misty say as she turned and headed to the parking lot.

When Gia drove up, her mother was outside watering the rosebushes in the front yard. "Where have you been?" Patricia asked. "Shelley's been here about fifteen minutes waiting on you."

The hiss of the running sprinkler system caught her attention. She watched as the water splashed on pavers.

"I went to the beach to clear my head," Gia said. "Where is she?"

"She's in the family room."

Gia rushed inside the house to greet her best friend. "I'm so sorry, Shelley," she said. "I was at South Beach and time slipped away from me. It'll only take me ten minutes to shower and slip on a sundress."

"You're good. I made a few phone calls while I was waiting. Principal Clinton wanted to see if I wanted to work. That woman knows I don't do summer school. I'm thankful she didn't make it mandatory." Shelley pushed a strand of her thick, glowing auburn hair behind her ears, revealing more of her makeup-free, tanned complexion.

Shelley was a high school history teacher who also loved to travel, which was why she didn't relish teaching summer classes.

Heading to the staircase, Gia said, "I can't wait to see this movie. I love Idris Elba." They'd made plans to catch a matinee and then have lunch afterward.

Fifteen minutes later, Gia returned downstairs saying, "I meant to tell you that I saw Trey for a quick minute yesterday."

"How did he look? I was in Charleston yesterday, so I missed his homecoming." Shelley rose up from the navy-and-gold striped chair, placing her purse on her shoulder.

"Haunted. He's still handsome, though. He just needs some time to adjust to being home."

"I'm glad he survived that horrific bombing."

"Me, too," Gia replied. "I don't think I've ever prayed so hard."

"His life has changed."

"It has," Gia agreed. "But Trey can adapt. It may take him a while, but I know him. He'll get over this hurdle."

They walked outside and headed to Shelley's car. "Your mom took me on a tour of your grandmother's house. The renovations are coming along beautifully."

"We still need to do the kitchen and finish the attic. It needs serious updating and all-new appliances. I need to find a job so I don't run through my savings to repay the loan." Gia opened the door and sat inside the vehicle, then closed the door behind her. "That's the money I set aside for my clinic."

"Everything's gonna work out fine," Shelley assured her. "You're gonna make so much money when y'all open the B and B. Just watch. It will pay for itself."

Gia grinned. "You're forever the optimist."

"You're the former cheerleader." Shelley turned the ignition and put the car into Drive. "In fact, you were captain, so don't stop cheering now. You got this, Gia. That witch will soon move on to the next woman she catches her husband with—remember last year when they were caught on camera arguing after she followed him to some hotel? It was all over *TMZ*."

"I know. I felt so bad for their children. It's a shame Chris and Cindy aren't thinking about them. I can only imagine their embarrassment. They're really sweet kids—they don't deserve this kind of drama in their lives."

"I'd be ready to ruin that man with all the stuff you got on him," Shelley uttered, "but I know you don't want to hurt the children."

"I really hope it doesn't come to that. Chris is still trying to get me to talk to him. I'm taking screenshots of everything. However, if Cindy tries to come for me again—I'm not holding back. Not this time."

TREY WOKE UP in a cold sweat. He gasped, panting in sheer terror. His stomach clenched tight as a wave of panic swept through him. His gaze bounced around the room, taking in his surroundings as he clamored to remember where he was.

Renee burst into the room. "Hey…you okay?"

"Did I wake you up?" Trey asked. "I hope I didn't wake Aunt Eleanor."

"You didn't," she responded. "I was in the kitchen getting a bottle of water when I heard you call out for help. I figured you might be having a nightmare."

Renee sat down at the foot of his bed. "Do you have them often?"

Trey felt a shudder of embarrassment, but he and Renee shared a special bond. She had always been his confidante, so he told her the truth. "I have them almost every night. My brain won't let go of what happened that day. I relive that feeling of being helpless out there on the ground with my entire team around me…dead."

Under Operation Freedom's Sentinel, Trey's battalion had been in Afghanistan's Helmand Province, tasked with raids and patrols targeting Taliban territories in an effort to repel their attacks on the Afghan government.

He gazed at Renee. "Don't say anything to Aunt Eleanor. She gets upset easily."

"I won't," she said. "Trey, I hope you know it wasn't your fault."

"I was responsible for them." His voice was low, and tormented. "I lost three good marines that day." His anguish was like a steel weight on his chest.

"It was a bomb," she interjected. "There was no way you could've known that an abandoned car on the side of the road contained explosives."

"We've seen cars like that alongside some of the roads before. I just feel like I should've sensed something wasn't quite right."

Renee took his hand in her own. "You were injured in that blast, as well. Cousin, there was only so much you could do. You almost died."

Trey could hear the earth-shattering explosion in his mind even now. It was like an earthquake. He involuntarily squeezed Renee's hand as he relived that life-altering moment. "I can still smell the burning fuel coming from what was left of our vehicle. The heat from the flames set off our ammunition." He shuddered inwardly. "It was popping off all around us."

His memory refused to let him escape the painful images. Fanned out around him were the dead, and some human body parts, too. He looked down and didn't see his legs. He felt them, but he couldn't see them.

But it was the sight of Laura Hudson's body

that knocked the wind out of Trey. Earlier that day, she had confided in Trey that she was scared—her intuition screamed that something bad was about to happen. He'd never seen Hudson afraid of anything.

"Sarge, I really don't want to die," she'd whispered. "You know after this tour, I'm retiring. I have two small kids and I don't want to miss a minute more of watching them grow up."

He'd reassured her that everything was going to be fine. "Any ideas on what you're going to do when you get out?" Trey asked in an attempt to distract her. He couldn't let her fears overtake her. He needed Hudson to keep it together.

"Maybe something on the government level. I don't care as long as it's safe and I'm home in time to cook dinner and help my babies with their homework."

As he lay there on the ground, Hudson's last words to Trey echoed in every corner of his mind.

Trey tightened his grip on the quilt as he continued to recount the events of that day. He wasn't one to wear his vulnerability on his sleeve, but he could always be himself with Renee. "Hudson was sitting beside me when the exploding car shattered the windows and tore a hole into our vehicle. Soon after, I heard a second explosion. There was a rocket. It decimated what was left."

He picked up his water bottle and took a sip. "Somewhere in the distance, I could hear the medevac helicopters. I remember thinking it was too late. By the time they landed, I'd be dead, too. Memories of my parents, of Aunt Eleanor and Leon flashed in my head just before everything went black." Trey paused a moment. "When I opened my eyes, two days had passed, and I was in the hospital in Germany."

"I'm so sorry, Trey." Renee's words cut into his thoughts. "You had to be so scared out there alone."

His gaze met hers. "My reaction at the time wasn't fear… I was annoyed. I guess I had a belief—no, it was more of an arrogance— that nothing was going to happen to us. And even if it did, we were prepared."

"I would've been frightened out of my mind."

"Renee, more than anything, I couldn't believe they got us." Trey shook his head in confusion. "It was supposed to be a simple patrol."

She blinked back unshed tears. "I wish I knew what to say—something that would make you feel better. I'm just so glad you're alive." A tear rolled down her cheek. "I know you're sad and hurting, but Trey…I need you to survive."

His head bowed and his body slumped in despair, Trey sighed heavily, filled with anguish. The hardest part for him was losing his team. And the feeling of helplessness in that moment.

"I need you to survive," Renee repeated. "Are you listening to me?"

His eyes filling with water, Trey gave a slight nod.

Wiping her face, Renee said, "I came down to make some chamomile tea. It helps me when I'm having a hard time sleeping. Have a cup with me?"

"Sure."

She stood up and crossed the hardwood floor in a brisk stride.

Trey's heart rate resumed its normal pace and the intense desolation he was feeling slowly dissipated. He knew it wouldn't go away completely; it would always be waiting in the shadows—this terrible grief and bitter, cold despair.

He reached into the drawer of his nightstand and pulled out a small bottle of rum. Trey quickly downed the contents.

"Here you go," Renee said when she returned ten minutes later. "I hope it'll help you rest better."

Trey pasted on a smile, pretending an ease he didn't truly feel. "Thank you."

He took a sip of the warm liquid. "This is good. Did you add honey?"

She nodded. "Granulated honey."

They talked about childhood memories as they finished off their tea.

Renee stood up, took the cup from Trey and said, "I don't know about you, but I'm getting sleepy. You need anything before I go to bed? I can sleep in here on the sofa. Just so you're not alone."

"I think I'm good," he answered. He was beginning to feel the effects of the alcohol.

"Good night, then."

When Renee left his room, he settled down, squeezed his eyes tightly closed and sought the sweet oblivion of sleep.

Atlanta, Georgia

GIA SAT IN a booth along with two athletic trainers volunteering their time at the annual Circle of Hope for Warriors Race. She raised her red, white and blue pom-poms, shaking them as the runners passed by.

She'd been volunteering for the past three years after learning about Circle of Hope for Warriors from her father, who'd been a dedicated supporter of the organization until his death. It was a way for Gia to honor and give back to veterans, military members and those who had fallen in sacrifice to this country.

"Gia, it's really nice of you to come all this way to help out," Linda, the woman beside her, said.

"I don't mind traveling," she responded. "Especially for events like this."

"Do you have family in the military?"

"I do," Gia said. "My late father was a marine and so is my brother, Braxton." She and Braxton had different mothers, but he'd spent most summers with Gia whenever their father was home on leave. "What about you?"

"My dad is in the air force." Pointing to the girl on the other side of her, Linda added, "Janice was in the navy."

Leaning forward, Gia thanked her for her service. "Just saying thank-you never seems to be enough."

"You're right, but you have no idea how much it's appreciated," Janice said.

Gia's mind centered on Trey. She couldn't help but wonder how he was doing.

They'd been friends in high school. They both loved the ocean and had spent a lot of time at the beach and watching movies about historical figures like Henry VIII and other royals. They'd also shared a love for thrillers and mysteries.

She'd never forget the day she heard about the

incident. Gia had gone to the beach for a run when her mother called and told her that Trey had been wounded. At the time, they weren't sure if he was going to make it. Gia had collapsed in sobs right there.

Once she'd composed herself, she had returned home, abandoning all thoughts of exercise. She'd spent the next day or so praying for Trey and recalling memories that she hoped would not be the last ones they shared.

Gia had phoned Leon earlier to check on Trey and to inquire when would be a good time to visit him. He'd promised to get back to her after talking to his brother.

She was elated that Trey was home on Polk Island. He'd survived a tragic bombing that had taken the lives of others. He'd suffered the loss of his limbs, and it was still too early to know the extent of his invisible wounds.

Gia wanted to support Trey through his recovery and rehabilitation. She cared for him—always had. *Probably more than I should.*

CHAPTER THREE

TREY LOVED HIS AUNT, but he was glad he'd been able to convince Rusty to take her home after two days. He knew she was only trying to help, but the "mother hen" behavior was beginning to get on Trey's nerves. She was constantly checking on him to see he'd taken his medicine or if he needed anything.

Since being discharged from the hospital, he didn't miss the round-the-clock nurse visits, lab work and doctors… He was finally free to rest without interruption now that he was home.

Trey maneuvered out of bed and into the wheelchair shortly after nine o'clock in the morning. He released a deep breath before wheeling himself into the bathroom to shower and prepare for the day ahead.

There wasn't much to look forward to, Trey thought as he brushed his teeth. He couldn't help but wonder why he'd bothered to get out of bed. He remembered a time when waking up each day was like a new adventure, but that was no more. The throbbing just below his knees was a bold reminder that it was time to take his medication. The origin of the pain was circulating in the part of his remaining limbs, although every now and then Trey experienced what his doctors called phantom limb sensations.

It took nearly all his remaining strength to navigate the wheelchair to the kitchen.

Grimacing, Trey prepared a bowl of cereal for breakfast. He finished that off, then reached for an apple from the fruit bowl on the counter. *Maybe I should've waited until today before sending Aunt Eleanor home.* He was already missing her cooking.

While he ate, Trey heard Renee moving about upstairs. Her off-key singing elicited a dry chuckle out of him.

He finished eating, stuck his bowl and spoon in the dishwasher and made his way to the living room. Trey's eyes traveled the room, landing on the bookshelf. He found a book he hadn't heard of, but the storyline looked interesting.

I might as well read. It's not like I have anything else to do.

He positioned his wheelchair near the huge picture window in the living room and opened the book.

When he glanced at the clock, an hour had passed without him noticing.

The sound of a car pulling into the driveway

caught his attention. He looked out the window and his lips spread into a grin.

Trey wheeled himself to the door, then unlocked it.

"I can't believe my eyes," he said. Intense pleasure washed over him at the sight of his cousin. "Jordin DuGrandpre Holbrooke. What are you doing here?"

She pulled her long dark hair to the side as she bent down to hug him. "I came to check on you, cousin. We're staying at the beach house for the week. My sister and her family are arriving later this evening. My brother will be coming up with Ryker on Friday with their families."

"Outstanding," he said. "I'm looking forward to seeing Austin." He couldn't remember the last time he'd seen Ryker. Jordin, Jaydin and Austin were siblings. Their father and Ryker's dad were brothers.

Renee descended the stairs. "I knew I'd heard voices. Hey, cousin."

Jordin gave her a hug. "I'm trying to remember the last time I saw you."

"It's been at least a couple of years... I think."

She nodded. "You're right. It was when we met up for dinner in New York."

"We had a great time that night."

Jordin laughed. "Yes, we did. Oh, I've been

hearing some great things about the boutique. They're talking about it all over Charleston."

Renee's mouth busted into a grin. "I'm glad to hear that."

"I'll definitely stop by later this afternoon to check it out," Jordin said.

"I hope you do. Right now, I have to run," Renee said. "I'm meeting a client who wants a custom gown."

The two women embraced again.

"How's she doing?" Jordin asked Trey after Renee walked out of the house. "The last time I saw her, she was engaged. I heard she called off the wedding."

"She seems fine, but then she's a Rothchild. You know how we do."

Jordin followed Trey to the living room.

Taking a seat on the sofa, Jordin said, "Which brings me to my next question… How are you?"

"I don't have a real answer for you. I'm just here going through the motions." He was tired of people asking because he just didn't have a response. He knew they were asking out of concern but wished they would just stop

"Well, you've been through quite an ordeal. I hope you know that we're all here for you, Trey. Why don't you consider talking to Bree? She's a psychologist. I'm sure she can refer you to someone."

"I know. I'm not one for sharing my feelings with complete strangers. I'm just focusing on taking it one minute at a time. That's about all I can handle right now."

"You have to do what's best for you," she said.

"Where's your husband and the children?"

"I left them at the house. Ethan wanted to get them settled. I'm supposed to be picking up some groceries. I told him I intended to stop by here to see you and check in with Leon and Aunt Eleanor."

"Do they know you're in town yet?"

Jordin grinned. "They're my next stop, so don't ruin my surprise."

"I won't. I'm happy you came by. I've missed you...the whole DuGrandpre clan."

"We have to get together. Maybe on Saturday? I'll host it at the beach house."

"I'm free," Trey said. "I'll be there."

He needed a nice distraction to take his mind off the memories he couldn't shake—just for a short while.

When Jordin walked out of the house, Trey's neighbor and childhood friend, Jay, was standing on the porch.

"I came to see if you needed anything from the store," he said.

"I could use a few things," Trey responded.

Jordin pulled out of the driveway and waved.

Trey waved back, then told Jay, "Can you pick up some flour, sugar, eggs and a bottle of rum, please?"

"Sounds like the ingredients for a rum cake."

"Yeah." He pulled out his wallet and handed Jay forty dollars. If it's not enough, let me know and I'll send it to you via Zelle or Cash App."

"We good," Jay said. "I'll be back shortly."

Trey thanked Jay with a tip when he returned and took the bag of groceries from him. "I appreciate you picking this up for me."

He took the food to the kitchen and put it away.

Then he carried the bottle of rum with him to his room, opened it and drank straight from the bottle.

He knew the danger of mixing alcohol with his medication, but he only drank enough to feel numb. He didn't want to feel the grief, the pain or the loneliness. The alcohol helped wrap him in a cocoon, where he didn't have to feel the anguish and the wretchedness anymore. Despair tore at his heart. He closed his eyes, mentally trying to block out the excruciating agony.

Trey took another swig of rum.

He glanced around the bedroom, his breath shallow and his senses dulled. Then he maneuvered himself over to the window and stared at the waves dancing back and forth in the ocean.

I would give anything to swim in that beautiful body of water one more time. He glanced down where his legs used to be. "I took so much for granted."

Tears slowly found their way down his cheeks, and Trey was conscious only of the low, tortured sob that came from him.

He wiped his face with the bottom of his T-shirt. "I'm so sorry. I'm sorry I couldn't save y'all. I'm sorry I didn't die…"

"Hi, Gia," Misty greeted on Tuesday morning. "What can I get for you?"

"My mother told me you have the best chocolate raspberry brownies, and she simply can't live without them. I was driving by and figured I'd stop and buy some for her."

Misty chuckled. "Perfect timing…they're fresh out of the oven."

"I'll take a half dozen," Gia said. "How's Trey doing?"

"Whenever we ask, Trey just says he's fine," she responded. "He doesn't seem to want to talk about how he's feeling. He's just fine."

"That sounds like him," Gia said. "I've never known him to complain or show much emotion. He's always internalized his feelings. Leon told me that when his parents died, Trey didn't cry. He was just quiet. About a week after the funeral, their uncle found him at the cemetery sobbing. He wanted to be so strong for everyone. As young as he was—he wanted to take care of Leon and Miss Eleanor."

"I can see that. He is very protective when it comes to his family." Misty lined a white box with wax paper, then placed the brownies inside. "He and Leon have that in common."

Gia agreed with that. "I'd like to visit with him whenever he's ready to have visitors."

"Have you spoken to him since he's been home?" Misty asked.

"Just for a few minutes, when they first arrived from the airport, but there was a lot going on."

"Seemed like the entire community showed up to welcome him."

"He's always been well thought of around here." Gia presented her debit card to Misty, then wrote down her phone number on a scrap of paper. "The next time you see Trey, please give him this. I'd love to talk to him." Gia was not only concerned for him—she also missed their friendship. She was willing to do whatever she could to help him adjust to his new normal.

"I sure will," Misty promised with a mischievous smile. "Now, don't forget about lunch. I still want to hear all about Leon's youth. Whenever I ask him—he won't say much about it."

"I don't have anything scheduled for tomorrow, if you have some time," Gia said. "However, I have to tell you Leon was very popular. All the girls were crazy about him and Trey, but they didn't really seem to notice. Well... Trey loved the attention, but Leon seemed to shy away from it."

"Was he socially awkward?"

Gia laughed. "Let's just leave it at shy."

"Can you do one o'clock for lunch tomorrow?" Misty inquired.

"See you then. I'll even bring my yearbooks."

Gia left the bakery smiling. She looked forward to getting to know Leon's wife and she hoped to hear from Trey at some point.

She knew he was too proud to ask for help. Trey had always been that way—very independent. It was a quality she liked in him, but she also recognized that the trauma he'd experienced would leave him marked for life in some way, like it had her father. Trey would need the tools and resources available to help him cope.

And Gia prayed he would readily accept the help offered.

"Maybe I should just stay home," Trey told Leon over the phone. "That beach house has steps. It'll be too much trouble to try and get my wheelchair up to the porch, not to mention back down them." He now regretted accepting Jordin's invite.

"Everybody is looking forward to seeing you. I'll get Ryker or Ethan to help me. Don't worry about it. We'll get you into the house. It's been a while since we've all been together. You can't miss this."

Trey didn't want to be a burden. It bothered him to need assistance just to get up a set of stairs. He didn't like asking or needing help from others. He was also worried that he'd frighten some of the children. He'd witnessed how some kids were afraid of amputees.

"C'mon Trey...please come."

"All right. I'll see you there. Renee and I are leaving in about an hour."

He found his cousin ready and waiting in the living room, dressed in a bright green sun-dress and silver sandals. Renee had her choco-late brown hair pulled back in a messy bun. She sat on the sofa, her legs crossed, going through her texts.

"I can't believe you're all set to leave," Trey said. "I'm usually having to wait on you."

"Boy, pleeze..."

He laughed. "What?"

"Trey, you used to stay in the mirror. You don't have much hair now, but you still make sure your waves are laid. I know you still sleep in a satin skull cap."

"Whatever…"

She stood up and grabbed her purse and keys. "C'mon, let's get out of here. I'm hungry."

Fifteen minutes later, they were on their way to the north side of the island where the luxury homes were located.

"I'm glad Etienne and Eleanor Louise decided to reopen their beach house," Renee said, referring to their aunt and a cousin who'd been named after Aunt Eleanor. "We used to have so much fun there when we were younger."

"Hopefully, we'll see more of our cousins. It's a shame they're right in Charleston and we only seem to get together for major life events."

"We get busy, I guess."

"I suppose we do," Trey responded.

Leon was outside waiting for them when Renee pulled into the circular driveway behind his SUV.

Trey was touched when he saw that a temporary ramp had been set up leading to the porch, relieving him of his initial concern about the stairs.

Opening the passenger-side door, Leon said, "See, you didn't have anything to worry about."

"I guess you're right, big brother."

When Trey was wheeled into the house, he

soon found himself the center of unwanted attention as some of the children surrounded him. His niece, Talei—Misty's daughter from her first marriage—was six. The others were his cousins' children. Kai and Amya had just turned eight, and Emery was also six years old.

"Trey, what happened to your legs?" Emery asked.

"Uncle Trey got hurt in the war," Talei told him. "He was in Afranastan."

He bit back a smile and didn't bother to correct her.

"Did it hurt?" Amya inquired, her expression one of concern.

"I can't lie to you— it hurt," he responded honestly. "Still does from time to time."

Hugging him, Talei whispered, "I'm so glad you're home and not in the war anymore." She kissed his cheek. "We have to give Uncle lots of love. He's a hero."

"Yeah…you're my hero," Amya said.

"Mine, too," her sister Kai said. "You're very brave."

His little cousins showed real concern for him, a gesture that touched Trey all the way to his soul. He felt unworthy of their open admiration. They didn't know he'd failed his team—that he'd led them into an ambush. It didn't matter that he was following orders from his superior. His instincts had been off, placing them all in danger. Trey's eyes watered but he blinked rapidly to keep the unshed tears from rolling down his cheeks.

Bree, Austin's wife, walked over, saying, "One thing I bet y'all didn't know about Trey is that he's a great storyteller. I'm sure if you ask him nicely—he'll tell you one."

"Please, Uncle," Talei pleaded.

He awarded Bree a grateful smile. He appreciated the tactful way she'd distracted the children from asking too many probing questions. Austin DuGrandpre was a lucky man to have such a beautiful and compassionate wife.

Turning his attention back to the kids, Trey began, "Once upon a time…there was a dog named Harry."

"Because he was hairy, I bet," said Kai.

"His name was *Harry*. H-A-R-R-Y."

"And he was hairy," she repeated. "H-A-I-R-Y."

"Hey, who's telling this story?" Trey asked. "Me or you?"

Kai folded her arms across her chest. "I'm just trying to help you out."

The girls burst into a round of giggles.

"Kai, why don't you continue the story for me?" Trey said. "I like the way this is going. We can all add to it."

"So… Harry liked hot dogs and—"

"French fries," Talei interjected. "Like me."

Emery held up his hand. "Harry liked candy, too. He loved gummy worms the most."

"Naw," Trey said. "Harry loved to eat real worms. He'd dig them up and gobble them down."

Frowning, Kai made a face, then uttered, "That's so gross. Ugh…"

Trey laughed.

"I think Harry liked to race cars. He'd sit on the corner and when a car was coming, he'd race it down the street," Emery said.

"Harry liked to play with the bunny rabbits," Talei contributed.

"But one day, Harry got lost," Amya said. "He was following this pink bunny and he ended up in a forest."

"While in the forest, Harry met…" Trey began.

"He met a dog named Bear!" Kai said.

Later when the kids were eating, Trey pulled Bree off to the side. "Thank you."

"We talked to them about what happened before you arrived. They were really concerned about you."

Her words surprised him. "They weren't scared?"

Bree shook her head. "Not at all. They have questions but we told them to just hold them until later. I didn't want to overwhelm you. I knew my son would have lots of questions about everything."

"Emery's gotten so big," Trey said. "I can hardly believe he's six now?"

"I know." Bree smiled.

Trey was grateful he was still able to connect with his younger cousins, especially since he might not ever have a family of his own. He'd hoped to be a father someday, but now he couldn't imagine burdening a wife with the task of caring for him and any children they might have—it wasn't fair. He shook the thought from his mind, then asked, "If the children ask, how much should I tell them?"

"Be honest, but don't dwell on the details," she said.

"Aunt Eleanor and Leon told me to reach out to you for some referrals for a therapist. I was given a few from the VA Hospital."

"Only do so when you're ready, Trey. Your wounds are still healing, and you've only been home for a week. You need time to adjust."

"Do you see many veterans?"

She nodded. "I have a few as patients."

"With injuries like mine?"

"More or less," Bree said.

They talked a few minutes more before she went to check on the children who had wandered outside, while the toddlers remained inside with their parents.

Trey took in his surroundings. Everyone was talking and laughing without a care in the world. He envied them. Every strange sound gave him a start, although he tried to pretend otherwise. Trey hated being jumpy like this. He didn't want anyone to worry about him.

"I am so glad you and your family decided to come back to the island," Leon said to Jordin as he slid over on the long bench to make room for Misty at the table. Misty sat down, placing their sixteen-month-old son, Leo, on her lap.

Jordin nodded. "We used to have some really good times here."

"Yes, we did," he agreed. "So many wonderful memories growing up."

Jordin took a sip of her lemonade. "We also got into a lot of trouble, too. Aunt Eleanor was always fussing and threatening to punish us."

Misty broke into a grin. "*Really?* This is the stuff I enjoy hearing about, but Leon doesn't like to share things like this with me."

"Okay, sweetheart. I don't talk about my childhood because I was awkward back then," Leon said with a glint of amusement. "But whenever the DuGrandpre clan was on the island—we stayed in trouble. We were always sneaking off to the beach without supervision."

Jordin laughed. "We kept my parents worried that something bad might happen to us. I didn't understand back then but now that I'm a mother—I get it. Poor Aunt Eleanor…she used to say we would be the death or her. Especially Trey."

"Yeah. He was always the one running out into the ocean without a care in the world," Leon interjected.

Trey shrugged. "Hey, I knew we were going to get in trouble, so I wanted to make sure it was worth the punishment." Although he'd had second thoughts before coming here, Trey was now glad he'd had a change of heart. Being surrounded by his family like this kept him from focusing on the haunting and troubling thoughts that often took over. The guilt that resided within him would never go away, but sharing old memories, he was enjoying himself for the first time since that fateful day.

Misty chuckled. "I can actually see the logic in that."

"She says that now," Leon said. "We'll see how she feels when Talei or Leo offers that as an explanation."

Rusty and Aunt Eleanor arrived in time to join the others on the patio where his cousins had lunch waiting.

"Who made this shrimp salad?" Misty inquired. "It's delicious."

"I did," Austin said. "It's kind of my specialty."

Bree agreed. "It's the only thing I let him prepare when it comes to cooking."

Aunt Eleanor sampled some. "Suga, you need to brand and put this on the market."

Trey and the others agreed.

Austin smiled. "Thank you. It's one of my mom's recipes."

Leon downed the last of his ice water. "How is your sister? I heard she opened a restaurant in New Orleans, right?"

"Yes, Aubrie opened Manoir Rouge last year, but she also has a restaurant in Charleston. You've heard of Manoir Bleu."

"Yeah, I've heard of it, but haven't been there," Leon said. "Now that I know she's the owner, Misty and I are going to have to check it out."

"Manoir Bleu has gotten great reviews." Misty leaned against him. "You can take me there for our next date night."

Leon planted a kiss on her cheek. "It's a date, sweetheart."

"It really does my heart good to see the two of you together," Aunt Eleanor stated. "I can't wait for Trey and Renee to find their soul mates."

"I don't think you should hold your breath,

Auntie," Trey responded. "I'm pretty sure there aren't a lot of women around who will find a man with no legs sexy." He'd already resigned himself to the fact that he was going to spend his life as a single man. Trey determined to find a way to be okay with that because he didn't feel like a whole man. Not anymore.

"You'd be surprised," Jordin said. "Good women want good men—they want someone like you."

All the women around the table agreed.

"Don't give up on love just yet," Jordin told him. "One day Ethan and I will have to tell you about the journey to our happily-ever-after. He didn't make it easy."

Ethan met her gaze. "My wife is right. I allowed my baggage at the time to come between us, but she refused to give up on me. I've learned that the DuGrandpre women are beyond stubborn."

"Yes, we are," Jordin said.

Trey laughed. He loved hearing about how his cousins had found their mates.

Laughter and more stories rang out around the room.

As he listened to his cousins talk about falling in love, Trey's mind traveled briefly to Gia. He wondered what she was doing. Both Leon and Misty had mentioned that she wanted to visit with him, but Trey didn't want her to see him just yet. He wasn't ready for visitors—maybe they could meet when the physical pain wasn't so bad.

Misty went back into the house with Leo, who'd fallen asleep in her lap.

"I'm glad Aunt Eleanor and Rusty finally got together after all these years," Jordin's twin sister, Jadin, said.

Rusty placed a kiss on his wife's forehead. "Ain't nobody happier than me. I've loved this woman since I was a teenager. I wouldn't give up because I knew in my heart that she was mine. Even when she married Walter Pittman. I was heartbroken, but she was the other half of me, and I *knew* it."

"Uncle Walt was a good man, and when he died—we didn't know if Aunt Eleanor would ever recover. But we knew you loved her," Trey said. "Everybody but Aunt Eleanor. We didn't know if she'd ever give you a chance."

"If Rusty had spoken up back then when we were in school, I might not have given Walter the time of day," Eleanor interjected. "Walter was a good husband. I can't take that from him, but so is Rusty. I'm blessed to have had two great men in my lifetime."

Misty returned and sat down beside her husband. She picked up her glass of water and took a sip. "I love this. Sitting here and talking about the way we all got together. It reminds me of just how blessed we are as couples."

"I guess Trey and I will just celebrate our singleness," Renee said with a laugh.

He agreed. "Single and proud of it."

After lunch, the children gathered in a newly renovated media room to watch a movie, while most of the adults moved outside to the deck facing the ocean.

Trey heard children shrieking from the media room, even amid the crash of waves and the fizz of foam. People on Jet Skis thundered past the house. He waved to a few people he recognized. On the beach, there was an elderly couple strolling and holding hands.

"Some things never change," Leon said. "Mr. and Mrs. McCoy walk the beach every Saturday around this time. Remember we used to see them when we were younger."

"They're definitely getting in their exercise," Trey said. "I'd give anything to be out there taking a walk, my shoes in my hands while the shells and rocks cut into my skin."

"I believe you'll be able to walk the strip again."

Trey glanced at his brother. "You don't have to try to make me feel better." Pointing downward, he added, "This is my reality."

"I meant through the use of prosthetics."

"I know, but it's just not going to be the same, Leon. Imagine what your life would look like if you were in this chair. You wouldn't want Misty raising your children, taking care of you and running the café."

Leon nodded in agreement. "No, I wouldn't, but we'd make it work."

"That's easy to say when you can stand up on your own."

Aunt Eleanor walked over to them. "Son, did you take your medicine?"

"Yes, ma'am."

"Okay, now. Make sure you do."

When Eleanor rejoined her husband, who was seated on the other side of the deck, Leon chuckled.

"I don't why she insists on treating me like a little boy," Trey complained.

"It's the same with me," Leon said.

"All right, you two," Misty cautioned in a low voice. You don't want Aunt Eleanor coming back over here."

"Naw, I don't," Trey said. "She'd probably snatch me out of this chair and toss me into the next year."

Leon laughed, then looked at his wife. "Aunt Eleanor used to threaten us by saying she'd knock us clean into the next year. We really believed it was possible."

"Remind me to stay away from her bad side," Misty stated.

They were joined by Jordin and Renee. "So," Jordin said, glancing between Trey and Renee, "do either of you see yourself taking another chance at love and getting married?"

"Maybe," Renee responded. "Eventually. I'm just going to take time to get to know that person. I rushed into my last relationship."

Trey shifted his position in his wheelchair. "Right now, I've got to learn how to navigate this new version of my life. I can't consider anything else."

"Trey, you've never had a problem with women. You've always been such a flirt."

He grinned and stroked his chin. "What can I say… *I am a good catch*."

Deep down, Trey wished he could believe his own words, but he'd meant it as a joke. He didn't think he'd ever feel whole again.

CHAPTER FOUR

GIA SPENT MOST of Saturday helping her mother hang curtains and cover the recently delivered bedroom sets with bedding. They had just finished up in the last guest room on the second floor.

Her eyes traveled the length of the room. "It's a really beautiful room, Mama."

Patricia nodded. "Since this is the largest room and the only one with a sitting area, we have to classify it as a suite."

Gia agreed. "I'm sure we'll get quite a few honeymooners requesting the one upstairs with the claw-foot bathtub big enough for two people." She exhaled a long sigh of contentment. "Everything is really coming together in this place." Being back at home meant a lot to Gia—more than she'd expected it would. She didn't realize how much she'd missed Polk Island and its community as a whole. The locals were her friends and family. This was where she belonged. Being in business with her mother was a delightful perk.

Patricia's features became more animated. "I can hardly wait for the grand opening."

"I've been thinking about that," Gia said. "We should plan to have it open and staffed in time for the new year. I don't want to rush the opening. Our busiest months will most likely be centered around holidays and the spring and summer, but then again, we get tourists to the island year-round."

"You're doing all this planning for the B and B and your PT facility... What are you doing for yourself?"

"Right now, I really need to focus on finding work so we can continue building our businesses." Gia eyed Patricia. "This is a priority for me. I'll have plenty of time to relax later. I need to keep building my clientele. My last two were very pleased with my work."

Gia was content with her life, and she wasn't stressed. She was comfortable being single and in her thirties. She was passionate about helping others. Gia loved her job because she often witnessed levels of perseverance and willpower she rarely saw in everyday life. She also experienced great joy in knowing she played a role in the restoration of her patients' quality of life.

Since coming home, Gia had worked with several clients in a private capacity and was currently working with a woman in Charleston who'd had hip replacement surgery. The treatment plan was only for twelve weeks. She hoped to continue picking up patients seeking private physical therapists. As her plan B, she'd also applied to the local hospital. If necessary, Gia would expand her job search to the hospitals in Charleston.

Step by step, she'd make her dream a reality.

"HAVE YOU BEEN in this shop yet?" Shelley asked, pausing in her steps and sticking her sunglasses in her auburn hair. They'd just walked out of the Polk Island Café, having met there for breakfast. "It's owned by Leon's cousin Renee—she's a fashion designer. She's got some really gorgeous clothing in her boutique—several private label collections that are pretty affordable, but she also has a couture line."

Gia glanced up at the signage. "RR Designs… My mom raves about this place, but I've avoided it intentionally," Gia responded. "You know I love to shop, but right now I have to rein myself in because I'm saving for the clinic."

"We can at least take a look. Don't worry, I won't let you buy anything." Shelley kept urging her until Gia gave in. "I'll even hold your credit card hostage."

As she walked around the store, a wave of disappointment washed over Gia each time she saw an item she wished to purchase. She avoided the clearance rack, fleeing temptation.

Gia sent a sharp glare in Shelley's direction. "I don't know why I let you talk me into coming inside this place. This is pure agony."

Out the corner of her eye, she glimpsed Eleanor and Renee in conversation and waved in greeting.

She walked over to the rack closest to the counter to check out the scarves. Her attention was drawn away from the accessories to their conversation.

"So, Trey is still refusing to take physical therapy." Renee sighed. "Auntie, he can be so stubborn at times."

Eleanor brushed away a curling strand of her salt-and-pepper hair. "Yeah, he sho' can. Ain't nothing changed about that."

"He's too proud to let anyone help him," Renee said. "I don't really feel comfortable leaving him alone in the house—he's still healing and he's taking meds…"

"I agree with you, but we can't force Trey to do something he don't wanna do. Sometimes I just wanna shake some sense into him."

Maybe Trey would be more comfortable working one-on-one at home. *This could be a great opportunity for me.* She preferred being a private physical therapist over working in a hospital or rehab center. Gia also relished the idea of spending time with her old friend.

He'd never called, but she hadn't really expected to hear from Trey so soon. He needed time to process what happened and grieve the loss of his limbs.

When Eleanor left the store, Gia followed, catching up with her outside.

"Miss Eleanor..."

She swiveled slowly. "Hey, suga. I'm sorry I didn't get a chance to talk to you in the store. I need to get back to the café to pick up some meals for Trey."

"That's why I wanted to speak with you. I'm a physical therapist and I believe I can help your nephew. Trey may be more comfortable doing PT one-on-one."

"All I know is that he refused it at the VA Hospital in Charleston."

"I could at least give it a shot," Gia offered. "I'm confident I can help rehabilitate Trey if given a chance. I've worked with people like him before—veterans suffering from survivor's guilt, PTSD and those who've lost limbs." She walked Eleanor next door to the café.

"I'll talk to Leon and get his thoughts on the matter. If he thinks you can help his brother, then we'll sit down and discuss it with Trey."

Giddy, Gia hugged her. "Thank you, Miss Eleanor."

"Don't thank me yet, suga. This idea may not make it down the road."

"Where'd you go?" Shelley asked when Gia returned to the boutique.

"I needed to speak with Miss Eleanor. I overheard her and Renee discussing Trey. He's refusing PT at the VA Hospital, so I offered my services."

Looking at her reflection in one of the full-length mirrors, Shelley held a vivid purple dress to her body. "That's actually a good idea—I hope you get the job."

"Me, too," Gia said. "I really need it."

Renee walked over, asking, "Did you two find something you'd like to try on?"

"Everything." Gia chuckled. "I love every item in here, but right now I have to save my money—so I'm going to have to pass."

"Well, I found a couple of pieces," Shelley said, "but I don't need to try them on."

"Just a heads-up," Renee informed them, "I'm going to be adding a couple of new items next week."

"I'll be back." Shelley handed Renee the clothing. "I'm going to get these for now."

They followed her to the counter.

"I've seen you around, but I don't think we've

met," Renee said to Gia. "Did you recently move to the island?"

"I'm Gia. I actually grew up here. Leon and I went to school together. My mom lives just on the next block—the brick house on the corner."

"You're Miss Patricia's daughter." Renee smiled. "I love your mother. She's a sweetheart."

"I think so, too. We're actually converting my grandmother's house into a B and B."

"She did mention that when she stopped in last week. I think it's a wonderful idea, especially since it will be the first one on Polk Island."

Renee handed Shelley her purchases. "It's really nice to meet you, Gia. I'm sure I'll see you around the island."

"For sure. And I'll definitely be back to shop. Your boutique is beautiful."

Smiling, Renee said, "I look forward to having you as a customer."

"AUNT ELEANOR, you wanted to see me?" Leon asked when he strode into the family room of his aunt's house, where she sat folding clothes the next day.

"I saw Gia Harris yesterday and she approached me about helping Trey with physical therapy. I told her that I'd mention it to you to get your thoughts."

"I think it's a great idea," Leon said, "but I'm not the one who needs to be convinced."

Eleanor heaved a soft sigh. "I know."

"Trey's stubborn. He's never liked going to the doctor and he's made it clear that he doesn't want PT."

"So, what we gwine do?"

Leon thought for a moment, then said, "Auntie, he's always liked Gia. In fact, he had a crush on her in high school."

Eleanor seemed surprised. "Really? She's a couple of years older than him."

"Age doesn't matter. When Trey was in eighth grade, all he talked about was Gia. That's why he always wanted to go to the games with me."

"I thought it was because he wanted to play ball when he got to high school."

"I'm sure that was part of it, too... When we pulled up to the café during his homecoming, Trey stopped to talk to Gia," Leon said. "I think she was the only person he really had a real conversation with."

She frowned in confusion. "I should remember that. It was just a couple of days ago."

Patting her hand, Leon said, "It's been a little more than a week, Auntie." He felt so helpless. There was nothing anyone could do but love and support her as the disease progressed.

His aunt had Alzheimer's. He hadn't told Trey

about their aunt's diagnosis yet because Eleanor hadn't wanted Trey worrying about her when he was in Afghanistan. Now that he was home, they were waiting for the right time to tell him. Leon hated keeping this secret from Trey.

Eleanor dismissed his words with a slight wave of her hand. "Did I tell you that I saw Gia today, or was it yesterday? Anyway, she asked about helping Trey with his physical therapy."

Leon gave a slight nod. "I actually think it's a good idea."

"I need to finish cooking. I'm making some dinner for Trey. Can you drive me over there? We can talk to him about Gia."

"Yes, ma'am. I'll take you. Why don't I help you in the kitchen?"

"Sure." Eleanor finished up the last of her folding, then placed the clothing neatly in the laundry basket before heading to the kitchen.

Leon helped her prepare the food. Rusty didn't really like her to cook when she was home alone. However, when Eleanor made up her mind to do something, there was no stopping her.

An hour later, the food was ready.

"Let me go freshen up and I'll be ready to go," Eleanor said.

While he waited, Leon sent Rusty a quick text

notifying him that his aunt was with him and that he'd make sure Eleanor was fine.

Ten minutes later, they were on their way.

"Trey, I brought you some fish, hush puppies, collards, and macaroni and cheese for dinner," Eleanor announced when she walked into the house behind Leon, who used his key to unlock the door. "Are you napping?"

"I've been up for a while," he answered as he wheeled himself into the foyer. "Leon, are you staying for dinner?"

"Sure…"

"It's more than enough." Eleanor bent down to plant a kiss on Trey's forehead. "How are you doing?"

"The pain is manageable," Trey stated, although his expression showed otherwise.

Leon could tell his brother was trying to put on a brave front. "The doctor said you could take two pills if necessary."

"I know," Trey responded, then changed the subject. "I'm getting better with getting in and out of my bed."

Leon let the subject of the medication drop for now.

They gathered in the dining room.

Eleanor retrieved two plates and silverware from the kitchen while Leon grabbed several bottles of water from the refrigerator.

"You're not eating, Auntie?" Trey asked.

She shook her head. "Rusty and I always have dinner together. Y'all go right ahead."

Leon blessed the food before they dived in.

"I ran into Gia today when I was at Renee's boutique earlier," Eleanor said. "Did you know she's a physical therapist? *Dr. Gia Harris.*"

"I heard." Trey's expression was blank. "And Leon's a firefighter."

Eleanor gave him a sharp look. "Don't freshmouth me, son. I don't wanna have to tell you about yourself."

Trey seemed to regret his words. "I'm sorry. I shouldn't have said that."

"What's up with you?" Leon asked, tamping down a flash of annoyance. "Why would you talk to Aunt Eleanor this way? She was just trying to help you."

Giving his brother a sullen look, Trey replied, "I already apologized."

The room was enveloped in tense silence.

When Trey was nearly finished with his meal, Eleanor said, "I just thought since you've known Gia a long time—why not let her help you?"

"She can't give me my legs back, Auntie. How can Gia help me?"

Eleanor glanced over at Leon, who said, "Physical therapy will make you stronger, Trey. It can aid you in regaining your independence.

We've known Gia a long time. I've heard that she's good at her job. Remember that football player they said wouldn't play ball again? The one who played for the Panthers. Gia was his physical therapist."

"That's great for that guy, but that's not my story," Trey said. "Unless she's a miracle worker, I'll never walk again because I lost my legs."

Trey's words were verbal punch to his gut. Leon couldn't find the words to respond. He felt his brother's pain—almost as if it were his own. He didn't like seeing his younger brother like this, but there was nothing they could do about it. He wanted to comfort Trey, but his brother was too proud to accept comforting—he had always been this way.

"Son, you can't lose hope," Eleanor said. "What you've been through is life-changing. That's for sure, but the day will come when you see that so much more will come out of what you've lost, suga."

"Auntie's right," Leon said. "And thanks to some of the latest technology, there is a real chance for you to walk again and do some of the other things you enjoy."

Trey appeared to be concentrating on his near empty plate.

Leon glanced at his aunt, who shrugged in resignation.

Wiping his mouth with his napkin, Trey sat back in the wheelchair. "I know you and Auntie are trying to help me… I just need y'all to understand that this is my new normal—I have no choice but to accept this. So, you see, there's no need for all this worrying. And no need to bother Gia."

"Misty and I would like to host a welcome home party for you this weekend at the café. It might do you some good to see your friends."

"Leon, you don't have to do anything like that."

"We want to do it, little brother."

Trey eyed his aunt, who wore a muddled expression on her face. "You okay, Auntie?"

She turned her attention to him. "When did y'all paint the kitchen?"

Leon noted the confused expression on Trey's face. Guilt snaked down his spine. He was sure his brother had noticed how his aunt seemed to struggle with remembering simple things such as the passage of time and also that she often repeated herself on occasion.

"We did it after the renovations, Auntie," he reminded her. "When we were getting the house ready for Trey."

"Oh, that's right," Eleanor murmured, but she still seemed perplexed.

The look on Trey's face was unmistakable. He had questions. It was only a matter of time when he would demand answers.

CHAPTER FIVE

ON SATURDAY AFTERNOON, Gia left the grocery store with the intent of going straight home. But the number of cars parked outside the bakery and café caught her attention. She paused on the street, waved to one of her neighbors and rolled down her window. "Is there a sale I don't know about?"

"The Rothchild family is hosting a welcome home gathering for Trey. You should stop in for a bit. They invited everyone."

Smiling, Gia said, "Maybe I will." She was eager to reconnect with him. She found an empty space and parked her car.

She walked inside the café, nodding at a few people.

Trey was seated in his wheelchair at a table near the door. He spotted Gia and gestured for her to join him.

"Thanks for coming, *Dr. Harris*," he said when she sat down at the table. "We didn't really get a chance to talk the last time I saw you."

She discreetly admired his handsome features, especially the way his mouth curled as if always on the edge of laughter. Trey's black hair had grown out some and lay in waves. The shadow of his beard gave him an even more manly aura.

"Well, that day was a busy one for you," Gia responded. She wished she'd chosen to put on a pair of jeans instead of the yoga pants she wore. Most of the people there were dressed in sundresses or nice pants. Gia had only intended to run out to the store for food. "Now that you've had some time to settle in, how are you doing?"

His perfectly shaped brows flickered a little before he replied, "I really don't have an answer to that question."

"I get it."

"I'm curious, though. What brought you back to the island?" Trey inquired. "I heard you were the top physical therapist to pro athletes."

She gave a polite smile. "I don't know about all that, but yes, I had a number of sports figures as patients. I'm back home because my mom and I decided to turn my grandmother's house into a B and B. I also want to open my own PT clinic."

He looked impressed. "Wow. You'd do well with both on this island."

"That's my thought, too. Patients won't have

to travel to Charleston for rehab. They will soon have a choice."

"How's your dad doing?" he asked. "I haven't seen Gunny around. I'd like to talk to him."

"Oh… I thought you knew… My father passed away a little over a year ago." Her eyes teared up, but she blinked to keep them from falling. "He would be so proud of you."

Trey looked stunned by the news. "Gia, I'm so sorry. I didn't know…"

"He was at home with us," she said. "We were watching television. Mom and I went to make popcorn and get drinks. When we returned to the living room—he was gone. I miss him dearly, but I know he's at peace."

She let her gaze travel the length of the café. "I was impressed with the number of people who came out to welcome you back home."

"I was surprised to see everyone," Trey agreed. "I reconnected with old classmates I hadn't seen in years."

A server set plates in front of them, saying, "Misty told me to bring these to your table. I'll be back with your drinks. Tea or lemonade?"

"I'll have half sweet tea and half lemonade," Gia answered.

"You can bring me one of those, too," Trey said. When the server left, Trey added, "I have to tell you that I never expected to see you.

Don't get me wrong. I'm thrilled. I just never thought it would happen."

"I would come home at least once a quarter through college. I guess we kept missing each other."

"I suppose so."

Gia's mouth salivated at the juicy burger and fries on her plate.

After whispering a quick blessing, she picked up the burger and took a big bite because her stomach demanded food now. Her burger tasted like a five-star meal. Gia savored every bite. She eyed him as he picked up a fry and placed it in his mouth. After he swallowed, the expression on his face changed abruptly. He squeezed his eyes shut and clenched his lips tight.

"What's your pain level right now?" Gia asked gently.

"About a seven," he managed to say. "It's phantom pain, according to my doctors." Trey pulled out a bottle of pills and took one. He downed his glass of water.

She hated to see him hurting. "Did anyone discuss a treatment called mirror therapy?"

"No, I don't think so…maybe…" Trey massaged his temples with both hands. "What is it?"

"The goal of mirror therapy is to trick the brain out of processing pain signals," she explained. "Instead, the brain receives new information that your missing limbs are there and functional—this restructuring may lessen your pain or stop it completely."

"Is it something I can do on my own?" he asked.

"It has always been considered a therapist-guided treatment," Gia responded, "but in my opinion, it's pretty simple and it's something you can do at home yourself—all you need is a mirror and the motivation to practice the treatment daily. I can email you the instructions if you're interested."

"I guess it won't hurt to try it."

Gia handed him her phone. "You can put your email under my contacts."

"Should I include my number?" he asked with a grin. The medication was taking effect. Trey's face was no longer a mask of private agony.

Gia recalled fondly how he would flirt with her growing up, but she never took him seriously. Trey was very popular and had girls of all ages chasing after him.

She used to tease him that he was going to end up in some serious drama because of his flirtatious manner. Trey would just laugh and say, "There's only one girl for me." He would never say any more than that, no matter how much she tried to cajole it out of him.

"Sure. I think you already have mine," she told him.

"I do. I haven't called because I'm still trying to adjust to being home."

"I get it."

"I planned to catch up with you though." Trey settled back in his wheelchair.

"It's really good to have you back at home." She pushed away from the table. "I'm afraid, I need to get going, but I'm glad I was able to spend some time with you."

Gia was well aware that Trey's gaze followed her as she walked up to Leon and Misty. "Thanks for letting me pop into the party without an invitation."

"Everyone was invited," Leon responded. "I saw you over there with Trey. How did it go?"

Gia glanced over her shoulder, then back at Leon. "He's not interested in PT, and I didn't want to force the issue. Trey's still in a lot of pain, although he tries to hide it. It may take some time for him to consider therapy." She glanced down at her watch. "I have some groceries in the car, so I better get going."

She exited the Polk Island Bakery & Café and walked to where she'd parked.

Gia drove to her mother's house, which was located across the street from the green-and-white house that had once belonged to her grandmother. She put away the groceries, then walked over to the B and B to join Patricia.

"Mama…you here?" Gia called out.

"I'm in the bedroom down here," Patricia answered.

She found her mother sticking paint samples across one of the walls.

"What color do you think we should go with?"

Gia assessed the array of paint swatches in detail. "I like the peach."

"I do, too."

"I'm sorry so much of this has fallen on you, Mama."

"Don't you worry about a thing. Ma'Dear left this house to you. You could've done whatever you wanted with it, but when I suggested the B and B, you were all in. We're partners. I know you've been busy looking for work. Besides, I love this part…the decorating."

Gia picked up a wallpaper sample. "I thought we decided to avoid putting up wallpaper."

"We did, but when I saw this one, I thought it would look really nice in the guest bathroom down here," Patricia said.

"I personally don't care for wallpaper but if you've got your mind set on it, try to limit it to just that one bathroom."

"Thanks, baby girl."

"Oh, I stopped by the café after I left the grocery store. They were having a party for Trey."

Patricia sat down on the edge of the king-size bed. "Did you get a chance to speak with him?"

"I did."

"How did things go?"

"It didn't," Gia responded. "He's not interested in physical therapy. I think he's still trying to process everything that transpired during his last tour in Afghanistan. Trey isn't dealing with what's happened to him—he's avoiding it."

"That poor boy…he's always been so full of life and always smiling and laughing. My heart aches for him."

"Mom, he can still have a great life. It's not over for Trey."

"Remember your daddy went through that period of avoidance."

"I try to imagine how I'd feel in Trey's situation and I can't. It's really hard to process."

"From where I'm standing, that man needs you."

"I made the offer," Gia said. "The ball is in his court now." Even if he remained adamant about refusing PT, she hoped they could at least remain friends.

Despite being two years younger than them, Trey was always around whenever they went to the movies, the shopping center—it didn't matter.

Now that he was home, Gia realized just how

much she'd missed their friendship. It saddened her that he'd returned so broken but being the daughter of a marine who'd seen firsthand the horrors of war, she understood that it would take some time for Trey to reenter civilian life, this time as a veteran with a disability.

TREY FLOUNDERED IN an agonizing maelstrom. He tossed and turned for what seemed like hours, yet sleep continued to evade him. He lay in bed, his mind racing. He'd heard the song of the water, calling for him since his return home. He wanted to answer but now those days were over.

Yet, the ocean continued to call.

Trey lowered his bed in order to transition into the wheelchair, then made his way to the sunroom. He stared out the large center window displaying a picturesque view of the ocean.

Each swell seemed to wave, welcoming him back to Polk Island.

The moonlight cut into the darkness of the night. Scattered stars twinkled and the fog appeared in a holding pattern offshore.

"I thought I heard you moving around down here." Trey glanced over his shoulder and saw Renee behind him, dressed in a tank top and pajama shorts. She stifled a yawn.

"I hope I didn't wake you up," he said.

"You didn't." Renee crossed the room and dropped down into one of the chairs. "I was up working on some new designs. It's something about being back here on the island that inspires me. I've been working on a new collection for beach weddings."

"All right, Ms. Fashion Designer. Congratulations."

"I'm excited," Renee responded. "Weddings here on the island are becoming very popular. I'm designing a line of wedding and bridesmaid dresses that are light and airy—perfect for tropical and…" She paused. "Trey…"

"Huh?"

"You zoned out on me. Am I boring you?"

"No, not at all," Trey said. "I was wishing I could run out there right now for a moonlight swim."

"I understand how you feel, especially because I know how much you love the water."

The familiar agonizing pain began to radiate around his knees and below. Trey leaned back in his chair as if to fight off the fiery burning sensation.

Renee gently massaged his shoulders, and he felt his body finally relax. "Are the pain pills helping?"

"My doctor told me I could take two every four hours—three if I needed it bad enough, but

I only try to take one," Trey said. "You know how much I hate taking medicine. When I saw a friend of Leon's earlier—she's a physical therapist—she told me about a treatment called mirror therapy. I'm thinking I might need to try it. She sent me the instructions in an email."

"It's supposed to do what?" Renee asked.

"Trick my brain into thinking I'm not in pain. She says it works for patients who are dealing with phantom limb pain. Right now, my mind is all jacked up. Too much going on physically and mentally."

"You should consider seeing someone," Renee suggested. "It might help. My therapist has helped me through a lot of my stuff."

He was surprised by her admission.

Reading his expression, Renee said, "There's nothing wrong with seeking therapy, cousin. I'm sure the VA can give you some referrals."

"They have," he told her. "I haven't even looked at the information. I'm not willing to share my feelings with strangers."

"You should… You don't know this, but I've always suffered from panic attacks. They can be so bad that they crippled me to the point that I couldn't function a couple of years ago. I couldn't leave home for days or drive. Kevin didn't understand what I was going through. He had political aspirations and my issues didn't line up with his plans, so that's why he cheated on me—at least that's the reason he gave me."

"Are you serious?" Trey's tone hardened.

"He wanted a woman without flaws, especially one without a chronic mental disorder."

"He didn't deserve you, Renee."

She smiled. "Thank you. I appreciate you saying that."

Renee stood up. "I think I'm going to have a cup of herbal tea to help me sleep."

"Would you make some for me?" he asked.

"Sure."

As soon as Renee left the room, Trey went back to his bedroom and took a drink from the bottle of rum he kept hidden in his nightstand.

With the refinement of a lame animal, Trey managed to pull himself up and out of the wheelchair and careened onto the bed. He released a deep sigh of exhaustion, hoping the herbal tea and rum would work its magic by dulling the pain that plagued him night and day.

"DID YOU GET a chance to talk with Gia about physical therapy?" Rusty asked when he and Eleanor visited Trey the next day.

"I did. She still gives off that cheerleader vibe." He chuckled. "She was cute in that outfit back in the day."

"The doctors say you need a physical therapist especially if you gwine want those artificial legs—I forget what they call them. You've known Gia forever, so I don't understand why you don't want her to help you. She knows what she's doing," Eleanor interjected.

"I'm good, Auntie."

"No, you're not."

Trey didn't argue with his aunt. He knew Eleanor only wanted the best for him, but she didn't understand what he was going through—none of them understood. His life was never going to be the same—even with the use of prosthetics. He would never be the same man—he didn't even deserve to be alive.

"I know you're wondering why you're still here," Rusty stated. "Son, you are alive because it wasn't your time to go. You haven't lived out your purpose in this world."

"Hudson deserved to live—she deserved to come home and raise her children." Trey cleared this throat. "That was her last tour. My team—they were outstanding marines. I was proud to serve with them. I would've been proud to die with them, too."

Eleanor teared up. "I hate it when you talk like that, Trey. Losing you would've just killed me, son."

He hadn't meant to upset her. "I'm just saying that our mission—it wasn't a dangerous one.

They should all be alive—not just me." Trey clenched his mouth tight. He didn't want to fall apart in front of them. "I failed them."

"No, you didn't. You did all you could do to protect your team," Rusty stated. "What you're feeling is survivor's guilt. I have a couple of friends who've dealt with it."

Wanting to change the subject, Trey reached over and took his aunt's hand in his own. "Auntie, how are you doing?"

"I'm fine."

Trey looked up at Rusty. "Is somebody gonna tell me what's really going on? I don't like being kept in the dark like this."

"Your aunt was diagnosed with early-onset Alzheimer's," the older man said.

"When?" Trey asked.

"Shortly after we got married."

A wave of hurt washed over him. "And nobody bothered to tell me. I'm still a member of this family or at least I thought I was…"

"Son, you were over in another country—I didn't want your focus on me," Eleanor said. "You had to keep a clear head. Don't be mad at nobody. I told them I would tell you myself when you came home. If you wanna be angry, then be mad at me."

"I can't get upset with you, Auntie, but I don't like being left out of something so important.

I need to know you're okay." Trey understood why no one said anything, but a part of him was angry with the family—especially Leon. His brother should've told him about their aunt. But then there were things he was keeping from Leon, as well.

"Suga, I'm fine. Some days are better than others," Eleanor said, "but I won't complain."

"Her new medication seems to work great," Rusty interjected. "Working on puzzles helps, as well."

"That's good to hear."

Eleanor and Rusty stayed for another hour. When they left, Trey went to his room to practice the mirror therapy.

He was grateful to Gia for the suggestion. The treatment didn't work as he'd hoped, but this was his first time trying it. He wasn't experiencing as much of the phantom limb pain as he was earlier. However, he still had to take meds to fight the pain radiating around and within the incisions.

He appreciated Gia's ability to offer a solution without expecting anything in return.

She'd texted once just to see how he was doing, but didn't mention PT.

Trey liked that—he didn't want to be pressured into doing anything.

And yet Gia had always been enthusiastic in

all her pursuits—from playing volleyball on the beach to watching a movie or playing a game of Scrabble with him. She possessed a bubbly personality and carried with her an energy that seemed to pulse in the air when he was near her…a vitality that drew him to her.

CHAPTER SIX

"I COULD HARDLY sleep last night. I'm a bit nervous about this interview at the hospital," Gia confessed to her mother over breakfast. "I'm sure they're going to check my references." Although she preferred being a private therapist, Gia was realistic about her options. She intended to do whatever she had to do to reach her goals.

"Just give them Chris Latham's number," her mother suggested. "He should give you a nice reference. He's walking around because of you. It's that wife of his who's causing all the trouble."

Frowning, Gia stirred uneasily in her chair. "I really hate to have him do anything for me." The last thing she wanted was to need his help at all. He was still reaching out to her, and she continued to ignore him. She had too much pride to beg Chris for a reference—she knew it would come at a price.

"I understand, but Chris needs to make this right. That's the least he can do."

Gia finished off her apple juice. "We'll see what happens, Mama."

"It'll work out because you're a good person, my sweet daughter."

She smiled at Patricia. "I think you may be a little biased."

"Don't worry. Your work will speak for itself. You got this."

"You're right. *I got this.*" She pushed away from the table, then carried her plate to the kitchen sink.

An hour later, Gia entered the administration section of the hospital. She heard the rush of blood pounding through her ears as she forced herself to walk up the steps to the third floor where Human Resources was located. Butterflies skittered around in Gia's belly, but she was determined to get through her interview like a pro.

The young woman behind the desk in the reception area smiled in greeting and said, "Gia Harris?"

"That's me."

"I'm Jill and I'll escort you to Interview Room B."

Gia followed her down the hallway to a small intimate room on the left. The only furniture inside was a circular table and a couple of chairs.

Smiling, she said, "Carol will join you shortly."

Gia sat in the chair, her fingers tense in her lap and her thoughts disquieting. Gia prayed that she wouldn't be asked any questions about Chris. During her previous interviews, a few of the interviewers seemed more interested in him than her actual work history.

Gia walked out of the room thirty minutes later feeling good about her conversation with the head of Human Resources.

She was surprised to run into Trey in the waiting area downstairs when she was on her way to the parking lot. "Hey, Trey…"

A spark of concern flashed in his eyes. "What are you doing here? Are you feeling okay?"

"I just finished up an interview for a job," she responded. "Are you here to see a doctor?"

He nodded. "A follow-up to see how my incisions are healing."

"And the other wounds?" Gia asked. "The ones that no one can see. What are you doing about them?"

Trey stared at her wordlessly.

"The reason I asked is because my dad suffered most from those —the wounds no one sees. They're the ones that take the longest to heal."

"I'll be fine." His voice edged toward uncharacteristic astonishment.

She cleared her throat, then said, "I know

you will. I just wonder if you *know* that you're gonna be fine?"

"You've never been able to keep your thoughts and opinions to yourself," Trey said.

"I guess I haven't learned that particular trick." Gia gave a slight shrug. "What can I say? I'm a communicator."

"Hey, you in a hurry to leave?" he asked.

"No, I don't have anywhere to be," she answered.

"Will you have lunch with me?" Trey questioned. Gia's memory traveled back through time, before Trey's voice matured from a higher pitch to the deep raspy tone now as he asked her to lunch. He was so cute back then. Now he was just grown and sexy. A sudden awareness overtook her, and Gia realized Trey was staring at her. "I couldn't have anything to eat this morning," he continued. "They want to redo some blood work."

"I'll wait down here for you," Gia said quickly. "I can drive you home afterward."

"Outstanding. I'll let Renee know that she doesn't have to come back to pick me up."

She sat down and picked up a magazine to read while she waited for Trey to finish up his appointment. Although she wished he'd change his mind about physical therapy, she wasn't going to force the issue. He really needed strength training. Observing him, Gia could tell that he exerted too much energy when he operated the wheelchair as he made his way to the elevator.

"What's wrong?" Gia asked when he returned forty-five minutes later. His expressive eyes were almost somber, and he looked irritated.

"I just ran into someone I know in the elevator and while I know he didn't mean any harm, I'm so tired of hearing of people telling me how happy they are to see me out and about. How I'm going to be all right."

"I know it may sound patronizing, but you're right, I'm sure that person didn't mean any harm." She'd heard similar sentiments from some of her patients, so his words didn't surprise her.

"I don't need someone giving me kudos for trying to live a normal existence," he uttered in frustration. "Then I got hit in the head with some woman's supersize purse. Maybe this wheelchair comes with an invisibility cloak that I don't know about?"

Gia held back her amusement. She didn't want to appear insensitive but the way he joked just now was like the teen she remembered.

Once they were in her vehicle, Trey asked, "Why do you drive an SUV equipped like this?" It had been converted to transport wheelchair-bound passengers, complete with a side-door ramp.

"So, I can transport my patients if necessary. Not all of them are able to drive."

"You put a lot into making sure your patients know they're important to you."

"I want all of them to feel like they're my first priority. I find this helps the healing process."

"Where would you like to eat?" Trey asked.

"The Salad Bar," Gia responded. "Is that okay with you?"

"Yeah," he said.

Inside the buffet-style restaurant, they stood in line to choose their choices of lettuce and toppings.

When they found a table, Trey said, "I hope you get that job."

"So do I."

A server appeared, asking, "Can I get you anything?"

Trey glanced at Gia, then said, "We're good. Thanks."

When she walked away to check on another table, he said, "I have to admit that I was surprised to hear that you're no longer working with athletes. Do you think you'll be happy working at our little hospital?"

Gia shrugged in nonchalance. "I wouldn't

have come back here if I was worried about that."

"I guess that makes sense." Trey picked up his knife and fork. "I've been practicing that mirror therapy."

She was surprised that he'd actually tried the technique. "And?"

"I have to say that the more I do it, the pain doesn't seem to be as bad as before."

"I'm glad," she said. *Maybe now you'll consider giving me a chance to see what else I can accomplish.*

The server returned with two glasses of water for them.

Leaning her elbow on the table, Gia rested her chin in her hand. "What have you been doing since you got back?"

"Just resting mostly."

"That's good," Gia said. "But you need to make sure you're not just lying in bed. You need to move about so that your joints don't get stiff. It's good to get out and get fresh air."

"I get that on my patio."

"So, you intend to just sit at home. Why?"

"I think it's pretty obvious," Trey replied tightly as his eyes deepened to a dark coffee brown. "I can't walk."

Gia frowned. "I get that, but what does that have to do with you going out?"

Trey's mouth worked for a moment, making no sound, and then he sighed in obvious frustration. "It's too complicated for me to leave the house. Just getting to my appointment today was a struggle. Trying to maneuver in this wheelchair... I get exhausted easily."

Gia wiped her mouth on the edge of her napkin. "That's why I want to help you, Trey. PT will strengthen your upper body. I'm just saying."

He chuckled. "I knew you were going to say that."

"I hope you know I'm not trying to pressure you into anything."

"If I thought that, I never would've asked you to have lunch with me," he told her.

Pleased that he still trusted her, Gia took a sip of her water. "I've really missed you."

Rubbing his chin, Trey smiled. "I missed you, too. Whenever I came home—I would stop by to see your mom. I missed you by two days once. You left the day before I arrived. I guess my timing's always been off where you're concerned."

There was a time when Gia had been more than willing to give Trey her heart, but at the time, she thought he'd be better off with someone his age or younger. She took a deep breath and looked around the restaurant to avoid his deep, probing gaze.

"I can't believe you have nothing to say all of a sudden." The amusement was back in his voice. "Still friends?" Trey stuck out his hand.

She put hers in it, the strength of his fingers pressing against hers. "Yes," she murmured. "We will always be friends."

AT HOME, TREY MUTTERED A string of profanities as he struggled to remove the clothing caught on the wheels of his wheelchair. It wasn't enough that he had to endure the stares of people— he expected it from children, but not adults or teens. Trey better understood the unique challenges wheelchair users had to contend with on a daily basis.

For some, a wheelchair offered mobility and freedom, but Trey hated being trapped in this piece of metal.

"Why me?" he yelled in frustration.

Tears rushed down his face and Trey sobbed. "Why did this have to happen to me? Why didn't You just let me die?"

Trey was trying to accept his life-changing circumstance, but he was struggling, and shame kept him from allowing others like his own brother to help him. All of his doctors suggested that he participate in a support group, but the idea didn't appeal to him. Trey fiercely guarded his emotions and kept them in check in front of others.

He was finally able to free the piece of clothing from beneath the wheel and navigate to the bathroom to wash his face. Trey didn't want Renee to come home with him looking broken— it was unbecoming of a marine.

Life in Afghanistan had consisted of threats, the weeding out of false information from officials who collaborated with the Taliban. Two weeks after Trey had arrived, his platoon surrounded a village known to harbor insurgents, but they'd fled before the marines arrived.

The platoon commander had ordered them to make regular patrols each day to the nearby and outlying villages. Some of the people appeared friendly while others were openly hostile.

Fighting against the Taliban wasn't an easy feat. In one instance, insurgents armed with rockets and other heavy weapons had attacked their outpost—a fight that went on for almost three hours before they were able to dominate and force the rebels to retreat. But in this very moment—Trey felt like he was in the toughest fight of his life.

He wheeled himself to his bed and maneuvered himself onto it.

And yet…he'd enjoyed having lunch with

Gia. She didn't seem to look at him any different than she had in the past, which had enabled him to relax during lunch.

Trey decided he didn't mind having her visit him sometime. Just the short time they'd spent together had ignited a yearning for more of her company.

"How did the interview go?" Patricia asked when Gia walked into the house. She'd been home for almost an hour but had sat in the SUV talking with a potential patient on her cell.

"I feel like it went well, but we'll see," she replied. "I just got off the phone with a woman who was referred by Mary—the woman who had the hip replacement."

"That's wonderful."

"I'm meeting with her tomorrow. She lives in Charleston, too."

"And lunch with Trey?"

She'd texted her mother earlier about her plans. Gia settled back in her seat, arms folded across her chest. "It was nice, but then I've always liked him. He's stubborn, though."

"I have no doubt you'll be able to get through to him."

"I'm not gonna hold my breath." Gia headed to the stairs. "I'm going up to change. Why don't you come to the beach with me?"

"I think I will," Patricia said. "I've been so focused on the renovations. I need a day for me. Even Sam is always telling me to take time to relax and rejuvenate."

"Your boyfriend's right. You've put all your energy into redoing Nana's house. It's time for you to relax and just have some fun."

They left the house a short time later and drove to the beach.

The coconut-scented sunscreen wafting around them, Gia carried a tote stuffed with towels, suntan lotion and two bottles of water. When they'd found a spot, Gia removed her top and shorts, revealing her strapless purple one-piece swimsuit. Sand squished between her toes as she sauntered to the end of the beach where the waves congregated with the shore.

The salty air tickled her nose. "It's so nice today. The weather's perfect."

Her mother stood beside her in a black one-piece swimsuit with a multicolored knee-length sarong. "The water's not too cold, either."

Using her foot, she splashed water around and then took a step in deeper. The saltwater reached to her calves. A piece of seaweed floated by, brushing against her.

A wave rolled to midthigh, then rose to her waist as Gia and her mother ventured farther out into the glossy softness of the ocean.

Her body merged into the sea, as if her skin and the water were one. The water's buoyancy had a way of lifting her spirits. Her entire body relaxed as she floated.

Patricia swam over to her. "I'm glad you asked me to join you. It feels so good to be in the water. Very relaxing."

Eyes closed, Gia was free to enjoy herself at least for a little while, and she took the opportunity to do so every chance she got. It helped to release the tension she felt whenever she thought of Chris Latham. The consequences of his wife's allegations had forced her to come home. As it turned out—it was the best decision Gia could've ever made in so many ways.

"I have a feeling that Trey is gonna come to his senses and hire you," Patricia said. "I know Leon and Eleanor will convince him."

"Mama, he's a grown man," Gia responded. "This has to be his choice. If Trey's not committed, then it won't work."

She stood up in the water. "Here comes another wave."

Gia burst into laughter as Patricia attempted to jump over it. Gia and her mother were very close, and she relished spending time with her.

She ran her fingers through her short curls, damp from the water, then glanced over her shoulder to the houses dotted across the road from the beach. Gia knew that the house directly behind her was Eleanor's house—the one where Trey lived with his cousin.

There was a part of her that yearned to visit him, but Gia dared not intrude unless she was invited.

"What are you thinking about?" Patricia asked. "Are you still worried about that interview?"

"No, not at all," she responded. Gia was actually thinking about Trey. On the outside, he seemed fine but inside, she presumed he was an emotional mess. The sad thing was, he wouldn't let anyone help him.

CHAPTER SEVEN

TREY SAT ON the patio enjoying the sunny weather and inhaling the fresh ocean air. There were people scattered in groups along the strip of sandy beach, but two people directly in his view captured his attention, holding it captive.

He watched Gia and her mother as they swam and frolicked in the ocean. She'd mentioned during lunch that she'd intended to spend the rest of her afternoon at South Beach. He longed to join them but forced the thought away from his mind.

Renee flung herself onto the lounge chair next to him. Shielding her eyes with her hand, she asked, "Are you spying on the Miss Patricia and her daughter?"

"I was enjoying the ocean view and just happened to see them out there," Trey stated

"She's beautiful, don't you think?"

Grinning, Trey glanced over at her. "Who? Miss Patricia?"

Renee laughed. "You know exactly who I'm referring to."

Trey turned back around. "Gia's pretty. She's the physical therapist Leon and Aunt Eleanor want me to work with."

"That's great, right? You'd probably be more comfortable with someone you know."

"Why don't we take a stroll?" Renee suggested. "You don't have to stay on this patio. You can get some fresh air."

"I'm good," he responded.

"It's not healthy for you to just stay here all day."

Trey's throat ached with defeat. "This is my new normal, Renee. This is my life now and I have to accept it."

"Physical therapy will only make you stronger."

Trey put up a hand to stop her from saying more. "Renee, don't… I've heard it from the doctors at Walter Reed, the doctors here, and from Leon and Aunt Eleanor. I even heard it from Gia earlier."

She broke into a grin. "So, that's who you had lunch with."

"Why are you home so early?" Trey asked, changing the subject. His cousin was nosy.

"I was hoping to catch you having a hot, torrid affair."

He laughed. "Only in my dreams."

"Between the two of us—we're pretty boring," Renee said.

"Speak for yourself." Trey returned his attention toward the ocean, looking for Gia and Patricia. When he didn't see them, he assumed they'd left. "I really miss being out there." His body yearned to be enveloped in the watery depths of the sea; he found it soothing and relaxing.

"I remember how you'd stay in the water for what seemed like hours. Aunt Eleanor would have to practically drag you out kicking and screaming."

Trey chuckled, despite how the memories of swimming in the ocean stung. He turned his wheelchair around to face her. "How was your day?"

"Busy," Renee responded. "I had two separate fittings for a couple of brides and their attendants. One was a bridezilla of course. She was so difficult that her maid of honor almost walked out. I had to talk her down." She stifled a yawn. "I'm so tired but if I lie down now, I won't be able to go back to sleep until late tonight."

"You don't have to worry about cooking," Trey said. "We can order a pizza or some wings. If you can stay awake long enough, we can watch a movie."

"I want pepperoni and sausage," Renee murmured. "I'm going up to take a quick shower."

"I'll order the pizza," Trey said.

Inside his bedroom, he pulled out a bottle of rum from his nightstand.

He took a long swig, allowing the liquor to warm his throat.

Sadly, he would probably live the rest of his life with only the companionship of friends and family. That bomb had not only taken the lives of his team but destroyed the very existence he'd once known, leaving a lasting effect that had driven Trey into a downward spiral. And it only seemed to end with a bottle of rum, vodka— whatever he could get his hands on.

His sole responsibility at the moment was to drown the pain by any means necessary.

He took another drink, then put the bottle away.

Twenty minutes later, he heard the sound of someone knocking on the front door. Before he could get across the room, Renee rushed down the stairs, saying, "I'll get it."

After she brought the pizza in, they watched a movie on the large television above the fireplace in the living room while eating and discussing the events of the day.

Renee cleaned up when they decided to call it a night three hours later.

"I'll see you in the morning," she told him as she ascended the stairs.

Trey returned to his room, closing the door behind him. He settled in bed, then took his medication.

His grief over his team was like an uninvited guest staying well beyond the point of wearing out its welcome. He didn't want this deep sense of sadness to become a permanent fixture in his life. Still, he refused to talk to a shrink. *Eventually, it will pass.*

Trey refused to accept the theory that he was suffering from depression. He didn't think he was the type of person who would get depressed, but even if that were the case—it was situational, and not permanent. Anyone who'd experienced what he had gone through would feel the same way. He knew a couple of marines who had to be discharged because of a depressive disorder. Before the bombing, he'd never dealt with bouts of sadness, loss of interest or any of the other symptoms. He just needed to numb his pain physically and emotionally.

He pulled out the rum and tilted the bottle to his mouth.

The effects of the liquor weren't what Trey expected. It usually helped to numb the pain of his grief and the sense of loss that was his constant companion.

Instead, he felt nauseous. Really nauseous.

He clumsily eased out of the bed and into his chair.

Trey wheeled himself to the bathroom but couldn't make it to the toilet in time. He grabbed the plastic bag out of the wastebasket, emptying the contents of his stomach inside.

He retched until nothing came out.

Trembling, Trey tied up the bag and placed it inside of another one. He brushed his teeth and washed his face.

His body felt weak, so weak that he was tempted to call out for Renee to come help him into the bed.

Trey allowed his pride to take over.

It took some doing, but he managed. He sat up, propped against two pillows. His throat was raw from puking and he'd developed a slight headache.

Trey moaned when the phone rang sharp in his ear. He answered automatically. "Hello…"

"You okay?" Leon asked. "You don't sound good."

"I'm fine. Just a little headache."

"I'm off tomorrow. If you're up to it, why don't you spend the day with me and the kids?"

Trey rubbed his temple with his left hand. "Can I give you a call in the morning? Hopefully my headache will be gone by then."

"Sure."

He heard the disappointment in Leon's voice. "I'll call you first thing tomorrow. My pain meds are kicking in." Trey pressed a hand over his face convulsively.

"Trey, you don't sound good. You sure you're all right?"

He felt drained, hollow, lifeless, but he wasn't going to tell his brother the truth. He didn't want Leon driving over so late at night. "I'm fine, Leon. You don't have to worry about me."

"WHAT DID YOUR brother say?" Misty asked when Leon hung up.

"That he'll give me an answer in the morning. I'm worried about Trey. He didn't sound well and the worst of it is that I think he's been drinking. I smelled it on him the last time I was at the house."

Misty looked surprised. "Are you sure? Maybe it's just the medication he's on."

Leon rejected the idea. "I know him. He's self-medicating with alcohol."

"Maybe you should give Renee a call?" Misty suggested. "See if she's noticed anything."

"That's a good idea." He grabbed his phone. "Hey, Renee, it's Leon…can you do me a favor?"

"Sure, what's up?" she replied sleepily.

"I think Trey's been drinking. When I called

him just now—he didn't sound too good. Would you mind checking on him for me?"

"Drinking? Are you sure? I was with him earlier. We ate pizza and watched a movie. He seemed fine to me," she said. "Maybe it's the pain pills."

"I've never heard him sound like he did a few minutes ago. The last time I was there—I could smell the alcohol on him."

"Okay, I'll go down there right now," she said.

"Do me a favor and don't say anything about this," Leon told her. "I'll talk to him tomorrow. I just want to make sure he's okay for now."

"I'll call you back."

"Thanks so much."

"It's no problem."

Misty climbed into bed and settled back against a set of pillows. "You know Trey isn't stupid. He's going to know you're behind Renee's wellness check."

Leon shrugged in nonchalance. "I'm fine with that. I almost lost my brother in Afghanistan. Now that he's home—I intend to make sure I don't lose him."

"KNOCK KNOCK…" RENEE EASED Trey's door open and stuck her head inside.

He gestured for her to come into the room.

He had a feeling that she was going to check on him. Trey knew Leon had called her.

"I just wanted to check on you before I call it a night," she said.

He noted the way her eyes appeared to be searching the bedroom. "Did Leon ask you to check on me?"

"I'm not gonna lie. He was worried about you, Trey."

"I'm fine."

"You don't look like you're okay," Renee stated. "I know how private you are, but you don't have to deal with this stuff alone. I've been where you are—keeping my pain, my fears—everything bottled up inside. I'm telling you it does more harm than good. Even if you won't talk to me...talk to your brother."

"I'm not deliberately shutting everyone out. I'm just trying to process everything that's happened. I can't do it with everybody constantly watching or checking on me—it's overwhelming. I need to do this alone. Why is that so hard to understand?"

Her eyes brightened with unshed tears. "I know we're cousins, but you and Leon have always been like brothers to me and Junior," she shared of herself and her own brother. "We've always looked up to y'all."

His heart filled with tenderness at her words.

"I feel the same way about you, Renee. I really need you to believe me when I tell you that I'm good. I just need some time. That's all."

She nodded.

"I love you, cousin," he said.

"Rest well," Renee responded. "I love you, too."

Trey knew she was going back upstairs to call Leon. If she couldn't convince his brother that all was well, he would see Leon tomorrow whether he wanted to or not.

CHAPTER EIGHT

WHEN LEON SHOWED up at the house the next day, it didn't surprise Trey at all, but he resented the intrusion. He wasn't a little boy, and he didn't need his big brother. Besides, he was upset with Leon for keeping him in the dark about their aunt.

"We need to talk."

Trey looked at Leon. "About what? *Aunt Eleanor?* About why you didn't tell me she has Alzheimer's? Don't you think I had a right to know? I mean… I'm still a member of this family."

"She asked me not to," his brother responded, "Auntie wanted you to hear it from her."

"And if she wasn't able to tell me?"

"Then I would've told you, Trey," Leon said. "Right now, I'm here to talk about your drinking. Alcohol and pills are not a good mix, little brother. I've smelled it on you, so don't bother to deny it."

"I don't drink that much. I'm not an alcoholic."

"You shouldn't be drinking at all."

Trey sighed, weary of the conversation already. "There's nothing to worry about. It's just been a couple of times. I needed to soothe my nerves."

Trey could see that Leon didn't believe him. "I can always tell when you're lying."

He met his brother's accusing eyes without flinching. "Since you seem to have all the answers," he uttered, "what do you think I should do?"

Leon lifted his chin, meeting Trey's angry gaze straight on. "How can you say that? All I've done is try to be supportive of you."

"Sounds to me like you're trying to be my parent."

Leon shook his head. "If you want to feel sorry for yourself—that's on you, Trey. You have some real issues and drinking isn't going to solve them. You're starting to attack the people who love you." He stood up. "I've tried so hard to be here for you, but you obviously don't want my help." Leon shook his head again sadly.

"Leon…don't leave," Trey said. "Look, I know you're right about everything. I'm sorry."

"You don't know how badly I want to help you through this." Leon put his hands to his face and sighed.

"That's just it. You can't. I need some time and space to process everything."

"But there are people who can—you refused help from the VA, from your doctor here…even Gia's offered her assistance. Trey, you talk about how we can't understand what you're going through. Let me tell you what your family is dealing with," Leon stated. "You can't imagine what it did to me to receive a call notifying me that you were wounded in action. The person who called couldn't tell me anything except that he wasn't a medical professional and couldn't offer any details. Here I was…scared, with no real answers. The mere thought of losing you… There are no words to describe what I was feeling. Not to mention what it would do to Aunt Eleanor." He sat back down in a nearby chair. "My wife had to step in and take over because I couldn't think straight."

A tear rolled down Leon's cheek. "Man, I thought I'd never see you again."

"Leon…" Trey's voice broke. He choked back his own tears. It tore at his emotions to see his brother like this. Leon had always been the strong one—his big brother.

"Don't," he interjected. "I need you to hear me out. Aunt Eleanor had to be sedated to keep her calm. She wanted to fly to Germany to be by your side, but we were advised to wait and travel to Walter Reed. They gave us this manual with instructions on travel, lodging…even what to bring you and what to expect. I found it helpful, but it just seemed to upset Auntie—she was so worried about you, Trey."

Guilt over his behavior washed over him. "I didn't know," Trey said, "but seeing you and her… I was happy even if you couldn't tell. I know Auntie gave everybody a fit."

Leon nodded. "You should've heard her going off when we were told they weren't flying us to Germany. She told Rusty she was going to pay for her own ticket because she had to be there for you."

"I'm surprised y'all were able to convince her otherwise."

"We didn't. Her doctor advised against it. Her blood pressure spiked. He didn't think it was wise."

Trey swallowed hard. He felt bad for worrying his aunt like that. "I really don't remember a whole lot of what happened there. I just opened my eyes one day and found out I was at Walter Reed."

"We knew you were in a lot of pain. Emotionally and physically. We were just relieved to be able to see you for ourselves."

"I'm really sorry. I have to admit that I never once considered how y'all were affected."

"I'm not discounting your feelings. I hope

you know that. You're the only brother I have. I want us to grow old together."

"I just wish the pain would go away," Trey blurted. "I want to write letters to the families... I don't have the words. Just saying I'm sorry isn't enough."

"The words will come to you. Give it some time," Leon advised.

"I drink to escape the pain. Not so much the physical pain..." Trey confessed. He was a bit embarrassed to admit it, but his thoughts often threatened to overtake him in those long hours of solitude at night. He wasn't so sure he could fight them off without the alcohol. "I know what you're thinking, so you don't have to say it."

"What can I do to help you?"

"Nothing. It's just something I have to work through."

"And the physical pain?"

Trey pointed to the mirror on the nightstand. "Gia told me about a treatment to help reduce the phantom limb pain."

"Does it work?" asked Leon.

"Yeah. It's called mirror therapy and it works. It's not as bad as it was before."

"Really?"

Trey nodded.

"That was nice of her, but I'm not surprised. Gia's always had a heart to help others."

He couldn't disagree. "I thought about calling her later. I'm thinking I should really consider physical therapy."

"It's a good idea, little brother."

"You're so predictable," Trey said. "I knew you would say that."

"You forgot to mention that I'm never wrong," Leon teased.

"That's because you've only been right a few times."

They burst into laughter.

Later, as he watched his brother drive away, Trey was glad he'd been able to clear the air with Leon. He'd meant what he said about reaching out to Gia. The technique she'd freely suggested to help with the pain, her support without expecting anything in return, and now hearing what his family had gone through only served to confirm that he owed it to not only them but to himself to work toward improving his quality of life.

GIA HUNG UP the phone. "That was the hospital," she told Patricia. "They offered me the job, but the salary is much lower than I expected. I told Carol I'd get back to her by the end of today."

"Sweetie, you don't have to accept that position. You just have to be patient that the right one will come along."

Her phone vibrated.

Gia answered it.

"This is Trey."

She broke into a smile. "How are you?"

"I'm okay," he responded. "Do you have some time in your schedule to come by the house this afternoon? I'd like to talk to you about PT."

"I don't have anything on my schedule. I can be there in about five to ten minutes."

"That's fine."

"Great," Gia said. I'll see you soon."

She hung up, shouting, *"Yes!"*

"What happened?" Patricia asked.

"That was Trey. He wants to discuss PT."

"That's wonderful. See… I told you that he'd come around."

Gia pressed a hand to her chest. "I'm actually stunned. Trey was adamant about not doing PT. I wonder what changed his mind."

"It doesn't matter," Patricia said. "You'd better get going before the man changes his mind."

Laughing, Gia picked up her tote. "See you later, Mama."

Trey was on the porch when she arrived.

"Thanks for coming so quickly," he said when she climbed out of her SUV.

"I have to admit that this is a call I wasn't expecting."

He chuckled. "I never intended to make it,

but I've been giving it a lot of thought. I realize things can only get better. Not worse."

She sat down in one of the white rocking chairs. "I realize this is a huge step for you, Trey."

"Okay…so let's discuss money first. I need to know if I can even afford you before I make this commitment."

"I will say that private pay physical therapy is more cost-effective compared to insurance-based PT. However, I'm licensed in South Carolina and in good standing, so your insurance shouldn't have a problem covering the costs, since it's medically necessary."

"That's good to know."

"Have you noticed any stiffness?"

"Yeah," Trey responded. "In my knees and in my hip."

"That needs to be addressed because contractures can become permanent, which would make it difficult to wear a prosthesis. I can show you some stretching and positioning exercises to help maintain normal range of motion."

"How soon can we get started?" he asked.

"How about Monday, after the long weekend? That will give me enough time to go over your medical history and get the necessary approvals from your insurance company."

He nodded. "That works for me."

Gia handed him a folder. "I brought some forms that need to be filled out."

"Okay," he said. "Gia… I want you to know that I appreciate you for not gloating."

"You're my friend. I want to see you living life to the fullest—the way you used to," she stated. "This is not a quick fix. It's just the beginning." Gia looked at him. "I'm so excited for you."

"Of course, you are," he said dryly. "I thought you'd outgrow some of this bubbly, cheer squad stuff."

She laughed. "It's in my blood, Trey. You can consider me your very own personal cheerleader."

RUSTY AND ELEANOR hosted a Fourth of July barbecue for family and a few close friends.

"I called Gia." Trey said when Leon joined him on the patio. "I called her the same day you and I talked. I have my first session on Monday. She wanted to wait until after the holiday. Get everything processed so there wouldn't be any delays."

Leon smiled. "That's great."

"She explained why I was experiencing all this stiffness. I need to do stretches every day. I realize that I should've been taking PT all along." Trey regretted taking so long to come to this decision. He would've been further along by now.

"At least you're starting on Monday. Better late than never."

"I may have made it harder on myself, though," Trey stated. "The only PT I had was at the hospital—they wouldn't have released me otherwise. The therapist there basically taught me how to roll in bed and move from there to the chair. They showed me some stretching and stuff, but I haven't been doing them."

"I'm sure they see cases like this a lot."

"I'm still trying to find my bearings. I just want to feel like myself. But then there are times when I don't want to feel anything."

To lighten the mood, Trey broke into a grin. "I wonder if I can get Gia to wear her high school cheerleading outfit instead of scrubs. She said she was my personal cheerleader."

"Some advice, little brother. Don't say that around her. You might get punched in the face."

"I wouldn't," he said. "It was just a joke."

Leon shook his head. "Naw, you were serious. I know you, remember."

They laughed.

Deep down Trey was more interested in being around Gia than enduring who knew how many hours of rigorous exercise. Although he'd already learned how to roll in bed, sit on the side and to move to the wheelchair, Trey decided that he could still benefit from PT in some way.

Mostly, he would get to spend time with Gia. Her enthusiastic nature was infectious. She made him laugh and she didn't pressure him to talk about his feelings. He could be himself with Gia—it had always been this way and he was glad it hadn't changed.

TREY WAS UP early Monday morning. He was ripped away from sleep in the middle of the night by the loud roar of thunder, which had prompted flashbacks to overtake him. Outside, trees swayed violently as the wind blew and the rain poured from the heavens like a girl sobbing over her first real heartbreak.

He started drinking at 4 a.m. hoping the alcohol would lull him back to sleep, but every angry, thunderous boom made him jumpy, a residual tremor left from that fateful day.

Trey slipped on earphones to listen to music. He sat up in bed bobbing his head to the rhythm but even that failed to soothe him.

He eyed the card on his nightstand. He'd received it the day before the Fourth of July holiday. Filled with words meant to be encouraging and signed by everyone in his platoon. However, there were three signatures missing: those of Jenkins, Hudson and Mitchell.

He released a deep sigh.

If only I could go back to that day.

Trey replayed it over and over in his mind, trying to connect the dots. *How could the insurgents get close enough to ambush us?* They had to have had help from some of the locals.

He drank from the bottle, determined to finish it off. Trey needed to get rid of the evidence in case Leon had Renee spying on him.

Now I'm being paranoid. My brother wouldn't do something like that to me.

The rain dissipated around 5:30 a.m.

Feeling somewhat at ease, Trey turned off his music and lay down, hoping to sleep for a couple of hours. He needed to have his mind right by the time Gia arrived.

CHAPTER NINE

"GOOD MORNING," GIA greeted brightly when Renee opened the door.

"Morning to you, too. I have to run, but Trey's in his room. I heard him moving about, so I know he's up."

Gia stepped inside and headed toward his bedroom then knocked on the door. "Trey, it's me."

"Come in," he called.

She studied his face after opening the door. Fatigue had settled in pockets under his eyes. "Are you feeling okay?"

"I'm f-fine…"

His words came out slurred.

"Have you been drinking?" Gia asked. A wave of disappointment washed over her.

"Yeah," Trey said. "I had a bad night."

"The storm?" She wasn't surprised that the heavy rain made him uncomfortable. The thunder left her a bit shaken as well, but with Trey dealing with PTSD—his fears were magnified.

He nodded.

Arms folded across her chest, Gia stated, "Alcohol isn't going to help you."

He grinned. "It makes me feel good."

"Did you call the VA Hospital like I suggested?"

Trey shook his head. "I don't need counseling, Gia. Right now, I just need to lie down. My incisions feel like they're on fire."

"Did you take the pain meds?"

"No. I was drinking."

Gia held back her frustration. "This is not the way I expected things to start. I know that you're hurting emotionally, too, but the healing has to start somewhere."

His facial features were contorted in anguish. "I'm trying."

"I know you are, but I'm gonna need you to try harder." She paused a moment, quietly assessing his condition. "Why don't you rest today? I'll come back tomorrow."

"For your information, I didn't intend for this to happen," Trey said.

"Take some aspirin. It should help with your headache. Before I leave, I want to check the wound area for swelling." Gia pulled his covers back, revealing his boxers.

"What if I weren't wearing anything?" he asked her.

"Then I hope you're not shy." She slipped on

a pair of gloves and deftly removed his bandages. "I'm going to rewrap your limbs with elastic bandages to help control swelling and help the incisions heal. I'm also going to put on shrinker socks. These will assist in shaping your amputated leg."

"How long do I wear them?"

"Anywhere from six to twelve months," Gia responded.

"Wow, that's tight," he uttered when she'd finished.

"They're supposed to fit snugly to apply pressure to the soft tissue of your limb." Gia straightened up, then removed the gloves. "Get some rest. We'll get started tomorrow. No excuses or exceptions."

"I didn't know you were so bossy."

Gia smiled. "You haven't seen anything yet."

She'd given him a pass this time because of what led to the drinking. The bad weather last night had triggered Trey—likely igniting flashbacks of the explosion. Like her father, he'd resorted to alcohol to help him relax.

She hoped tomorrow would be a better day for him.

"GOOD MORNING, TREY," Gia said the next morning, entering his bedroom without knocking.

"Is it?" he asked, shielding his eyes from

the sun when she drew back the curtains and opened the blinds. "What are you doing?"

"Letting in some sunlight and fresh air. Looks like you're dealing with another hangover?"

Trey didn't answer. He felt achy and exhausted. Nightmares had plagued him again last night until he'd reached for the bottle of rum. He drank until he couldn't keep his eyes open.

"Get dressed," Gia said. "It's time to do your stretching exercises, unless you prefer to do them in your underwear."

He groaned. "I don't really feel like it." Trey felt as hollow as his voice sounded.

"Trey, you committed to this regimen."

"I'm just not up to it right now," he snapped. He thought he was ready for PT but now Trey wasn't sure. Was it really worth all the pain he'd have to endure? Maybe it was just too soon. He needed more time.

Gia lifted her chin, meeting his icy gaze straight on. "What you're not gonna do is talk to me like that," she countered. "I know what you're trying to do, Trey. You want me to walk away. To give up on you, but that's not gonna happen."

She headed to the door. "I'll be in the living room *waiting* on you. But first I'll make you a cup of red ginseng tea. It should help you recover from your hangover."

Trey sat up in bed. Gia meant what she said. He knew she'd be outside his bedroom waiting.

He made his way into his wheelchair and went to the bathroom, regretting his decision to take physical therapy in the first place. But then he thought about his family, and Trey didn't want to let them down.

He didn't want to let Gia down, either.

RENEE WAS IN the kitchen when Gia entered. "Was Trey up?" She was thrilled her cousin had decided to finally agree to physical therapy.

"Not really," Gia responded, "but I made it clear that I'm not leaving. I gave him a pass yesterday, but not this time."

"What happened yesterday?" Renee asked in confusion. "He didn't have his session?" She'd assumed the therapy had gone well when Trey didn't mention it. But then again, she'd gotten in late the night before, so they didn't have too much of a conversation.

"He wasn't up to it." Gia pointed to one of the mugs. "Do you mind if I make a cup of tea? It's for Trey."

"Sure, that's fine. I need to speak to him before I leave for work." Renee walked out of the kitchen. She was going to talk some sense into Trey.

He had just gotten out of the shower when she burst into his room.

A towel over his lap, Trey demanded, "Hey, can a man get some privacy around here?"

Renee glared at him. "I can't believe you…"

"What?"

"All Gia's trying to do is help you. She told me you didn't do your PT session yesterday and then you weren't even prepared this morning. Why are you acting like this?"

"I had a bad night, Renee," he responded.

"I love you dearly," she said, "but if you're going to act like this, then you don't need to waste Gia's time. She could be working with a patient who actually wants her help." Placing both hands on her hips, she ordered, "You're a *marine*. Act like one!"

RENEE'S WORDS HAD the desired effect on Trey. "Rah…" he muttered. His cousin was right. Despite all that had happened, he was still a marine. That would never change. His actions needed to reflect this truth.

"If you'd give me some privacy, I can get dressed," Trey said begrudgingly.

"Good. Don't keep Gia waiting too long. I'm about to head to the boutique, but I expect to hear all about how hard she worked you during PT when I get home later this evening."

"I'm sure my body will be protesting in pure agony," he said.

"You got this, cousin."

He gave her a grateful smile. "Thank you, Renee." She had every right to be irritated with him—Gia, as well. He was being difficult. He felt bad about his actions and vowed to turn things around from this moment forward.

"See you later tonight. I shouldn't be too late." Renee left the room, closing the door behind her.

A few moments later, Trey wheeled himself into the living room. "Let's get started."

Seated on the couch, Gia handed him the mug. "Drink this while I check your incisions."

She had a firm but gentle touch.

"You're still a bit swollen. Are you icing like you're supposed to?"

"I am," Trey said.

She picked up a black bag and unzipped it. "I'm going to change your compression bandages."

When she was done, Gia explained, "The first phase of this therapy is pre-prosthetic training. We focus on your range of motion, knee flexion, stretching and strength training." To help with manage his pain, she explained they'd also do manual therapy, which included joint manipulation and soft tissue mobilization.

"I read in your medical report that you told

the doctors at Walter Reed you didn't want to be fitted for a prosthesis."

"Not at that time," Trey said, trying not to flinch as she had him perform a couple of stretches. "I was in a lot of p-pain."

"I think you should reconsider your decision. Most people who've had transtibial amputations do well with them."

"Is it too late?" Trey asked.

"No, when your incisions are pretty much healed, you can have it done then. You're gonna also have to have a sufficient amount of strength to be able to walk with a prosthesis. Right now, the immediate goal is to get you to master wheelchair mobility."

Trey met her gaze. "Do you really think I'll be able to walk again?" He trusted Gia to tell him the straight truth. He didn't want the possibilities—he wanted a more definitive answer.

"I do. You may need to use an assistive device such as a cane, but yes…you'll be able to walk and become more independent."

"I guess we'd better get busy then," Trey said. He was hopeful for the first time since the incident. Just the idea of being able to stand up and walk around the house, walk on the beach… A thread of excitement snaked down his back.

Grinning, Gia replied, "I've been waiting on you."

Halfway through the hour, Trey was in pain and ready to quit.

"C'mon…it pays to be a winner," Gia said.

He looked over at her and smiled. He'd used that same phrase to push his teams to their maximum potential during physical training on base.

With renewed resolve, he pressed through the rest of the session.

TREY SURVIVED THE first two weeks of grueling physical therapy. He found himself looking forward to Tuesdays and Thursdays—days he didn't have PT.

He kept watching the clock because he was looking forward to his visits with Leon and the family. He'd wanted to order dinner, but Misty volunteered to cook—an offer he wasn't about to turn down.

Leon used his key to enter.

Talei was the first one inside, pushing past Leon. "*Osiyo*, Uncle."

"Hello, cutie," he said, hugging her. "I'm so glad you came to see me."

"I missed you." Pointing to the bandages below his knees, she asked, "Does it still hurt?"

"Sometimes," he told her. "But it's getting better."

"Will you come see me dance at the powwow in Charleston?" Talei asked.

"I'll do my best to attend." Deep down, Trey wanted to be there for his niece but wanted to avoid the displays of sympathy he often glimpsed in the faces of strangers.

Talei interrupted his thoughts. "Do you want to play a game with me?"

Trey smiled. "Sure. What are we playing?" He loved being around his niece. She always brought a smile to his face.

Talei broke into a wide grin. "Go Fish."

"I hope you're ready to lose."

She shook her head. "I'm not gonna lose, Uncle. I beat Dad all the time."

"I used to beat your dad all the time, too."

"Sweetie, don't believe that," Leon said from the doorway of the living room.

Talei retrieved a deck of cards from her backpack.

Trey shuffled them, then dealt seven cards to them both. He placed the remaining cards face down in a pile.

"Talei, you can go first."

She smiled. "Uncle, give me all your fours…"

Thirty minutes later, when they were at the dinner table, Leon leaned over and asked in a whisper, "How many times did you let her win?"

"Let her win?" Trey repeated. "Only the first time. Talei was on it tonight."

"I hear Gia's not taking it easy on you at all."

"She's not," he confirmed. "As much as I enjoy seeing her three days a week…man, I can't wait for her to go home."

Leon chuckled. "Whatever she's doing must be working. You're looking better."

"I'm definitely getting stronger," Trey said. "And I can work this chair without wearing myself out."

He sampled the roast beef. "Misty, this is delicious."

"Thank you. I'm glad you're enjoying it," she said.

"More potatoes, Mommy…please," Talei said.

Misty spooned some onto her plate. "Here you go."

"*Wado.*"

"*Hawa*, sweetie."

Trey knew that Talei had thanked her mother in Cherokee. "*Hawa* means you're welcome?" he asked. Misty's mother, Oma, was full-blooded Cherokee and had taught her daughter and granddaughter the Tsalagi language. A former performer in powwows, Oma had also passed on her love of dancing to both Misty and Talei.

Misty nodded. "Yes, it does."

He spent the next couple of hours talking with Leon and Misty while playing with Leo and

Talei. Trey was grateful for the company. This was one of the rare times he didn't want to be home alone with his thoughts.

He'd managed to get through the days and nights without so much as a drink in the past twelve days. Probably because Gia worked him to the point of near exhaustion. Trey hadn't realized just how out of shape he'd gotten, but he wasn't going to give up. He didn't want to disappoint Gia or himself.

After his brother left with Misty and the children, Trey went to his room.

He'd just prepared for bed and turned on the television when his cell phone rang.

Just as he answered, news flashed across the screen of another explosive ambush in Afghanistan. Trey began to shake as the fearful images built in his mind.

"Hello… Hello… Rothchild…" a familiar voice on the phone shouted.

Numb, Trey said, "Greg…tell me what happened." His stomach was clenched tight.

"I was hoping to reach you before you saw it on the news. They found the insurgents responsible."

"It says two people died."

"Trey…"

"Who? Where they from Whiskey Company? *Just tell me.*"

The room seemed to do a slow spin and he began to tremble.

"Yeah."

"Who?" Trey demanded.

"Barco and Sykes."

Trey uttered a string of profanities as a wave of profound grief washed over him.

"I'm sorry, brother."

Tears ran down his face. He swiped at them. "You said they found the ones responsible?"

"Yeah. They're the same ones who took credit for what happened to you and the others."

It didn't make Trey feel any better. "Barco's only been married for a couple of years. He just became a father in February. It ain't right…"

"I know this doesn't help, but at least they did take down the insurgents in that area. They were being helped by one of the locals."

After the call, Trey sat there for hours just staring off into space. He felt a numbness spreading within.

A SHADOW OF annoyance passed through Gia when she took one glance at Trey, studying him. "You've been drinking again."

She could tell he'd detected the hint of censure in her tone. "A-And…" Trey slurred. "So w-what…" Pointing to the door, Trey said, "Then you can leave."

Gia sensed there was something more going on with him, prompting his rude behavior. "What's really going on with you? I'm not leaving, so you might as well talk to me."

"Did you hear about the attack yesterday in Afghanistan where two marines died?"

"Yes..." she responded cautiously. A wave of apprehension flowed through Gia. She dreaded hearing what Trey was about to tell her.

"They were my brothers. From my platoon." Water filled his eyes. "I wake up each morning thinking this has been a terrible dream. I can still feel the shock of the explosion. I remember waking up in the hospital from an induced coma...taking one look at the bandages and crying. I'd lost my legs, my entire team. Just when I started to feel just a measure of normalcy—I lose two more brothers. You can't understand what that feels like, Gia."

"I haven't experienced what you have, but Trey, I do understand it because my father went through something similar. He lost his best friend during the war and the use of his arm. One thing's for sure—getting drunk won't help. Too much alcohol makes it harder to cope with stress and your trauma memories. Getting drunk can actually increase some PTSD symptoms."

"It's the only thing that makes me feel better."

"Is it that you feel better or feel nothing at all?" Gia challenged. "Be honest with yourself."

Rubbing his temple, Trey grimaced. "I have a headache."

"I'm sure you do." Gia headed toward the kitchen. "I'll get you a tall glass of water."

"Thank you," she heard him call.

When Gia returned, she said, "I'm getting rid of every bottle of alcohol on this floor."

"You can't throw away my stuff."

"I'm not throwing it away—just giving it to Renee for safekeeping." She didn't want Trey drinking each time he had to face his trauma. He had to find a better way to respond.

A few minutes later, Gia sat down on the sofa. "Talk to me, Trey. What happened after you realized your life was going to be different?"

"As far as I was concerned, it was over," he stated. "I couldn't see past all that happened. After I was flown to Landstuhl, Germany, I was there for a few days when this marine—he was an amputee—came into my room. I knew he was there to try to offer me something I was lacking…hope."

"You must have had a glimmer of hope," Gia said. "Or you wouldn't be here today."

"I guess he planted the seed. It just hasn't grown."

"My dad was flown to Walter Reed when

he was injured. He told me about the C-17 and how it's equipped with medical staff and double bunks on both sides."

Trey nodded. "They had me in the back of the plane. That's where they put the critical care patients. I have to say the CCAT team—they were professional and took good care of us."

"CCAT," Gia repeated.

"Critical care air transport team," he explained. "They had me wrapped so tight in blankets—I felt like I was in a cocoon. I do remember the plane being really cold..."

Gia smiled. "I remember my dad saying it was like a refrigerator. He talked about the men and women on the flight buried under quilts decorated with flags, eagles—symbols of patriotism. All reminders of how he'd ended up in the war."

She shifted her position on the sofa. "I was in college studying psychology at the time. When I came home, I could tell Dad was self-medicating with alcohol. He refused to see a therapist. My dad and I were very close, but he shut me out. At one point, I wasn't sure my parents' marriage would survive."

"I guess you and your mom were able to get him some help."

"Actually, it was my dad who made the decision that he needed help. One day he suddenly realized how he'd changed after the incident. He addressed his trauma and decided he needed therapy to recover."

"Did it work?" Trey asked.

"It did," Gia responded. "You have to decide what happens next. My question to you, Trey… are you really ready to commit to physical therapy? I ask this because it's not going to be easy, but I promise you that it's worth the pain you're gonna feel."

He groaned, then said, "Let's do this. I'm as ready as I'll ever be."

Pleased she'd been able to get through to him, Gia responded, "Then let's start with some stretching."

CHAPTER TEN

TREY WAS A JUMPY, fidgety, shaky mess.

Gia seemed to be on a mission to make him feel worse than he already did. On top of that, she'd taken all the bottles of rum, brandy and vodka upstairs. Without booze, he was unable to escape the unwanted thoughts, the vivid images recorded in his mind or the nightmares. Guilt seeped from his pores whenever he thought about his team—which was all the time.

I would give anything to go back in time to save them.

We were on patrol. How did I miss the danger signals?

Why didn't I notice that something wasn't quite right?

There had to be a timing device on the vehicle, but there had to be someone close by to fire that rocket.

They wanted us dead.

"That's enough for today," Gia said, pulling him out of his reverie. "Trey, you did a great job despite the rough start. I appreciate your opening up to me."

She had always been a good listener. Maybe that was why it'd been easy for him to open up to her earlier. "Thank you for listening. I guess I just needed to purge. I appreciate you telling me about your father. I had no idea."

"I know. Dad kept mostly to himself after that last tour. After therapy, he started to resume activities he loved and spent time with friends... Trey, I'm here if you ever need to talk about anything. We're still friends." She adjusted the ice packs on his knees. "I'll see you on Monday. I hope you have a good weekend."

"You, too," Trey said. "You have any special plans?"

"I'm going to a wedding in Savannah..." Gia groaned. "I forgot... I still need to find a formal gown."

"Reach out to Renee," he suggested. "I'm sure she'll be able to help you. If she doesn't have it—she'll make one for you."

"I'll stop by after I see my next patient. I really hope she has something on the rack I can buy."

Gia picked up the roomy tote off the sofa and headed to the door. "See you later."

"Good luck," Trey called out.

"Thanks," she responded on her way out.

Trey was too tired to move at the moment. His muscles ached; he felt as if his breath was cut off.

The tension in his body relaxed as his pain medication began working.

He'd just been with her, and yet Gia floated into his mind. Despite his rudeness, she'd listened to him and tried to comfort him as a friend. A smile tugged at Trey's lips. She'd wasted no time setting him straight. He loved a woman who spoke her mind and had no problem standing up for herself. He found himself drawn to her even more. No woman had ever made him feel like Gia did—her faith in him seemed immeasurable even when he lacked it in himself. She had always been his cheerleader.

He was glad to have her back in his life.

"HEY, YOU," RENEE greeted when Gia entered the boutique that afternoon. "You look a bit frazzled."

"I really need your help. I need the perfect dress for a friend's wedding tomorrow."

"What do you have in mind?"

"Formal," Gia said. "And it has to be white. For some reason, the bride wants all of the wedding guests to wear white."

She knew Renee and Trey were close, so she decided his cousin should be aware of his drinking. "By the way," Gia stated. "I don't know if you know, but Trey's been drinking. I took his stash and put it upstairs in the linen closet near your bedroom. Renee, he shouldn't be drinking any alcohol. For one, he's taking meds, and two, it could worsen his PTSD symptoms."

"I know. Leon talked to him about it," Renee said. "I looked around the main level, but I couldn't find where he was getting it. I'm pretty sure Jay from next door must be the one buying it for him. Trey mentions that Jay does come by the house to see if he needs anything."

"Maybe you can ask your neighbor not to buy any more alcohol."

Renee nodded. "I feel terrible. I just had no idea. I've been so busy focusing on my new line and a couple of upcoming weddings."

"It's not your fault," Gia assured her. "Trey's apparently been doing it behind your back anyway." Shaking her head, she added, "He had bottles hidden in his nightstand, closet—even in the bathroom. I think I found them all. I have to admit I was a bit surprised to find so many bottles."

"Do you think I should check his room from time to time?" Renee inquired.

"I don't want there to be friction between you two. Let Leon handle Trey," Gia suggested. "I'm hoping I was able to get through to him this morning, but we'll see."

As if something clicked in Renee's mind, she said, "You know… I think I have the perfect dress for you."

Renee walked to the back of her shop and returned with a white dress. "What do you think of this?"

"It's beautiful," Gia said.

"Try it on," Renee suggested.

She went into a nearby dressing room and slipped out of her clothes. Gia put on the gown, then smiled at her reflection. The floor-length, one-shoulder charmeuse evening gown with cascading ruffles fit as if it had been made just for her. She turned her back to the mirror and glanced over her shoulder to view the back.

It was perfect.

She walked out of the fitting room, saying, "*I love it*. I'll get it."

"Do you have time for lunch?" Renee asked when Gia changed back into her clothes in a booth. "I'm starving."

"Actually, I'm pretty hungry myself."

They walked next door to the café and sat down in a booth.

"I'll have a turkey club," Renee told their server.

"Chef's salad for me," Gia said, "Ranch on the side, please."

Renee's phone began to vibrate. She glanced down and sighed. "This woman is getting on my last nerve."

Gia chuckled. "Do you have a bridezilla?"

"I do, but this isn't her. In fact, you know the person I'm talking about—Cindy Latham. I'm designing a gown for her and when I tell you that this woman is so picky, and she has no idea what she wants—she keeps changing her mind. If she keeps it up, I won't be able to finish her dress by the deadline."

"Cindy *is* something else," Gia stated without emotion. "She was worse than Chris and he was the one who was my patient." She hoped to never see the woman again in her life.

"I can only imagine what that was like," Renee responded. "The first time I met him, while his wife was in the dressing room, the man had the nerve to flirt with me. Chris actually invited me to meet him for a private dinner in a hotel suite."

"Same here," Gia admitted. She wasn't surprised to hear this. Chris's reputation as a womanizer was well known. "When I was working with him, he was constantly trying to seduce me. When his wife caught him—he had the nerve to tell her I was the one trying to seduce him. She's the reason I was blackballed in Charlotte. Cindy told all of my clients that I was after her husband. She even called the clinic I worked with."

Renee frowned. "Is that why you came home to the island? Because of that jerk?"

"Yes. The only other person who knows about this is my mom."

Renee covered Gia's hand with her own. "Your secret is safe with me. As for Mrs. Latham, I'm not sure I want to work with her."

"Girl, get your money. I'm not worried about Cindy. If she tries to start this mess up again… the truth will come out. Trust me… I have receipts."

Renee smiled. "I'm sure you do. He isn't discreet at all."

When they finished eating, Gia said. "This is my treat. I wouldn't have such a beautiful gown if it wasn't for you. I love my dress."

Gia signaled for the server to bring their check.

"Thanks for lunch," Renee said. "At least let me leave the tip."

When they walked out, Gia suggested, "We should do a girls' night out with Misty and my friend Shelley."

"Just let me know when and where, and I'm there."

THE FOLLOWING MONDAY, Gia surprised Trey with a bag of his favorite chocolate chip cookies.

"Is this a bribe?" The warmth of his smile echoed in his voice.

"Think of it more like a reward," she responded. Studying him, Gia added, "You look relaxed."

"I went to bed and didn't wake up until this morning. No nightmares. First time that's happened without drinking."

"That's wonderful, Trey."

"You want me to start with stretching?"

"Yes." It thrilled her to see glimpses of the Trey she remembered. At one point she'd feared he'd lost all hope but looking at that shimmer of excitement in his eyes, she was certain something had changed.

"How was the wedding?" he asked.

"Expensive and very glitzy. The bride wore a silver wedding dress while all the guests wore white. It was nice, but I would never spend that kind of money for a wedding." Gia eyed him. "How was *your* weekend?"

"Outstanding. I sat on the patio and read my book, did some people-watching and listened to music. On Sunday, Renee and I had dinner with Rusty and Aunt Eleanor."

"I'm glad you left the house," she said. "A change of scenery helps you mentally."

"Do you have any more patients today?" Trey asked.

"Nope, I'm free. What's up?"

"Do you mind hanging around a little longer? I'd rather not be alone. I'm enjoying this feeling of being relaxed and I don't want it to end… Not yet. I can order something to eat."

"Why don't I just cook?" Gia suggested.

"Really?" Trey asked, grinning.

Gia chuckled. "You can wipe that grin off your face. I've been known to cook a meal or two."

"I remember that time when you tried to fry fish."

"I was eighteen, and I didn't know I was supposed to coat it." Gia laughed at the memory.

In the kitchen, she looked to see what was in the refrigerator and the cabinets. "Looks like you have everything I need to make a quick casserole. What do you think about Southwestern chicken?"

"Sure. I'll do what I can to help."

She was thrilled to be spending time with Trey outside of their sessions. Trey had always been a lot of fun to be around. Gia loved that charismatic smile, the mischievous twinkle in his gaze as he teased her. She missed this side of Trey, but tonight there was a glimpse of his former self.

After placing the casserole dish in the oven, Gia suggested, "It's a nice evening—do you want to go sit on the patio?"

"Sure."

Outside, Gia sat down in a chair closest to where Trey parked his wheelchair.

"Sometimes, the quiet becomes almost unbearable," he stated. "Especially when the memories of them replay in my brain over and over."

"It takes time," Gia reassured him. "It's normal to have upsetting memories after what you've been through, but you can't live in that space. You have to find a way to fight against those feelings and move forward."

"Is it normal to not want to feel anything?"

"Avoidance is a common reaction to trauma," Gia explained. "When my dad came home from the Gulf War, he wouldn't talk about anything. He wasn't much of a drinker, but suddenly he always had a bottle of Jack Daniels in his hand. My mom used to call me crying and it bothered me that I couldn't do anything to help." Gia felt her eyes fill with tears. "Braxton and Dad weren't getting along at that time, I'd never felt so helpless." She didn't like thinking back to that dark period. Instead, Gia wanted to focus on the good times they'd shared as a family.

"I want you to know that it was your father who inspired me to join the Marines."

That surprised Gia. "I didn't know that."

"I looked up to him." Trey chuckled. "Whenever your dad was home, he would come to the park and challenge us to a game of basketball or football…whatever we were playing at the time. Your brother used to always get upset whenever Mr. Eugene didn't pick him. He liked to alternate players, so that we all had a chance to play on his team."

"Braxton wanted to win," Gia said. "He knew that with Dad, he had a chance at it."

"Is he still in the Marines?"

"As far as I know," she replied with a slight shrug. "We haven't heard from my brother since the day we buried Dad. Mom and I reached out a couple of times but never heard back."

"Really?"

"I think Braxton took our father's death very hard. He's always wanted Dad to himself. I think it's because of his parents' divorce. I had Dad full-time, but Braxton only had snippets of time with him." Gia knew her father loved his son as much as he loved her. He and Braxton would've had a closer relationship if it weren't for his mother's interference. Gia hated the separation she felt from him but hoped in time Braxton would one day come back around.

She stood up. "I need to check on our dinner. Burning it will not leave a good impression."

"Yeah, because you know I'll talk about you. What's it called again?"

"Southwestern casserole."

Trey's smiled widened in approval. "It smells wonderful, but I'll have to see how it tastes."

Gia removed it from the oven and sat it on the counter. "You do remember I'm your physical therapist."

Trey laughed.

Five minutes later, they were seated at the table, prepared to eat.

"This looks and smells so great," Trey murmured. He scooped some up and stuck it in his mouth.

Gia smiled when Trey nodded in approval.

He wiped his mouth on his napkin. "This is delicious."

"Thank you," she said. "This is the least I can do after our session earlier. I'm letting you know that I'm not cooking for you after each workout."

"Why not?"

Gia quirked a brow. "Cooking isn't included in my fee."

"Thank you for dinner and your company," he told her. "Seriously…thank you for everything. I know I've been a jerk… I'm really sorry."

She could see the sincerity in his gaze. "We're not gonna look back in the rearview mirror, Trey."

"I appreciate that."

"You're making progress. I'm so proud of you," Gia said.

She kept him company until Renee came home. She wanted to make sure Trey was okay and that he didn't resort to alcohol. Although she'd taken all the bottles she'd found upstairs, he was smart enough to purchase more and have it delivered the same way he'd done in the past.

"I'm not going to drink, if that's what you're worried about," Trey said, cutting into her thoughts. "I give you my word."

Gia awarded him a smile. "I believe you."

Although she didn't really want to leave, Gia felt comfortable doing so now that his cousin was home. Trey seemed in good spirits when she left. He was progressing well in his rehabilitation. She hoped that Trey would continue to remain positive about his future.

Gia felt a certain sadness as she neared her house. She already missed Trey's laughter, that sexy grin of his and the mischievous twinkle he'd get in his eyes whenever he teased her.

She felt that familiar, eager affection she'd felt for him when they were in school. It was as if nothing had changed over the years. She remembered the first and only kiss they'd shared during his freshman year. Although she was a junior at the time—he'd been the first to kiss

Gia. The first to hold her in his arms and the first to make her feel as if her blood was on fire.

I can't get distracted.

She made a mental note that while Trey was her friend, he was currently her patient—there were certain boundaries she could not cross.

TREY HATED TO see Gia leave. He hated the quiet—especially feeling the way he did: anxious, jumpy and filled with a deep sense of dread.

Alone, he felt bereft and distant. Trey considered reaching out to Rusty or Leon, but he didn't want to lay his problems on them. He refused to unburden himself with Rence, who'd just gotten home and was upstairs in her room. She worked long hours at the boutique and Trey didn't want to invade her space with his issues.

How am I supposed to live like this?

Trey glanced around as if he expected an answer. He sat there in the living room a moment before wheeling himself to his bedroom.

Once he was settled in bed, Trey's mind traveled back to a time after his arrival to Camp Pendleton. He and his friend Greg Bowman had made the trip from Camp Lejeune, North Carolina, to Oceanside, California, together.

They were both excited about living in California, spending free time at the beach, trips to

San Diego and Los Angeles. They had lots of plans to enjoy life.

Trey vividly recalled pulling up at the guard station entry point, going through the motorized barrier and following the directions to the Installation Personnel Administration Center.

Back then, they had no idea what the future held for him.

His cell phone rang. He saw Greg's name on the screen.

"Hey, I was just thinking about you," Trey said. "I was thinking about when we first arrived at Camp Pendleton."

Greg laughed. "We had some good times."

"Yeah, we did," Trey responded.

"Brother, how you doing?"

"Taking it day by day. Some days are better than others."

Trey spent the next hour talking with his friend about life at Camp Pendleton. He still vividly remembered the first day they arrived. Trey had parked and he and Greg had stepped out of the car wearing their khaki shirts and ties with green trousers, then headed into the building together.

"I just got my promotion," Greg told him on the phone.

"Outstanding," Trey said. "All right, Staff

Sergeant Bowman. *Congratulations*, bro. You deserve it."

Trey had planned to make the marines a career accomplishment, although Greg had always said he would stay in until he married and had a family. Greg had grown up fatherless because his dad died while serving the military. He vowed never to put his children through that kind of heartache.

Suddenly Trey felt sleepy. He stifled a yawn.

"Sounds like you're getting tired," Greg said. "I'll call you later in the week to check in."

"Stay out of trouble, Staff Sergeant."

Trey hung up the phone.

He yawned a second time and stretched.

He heard Renee coming down the stairs. When she knocked on his door, Trey released a sigh of relief.

"Come in…"

"You want to watch a movie?" she asked.

"Only if you let me choose it. That last one you picked really sucked."

Renee plopped down on the sofa in his room. "Boy pleeze…you're the one who picked out that wannabe comedy mess…"

Trey was glad to have the company; he needed to hear another person's voice in the house. It kept him from thinking too much.

CHAPTER ELEVEN

"You're healing nicely," Gia said as she massaged around Trey's incisions. "But I can tell something's on your mind,"

Trey met her gaze—dark, sympathetic—as it lingered on him. She seemed to be attempting to look inside his soul. He hated that. He hated her sympathy and broke eye contact with her, not wanting to see any more compassion in the depths of her eyes. He had enough self-pity. Trey didn't need anyone else's.

"Trey…" Gia prompted.

"I was thinking about Laura Hudson. And how she was planning to retire. She just wanted to go home and raise her two children. I've started writing letters of condolences to their families," Trey said. "It's the hardest thing I've ever had to do."

"Is there anything I can do?" Gia asked.

He gave her a sidelong glance. "Can you proofread them for me?" Trey wanted to make sure his sincerity and respect was conveyed in each letter to the families. It had taken him at least six or seven drafts before he was satisfied with each letter. Each note highlighted his unique experiences with each member of his team. Their sacrifice deserved more than some general form letter.

"Sure," she responded with a smile. "It's very nice of you to do this."

"I wish there was something more I could do for the families," Trey said. "I just want everyone to know they are the true heroes." Trey looked at Gia. "Mitchell was a photographer. When we arrived in Helmand, our area was villages made of mud brick houses surrounded by pomegranate orchards, rows of grapes and poppy fields. Some didn't have running water or electricity. Mitchell took some great pictures—they're worthy of being featured in a magazine." He paused a moment, then said, "Now, Jenkins, he was funny. He could've been a comedian. He kept us laughing all the time."

"You have some wonderful memories of your time with them."

"I do," Trey agreed. "Hudson was tough as nails, but she knew when to turn it off. She could be girly when she needed to be, but she was a true marine."

"If they were here, I'm sure they would have some pretty nice things to say about you."

Shadows loomed in his heart, shifting his

mood to sadness. "That's just it, Gia. They're not here."

"Misty mentioned that she invited you to the powwow taking place next Saturday in Charleston. Are you going?"

"I haven't made up my mind yet."

"Although you didn't ask for my opinion— I'm giving it anyway," Gia stated. "You really should go. Both Misty and Talei are performing."

"I'd love to see that little girl dance. Talei is so adorable. She and Leo draw pictures for me every week." Just thinking about his niece lightened his mood once more. Trey really didn't want to disappoint Talei.

"I saw some of them on the coffee table," she responded. "You should put them in an album or something."

"I really like that idea." Trey glanced at Gia. "Do you want children?"

"I do. With a husband, as well."

They laughed, then he was suddenly somber.

"Are you thinking about your team again?" she asked.

"Actually, I was thinking about all the things I wanted to do with my family. Teach my children to swim…play sports…" The thought made him feel resigned once again.

"You don't have to give up on that dream," her tone firm but encouraging.

"I can't even take myself to the beach, much less the ocean. You have no idea how much I miss swimming out there."

"Oh, I can imagine," she murmured. "I love the water, too."

"Sometimes it feels like pure torture just sitting on the patio or looking out the window and watching people on the beach enjoying themselves."

"It won't always be this way for you," Gia reassured him. "You have options."

"You mean prosthetics?"

She nodded. "There are some which will enable you to swim like a fish."

"I don't want to get my hopes up." He couldn't bear the disappointment.

"I wouldn't do that to you. Pretty soon we'll get started on shaping your stumps to fit prosthetics. We're going to get you walking again."

Trey smiled. "You're still a cheerleader."

She raised her arms and said, "Go team. Maybe I should bring my pom-poms next time."

"Only if you're wearing a cheer uniform."

Gia shook her head good-naturedly. "I believe you have some type of fetish, Mr. Rothchild," she said as she placed the elastic socks back on his limbs.

Trey held up his hands in a placating gesture. "I'm just joking." Each time he saw her, the pull was stronger. He watched as she packed up her supplies and equipment and tried to come up with a reason for her to stay.

"Great job today, Trey."

"Thanks."

She studied him. "Are you okay?"

"I'm good," he responded, then winked at her mischievously. "Don't forget your outfit and gear on Wednesday."

Laughing, Gia walked out the door.

She had no idea how empty the house suddenly felt without her.

WHEN GIA ARRIVED on Wednesday morning, she was pleasantly surprised to find Trey dressed and ready for his session.

"I've already done my stretching."

Gia reached into her tote. "I brought you some brochures on the Harmony prosthesis. Just for you to have the information. That's the one recommended by your doctor."

"Thanks." He placed them on the coffee table. "I'll look at them when we finish."

At the end of the session, two hours later, Gia iced his knees.

Scanning his face, she asked, "You looked tired. How did you sleep last night?"

"I did okay, but I kept waking up."

Her heart went out to him—she cared about him. But Gia had to bury that under layers of professional distance. And yet it was a struggle to see him in so much pain and not want to offer comfort. "Any dreams?" she asked.

"Not that I can remember." Trey looked up at her. "You know…after the way you just tortured me—you should at least buy me lunch."

"You're right." Gia said. She couldn't control her feelings around him. Not like before. And Trey wasn't anything like Chris, so Gia didn't have to worry about him pressing her into something more than friendship. "How about the café?"

"I'll shower and change."

While she waited for him, Gia scanned through several real estate listings and saved some to explore later. She was searching for a building to house her clinic. A thread of excitement rushed through her at the thought of her dream coming to fruition. The bed-and-breakfast would open by year-end. Now Gia wanted to focus on her clinic, which meant she couldn't afford any distractions.

She heard the sound of the shower and forced her thoughts from wandering to a place she didn't dare tread. As much as she didn't want to acknowledge it—she was attracted to Trey. Nothing could come of her attraction, though.

Gia willingly spent time with him because they were friends and, right now, he needed her. In truth, she knew there was more to it. She felt an overwhelming need to be near him. And when she was, she drank in the comfort of being with a man she respected and cared deeply for.

She couldn't cross the ethical boundary between patient and physical therapist. She was thankful that Trey respected boundaries—a quality she loved about him.

CHAPTER TWELVE

THE POWWOW WAS the first Saturday in August.

Gia followed as Trey wheeled himself outside and down the ramp to the sidewalk. Trey had been given a grant from the VA to purchase an SUV that was wheelchair accessible, and he insisted that they take it to the powwow. "Now whenever you have to transport me—we'll do it in my vehicle."

"No problem." She assisted him up the rear entry ramp.

Logically Trey knew getting out of the house was a step forward—he couldn't stay in the house lost in the past forever. Still, he wasn't at all sure he was ready to face anyone.

Once Gia was in the driver's seat, she said, "I'm really excited. I've never been to a powwow before. I have no idea what to expect."

"According to Misty, it's spiritual more than entertainment," he responded. "She says that it's a place for Natives to strengthen bonds and to honor and preserve their culture. Oh, and we're not supposed to take pictures."

"I'm glad you told me that," Gia said with a chuckle. "I was camera-ready."

They arrived an hour after it began.

Leon had Leo with him when they met him near the food area.

Gia looked awestruck by her surroundings. "Oh, wow…the dancers look amazing. Their outfits look so authentic."

"That's because they are," Leon stated. "Some of them were passed down from generation to generation." Trey noticed her steps slow as she admired their clothing. "Talei is wearing the dress Misty wore when she performed in her first powwow, which was made by my mother-in-law," Leon continued. "Some dancers have new regalia designed using the feathers, beads and ribbons passed down from older generations."

He led them to the area where they would be sitting. "Talei will be dancing in about fifteen minutes."

"Where is she?" Trey asked, his eyes searching.

Pointing, his brother said, "She's over there near the entrance. Talei's behind the head dancer."

"Oh, she looks so adorable," Gia exclaimed. His niece wore a vibrant red dress with yellow and white ribbons sewn around the bottom.

"Did Misty do her hair? I love the way the ribbons and feathers are entwined in her braids."

"Actually, Oma did it. Misty's mom."

"I noticed when we came in there were several women brushing and braiding hair for each other."

"There's a teaching that speaks about how the single strands of hair are weak," Oma said as she joined them. "But when you pull all the hair together in a braid, the hair is strong—this reaffirms the sacredness of family and tribe."

Leon made the introductions. "This is my mother-in-law, Oma Brightwater."

Oma embraced Gia, then planted a kiss on Trey's cheek. "I'm so glad y'all decided to come."

"Misty, what do you call what you're wearing?" Trey inquired when she walked up.

She was dressed in a long buckskin dress adorned with beads, shells and ribbons, and carried a shawl draped over her arm, along with a feathered fan in her hand. She wore fully beaded moccasins to match the top of her dress and an eagle feather in her hair.

"This is what the traditional dancers wear," she answered.

They watched Talei dance with the other young ones.

Trey was filled with pride watching his six-year-old niece dance. He was amazed by another boy his niece's age who performed a ground blessing dance.

Afterward, Misty went to line up with the other dancers in her category.

"I'd better go back to my tent," Oma stated. "I have someone watching over everything, but if there's too many customers at one time, she gets overwhelmed."

"It's very nice meeting you," Gia said.

"Same here."

A man walking by gave a slight nod to Trey. "Semper Fi, brother."

"Oorah," Trey responded. He pulled at the neck of his shirt. He was uncomfortable with the attention from other veterans and attendees. Maybe he shouldn't have worn this T-shirt with the Marines insignia emblazoned across the front.

Grinning, Talei came running over.

"Osiyo," she greeted. She hugged Trey, then Gia.

"Uncle, did you see me dance?"

"I sure did, cutie," Trey responded, giving one of her braids a gentle tug. "You were outstanding!"

Fingering the ribbons on her sleeve, she asked, "You like my dress?"

"I love it," Gia interjected. "I heard that your

grandmother made it for your mom and that she wore it for her first dance."

"Mommy says it's a part of our history. I have to change now so that I won't mess it up," Talei said. "Miss Gia, can you take me to the bathroom—Mommy has to dance and Dad's feeding Leo. He's taking too long and I wanna eat a hot dog."

"Sure," Gia responded. "Do you have your clothes with you?"

Talei held up her backpack. "They're in here."

"I'm fine," Trey said. "In fact, I'm going to the food tent with Leon and Leo. Gia, you want anything to eat?" He glanced at Talei. "I already know cutie here wants a hot dog and French fries. She's going to wake up one day to find she's turned into a hot dog."

Talei giggled. "It's my favorite food, but I do like spaghetti and macaroni and cheese, too."

Gia looked down at Talei. "Are the hot dogs really good here?"

The little girl nodded. "Yes, but you gotta get the French fries to eat with it."

"I'll have what she's having," she told Trey, and he smiled. "Hot dogs and French fries all around, then."

Trey ordered their food, then navigated to the table where Leon sat with his son.

Leo immediately wanted to sit in his uncle's lap.

"I appreciate Gia taking Talei to change clothes. She was too impatient to wait for Oma or her mom," Leon said.

"She said she was hungry." Trey planted a kiss on Leo's forehead. "How's my little nephew doing?"

"Apparently tired of his daddy," Leon chuckled.

"He just wants some love from his uncle. That's all."

Leo looked up and said, "Fries…"

Trey looked at his brother and they both burst into laughter. "I think I'm being manipulated by a toddler."

A worker brought over a tray laden with drinks, hot dogs and French fries.

"Wado," Leon said.

"Hawa."

Turning back to face Trey, he asked, "Gia easing up on you some?"

"What do you think?"

Leon laughed. "That's who you need—someone who isn't going to take your stuff."

"She can definitely hold her own," Trey stated matter-of-factly. "It's one of the qualities I like about her."

"Gia's good for you."

"I think so, too."

Grinning, Leon said, "Uh-huh."

"What?"

"I'm just going to leave it there, but don't think I've forgotten how you crushed on her back in high school."

GIA TOOK TALEI by the hand as they headed to the bathroom.

"Uncle is so funny."

"Yes, he is," she responded.

"Mommy is teaching me the healing dance and I'm gonna do it for him. Not today, I'm still learning how to do it," Talei said. "But don't tell him. It's a surprise."

"I won't say a word," Gia promised.

Talei slipped on a red-and-white dress with a fringe bottom and changed into a pair of red moccasins.

"Did your grandmother make this dress, as well?"

"Yes, and the shoes. She has a bunch of clothes and shoes and blankets. You wanna see?"

"I would love to, but I know you're hungry, so let's eat first."

They left the bathroom to join the others.

Talei sat next to Leon while Gia dropped down on the bench across from them.

Trey handed her a paper tray containing her food.

Gia took a bite of her hot dog. "Mmm…this *is* delicious."

"I told you so," Talei said.

"You were right." She glanced over at Trey and winked.

After lunch they went back to watch the rest of the competition. It was time for the male dancers to perform.

"I'm really feeling this music," Trey said. "I love watching the drummers."

"They're really good," Gia agreed.

"Y'all missed the intertribal dance in the beginning," Leon said. "Y'all could've participated."

"You went out there and did what?" Trey asked.

"Just watch and follow what they do."

"I hate I missed that." Trey felt a bit drained of energy, but he was having fun with his family and Gia.

"We're meeting Jordin, Jadin and their spouses for dinner after this," Leon announced. "Why don't you two join us?"

Trey glanced over at Gia. "What do you think? You want to go?"

"Sure," she responded, "But how are you feeling?"

"I'm good."

When they were back in the vehicle, Gia said, "It's been a long day for you. Are you sure you want to go to dinner?"

"I'm fine," Trey stated. "Hungry, though. That

hot dog didn't do much for me. I had no idea how long we'd be out here." He was tired but wasn't ready to go home. He was having a great time.

"I imagine it varies with the number of entrants."

"You're probably right," Trey stated.

"We'll be at the restaurant shortly," she pointed out. "Jadin and Jordin...they're the twins that used to come to the island during the summer when we were younger, right?"

Trey nodded.

"We all hung out together one summer," Gia said. "I think it was our sophomore year. It'll be nice to see them again."

GIA DROVE TO the French Quarter Restaurant on Bay Street, located in the historic district of Charleston.

She parked the car, climbed out, then opened the door and lowered the ramp for Trey.

Horse-drawn carriages, locals and tourists strolled along the cobblestoned streets. Gia had always admired the city's architecture, colorful gardens, historic alleys and courtyards, some dating all the way back to the colonial era.

"This is a beautiful place, but I'm not exactly a fan of cobblestone right now," Trey uttered.

"Let me push you," Gia offered. "I love Charleston, but there's a beauty to Polk Island that this city can't come close to."

"I agree. There was a time when people had to take a ferry to go there, but now we can just drive across the bridge."

They entered the restaurant.

"There's a reservation under Leon Roth-child," Trey said to the hostess. "I think we're the first to arrive."

"Party of eight?"

"Yes," he said.

Minutes later, Jadin and her husband, Landon, walked inside, followed by Jordin and Ethan.

Trey broke into a grin. "Hey, cousins."

He made introductions.

"Gia, I remember you," Jordin said. "It's good to see you again."

"Oh, yeah," Jadin murmured. "We spent most of the summer at your grandmother's house when we weren't at the beach. Braxton's your brother."

Gia smiled. "You remember him?" Whenever her father was on leave, he always made sure to spend time with Braxton. Her father always made sure his son spent part of the summer with them on Polk Island, regardless of whether he was home or at his duty station.

"He was my boyfriend for about ten days." Jadin chuckled. "We promised to keep in touch, but then I never heard anything from him."

"I had no idea," Gia stated.

"I knew because she talked about that boy day and night," Jordin interjected.

Landon placed his arm across Jadin's chair. "Well, it's his loss."

"That's right, babe," she said.

Leon and Misty entered the restaurant. "Sorry we're late. We dropped the kids off at my mother's house, then had to turn around and go back because Leo's favorite toy was in the car. They're staying with her until Tuesday."

"Three days without the children...whatever will we do?" Leon said with a wink.

Trey sat there smiling.

Gia could tell from the expression on his face that it thrilled him to the core to see his brother in love with a wonderful woman and raising two beautiful children. She also glimpsed a glimmer of sadness in his gaze. She knew it was because Trey wanted this for himself, but he felt it was beyond his grasp.

She gently cupped his shoulder, then leaned down and whispered, "You're going to be a great husband and father one day."

"Forever the cheerleader," he whispered back.

THE FOLLOWING MONDAY, Gia surprised Trey by taking him to the beach. The closest she could get was the front row of the parking lot. They sat in the vehicle with the windows rolled down.

"This is such a nice view," Trey said. "There's something calming about being near a body of water," he said in a low, deep voice. "I could stare at it all day."

"Me, too," she murmured.

As he watched the waves roll in, Trey's body relaxed like it never had before. He enjoyed listening to the surf and inhaling the salty air. He felt an ease he hadn't felt in a long time. "This was a good idea. I'm glad we came here." He used to love just walking on the beach. Being here with the sun shining down on him, casting its reflection on the water. "If it were possible, I'd spend every waking minute in the ocean. I love it that much. Being back here only reminds me of how much I missed the island."

"You can still enjoy the water," she replied. "A pool, especially a warm one, can offer relief from aches and pains. I've seen amazing results from a range of individuals with disabilities— especially amputees."

"Really?"

She nodded. "I did my internship at Walter Reed with the director of the aquatic therapy program. After patient's wounds heal and before they go through prosthetic rehab, we used to put them through intense cardiovascular workouts with aqua therapy. I can do the same with you."

Feeling hopeful, he asked, "Where would we do these workouts?"

"We can use the pool at the wellness center in Charleston. It's just across the bridge. Are you interested?"

"I am," Trey responded. "I'd like to try it."

"Great. I'll call and check the schedule. It shouldn't be a problem, though." She made a note in her phone. "I don't know about you, but I'm hungry," she said. "Are you up to having some lunch? We can go to the café."

"Sure," Trey said. "I think my aunt's there today. It'll be nice to see her."

Gia started the car, backed out of the parking space and drove the short distance to the Polk Island Café.

Trey's nerves grew taut when she opened the rear entry door. He could smell the wonderful scents filtering the air and glimpsed both the locals and visitors going in and out of the café entrance. As a full onslaught of nerves struck Trey, his arms quit moving and the wheelchair came to a halt. He couldn't explain why but a wave of exhaustion washed over him.

"Are you feeling tired?" Gia inquired. "I can push you the rest of the way."

He shook his head. "No, I'm fine."

She stepped around the wheelchair to open the door for him.

Eleanor greeted and escorted them to a table.

"I didn't know you still worked here, Miss Eleanor," Gia said.

"I still come help out where I can. I get tired of being at home all day. You know I like to keep busy," she responded.

"Come hang out with me some time," Trey said. "Maybe you can convince Gia to ease up on me."

She chuckled. "I know my boy can handle anything that comes his way. Gia, you do whatever you have to do, suga."

Trey pretended his feelings were hurt. "Hey, you're supposed to be on my side."

"I am, son. You know that."

Trey planted a kiss on her hand. "I do."

When Eleanor walked away, he said, "I worry about her."

"Is she ill?"

"She has early-onset Alzheimer's." He was still processing this news about his aunt. Trey didn't like the fact that everyone had kept her diagnosis from him, but he was no longer angry. He understood their reasons, but he would've preferred finding out with the rest of the family.

Looking shocked, Gia uttered, "I had no idea. I just assumed she chose to retire after she married Rusty." She glanced over her shoulder to where Eleanor stood. "She's in good hands, though. I know how much you and Leon care for her. Then she has Rusty and a lot of people who love and cherish her."

"I wish I could do more for her," Trey said. "She sacrificed a lot for me and Leon. Aunt Eleanor always treated us like we were her own. I wish I could do more for her. It's frustrating that I can't even drive her around town or to her doctor appointments."

"But, you can go to them with her," Gia said gently. "If things had turned out differently— you would still be active in the marines."

"You're right. I would've been in California, but I'd probably come home more if that were the case."

He drank in the comfort of Gia's closeness. His feelings for her were intensifying. Trey found that she consumed most of his thoughts these days. It wasn't surprising, since Gia was all he used to think about through his high school years.

She opened her menu. "I don't know why I'm looking at this. I pretty much know it by heart, but every now and then Josh will add a new entrée."

As she spoke, his eyes traveled to her lips and lingered there.

When she looked up from her menu, he averted his gaze.

"You know what you're getting?" she asked.

"I know exactly what I want."

Trey thought he detected a glimmer of surprise in her gaze, as if she'd caught the hidden meaning behind his words.

As soon as she arrived home, Gia made a few phone calls to locate the perfect place for Trey's water rehab. Because he loved the water so much, she knew that putting him in a pool could lead to a change in his mood. He'd be able to move more freely, which could make him feel like his old self. Aquatic therapy could also help Trey manage his PTSD symptoms.

Gia threw up an arm in victory when she was told that she could use the wellness center pool. It was perfect because of the 96-degree water, and the hydrostatic pressure aided in increasing circulation and flexibility.

She noticed that Trey always made sure that he knew where all the exits were located. It was as if he had a constant escape plan in the works. The wellness center pool was housed within floor-to-ceiling glass walls, which might provide him with a sense of security.

Gia lay back on her bed.

She felt like something in their relationship

had shifted during lunch. It wasn't something she could put a finger on, but it was a feeling.

Get it together, girl. There's nothing wrong with being friends with Trey. You've known him a long time.

Still, it was a challenge to stay detached when he focused his gorgeous, dark brown eyes on her; when the fresh male scent of him circulated in the air around her, his energy filling the four corners of the room.

It's crazy, the kind of tension his mere presence ignites in me.

She was far too aware of him as a handsome man, when she needed to look at him objectively as her patient. Gia had to make sure the boundaries were clear when it came to the two of them.

CHAPTER THIRTEEN

THE NEXT DAY, Gia drove Trey to the historic section of the island after therapy at his request. Once she got him out of the vehicle and into his wheelchair, they looked up at the skeletal remains of Polk Rothchild's house.

"The original houses were built from a mixture of lime, shells and water," Trey said. "The cyclone that hit the island in the late 1800s did major damage to the houses on this street. Instead of rebuilding here, they decided to move to the south side of the island."

Looking around, Gia said, "It's amazing how the Praise House wasn't touched. Just the other four houses along this street." The church, made of the same mix of shells, lime and water, had a firm foundation, set for generations to come.

"My family has always talked about building up this area, but I don't know what happened."

Gia glanced up at the sign that read Polk Island Praise House. "When I was little, I used to dream of getting married here."

Trey was surprised by her words. "Really?"

Gia nodded. "Why do you look so shocked?"

"I thought all girls dreamed of huge, fancy weddings in big churches."

"Not me. I've always wanted something intimate and romantic. I dreamed of getting married surrounded by my family and a few close friends. It's about me and the man I marry— celebrating our love and the beginning of a life together." Gia smiled. "What about you?"

Trey gave a slight nod. "At one time, I considered marriage, but now…no."

"When you were younger, you used to go around saying that you were going to be a bachelor for life."

"I was just saying that to mess with you, Gia."

"I keep telling you that you can still have a full life with a wife and family."

He shook his head. "I don't want to be a burden to anyone."

"You wouldn't be," Gia responded. "Not for the right woman. You have to know that she wouldn't see loving you as a burden."

Their gazes met and held.

Clearing his throat noisily, Trey said, "Aunt Eleanor's mentioned a few times that people have come to her asking about the Praise House. Maybe it's something the family should think about—renovating it."

"I think it's a great idea. You need a project,

and this is something you'd love—I can hear the passion in your voice and a strong sense of pride whenever you talk about your history. This island that we all love was the vision of your ancestor Polk Rothchild and his brother Hoss."

"I often wonder what they'd say if they were here today," Trey responded. "We have such a diverse community now. I think they'd be pleased. Did you know that the pastor who took over when Polk was too ill to preach came from Canada?"

"I didn't know that. How did they cross paths?"

"It was actually through Hoss. He was a tailor and he'd made some suits for this man. When he found out Polk was sick—he sent for the reverend."

Gia glanced over at the Praise House. "That church may be small but it's still functional. Don't just let it sit and rot away. It's too beautiful and a very important part of your legacy."

He smiled. "I'll talk to Aunt Eleanor and the rest of the family. If they agree, then that's what we'll do."

TREY WORKED ON a proposal for the Praise House. He searched his memory for all he'd been told about the history. He'd even had Renee bring down boxes from the attic containing old maps and notes from the past.

His excitement for this project placed a temporary restraint on troubling thoughts, because he was able to focus on his ideas. When he had everything, he needed, he called a family meeting.

The phone rang.

"I'm just calling to wish you good luck," Gia said when Trey answered.

"Thanks. I actually feel really good about this project. I haven't felt this way in a while."

An hour later, Leon, Misty and Eleanor sat in the living room facing Trey, who was parked in front of the fireplace.

"I want to say thanks for coming over. I promise I won't take up too much of your time."

Leon chuckled. "It sounded important."

Aunt Eleanor sat down on the sofa beside Leon. "We haven't had a family meeting in a long time."

Renee entered the house. "I hope I haven't missed anything. I had a last-minute customer walk into the boutique."

"We're just getting started," Trey assured her. "Auntie, you once mentioned how people often ask you about wanting to have their weddings at the Praise House. I was thinking we should renovate it and open it up for weddings, maybe even for Sunday services."

"I actually think that's a wonderful idea," Misty said with a huge smile.

"A couple of pastors have asked about it over the years," Leon added. "I told them they could rent the church, but we would never sell it. The building is to remain in the family. It's an important thread in our Rothchild tapestry."

Eleanor shifted in her seat. "I agree. The Praise House is to stay under family ownership. All the property on that street belongs to us."

Trey glanced over at Renee. "I spoke to your dad earlier."

"What did he have to say about it?"

"Uncle Howard pretty much said the same thing," Trey stated.

"Renee, what are your thoughts?" Eleanor inquired.

"I'm in total agreement," she said, her tone enthusiastic. "I've always thought that we should restore the houses—I think the island should have a museum dedicated to Polk and Hoss Rothchild. It wouldn't exist if it hadn't been for them. Our history shouldn't be buried in the ashes. We need to rebuild the foundation of our legacy. Maybe tear down what's left of those houses, build a museum on the land and place some of the remnants in there."

"That's a great idea," Trey stated. "I really like the idea of a museum."

"Did you talk to my sister?" Eleanor asked him. "We can't leave her out of this decision. We'd never hear the end of it."

"Aunt Maggie said she liked the idea of turning the houses on that street into historic landmarks. I'll suggest the museum to her."

"Looks like everyone is in agreement," Leon said. "Now, who wants to spearhead this?"

"I'm willing," Trey responded. "I'm looking for a project to keep my mind busy. Maybe then I can focus on something positive for once."

For the first time in months, Trey felt the familiar feeling of pure satisfaction, and a sense of pride in the work he'd done so far. It made him feel good to be able to do something other than feel the anguish of all he'd lost.

"What do you need from us?" Aunt Eleanor asked.

"I need copies of all the birth records. We're going to need any important documents, such as deeds…whatever. I want to have it written down—we'll use that as a guide for setting up the museums."

"Let me know what you want me to do," Leon said.

"When I sort out everything, I'll get in touch with you," Trey said.

"This is a worthy project," Renee told him.

"My schedule's pretty full but I'll help when I can."

Trey gave her a grateful smile. "Our legacy will live on for generations, thanks to all of you."

"All of *us*," Leon corrected.

GIA SAT ON her yoga mat with her legs spread-eagled. "Mama, how you holding up?"

"I'm fine." Patricia wiped the beads of perspiration off her forehead with a small towel. With the assistance of a nearby chair, she rose up off the floor.

Gia held a bottle of water to her lips and finished off the cool liquid. "You did great today."

"Thanks, sweetie."

Patricia sat down in the chair. "How are things going with Trey?"

"We're getting along great." Gia grinned. "Although he complains that I'm a beast of a physical therapist."

"You are."

"Mama…"

"After my knee replacement, you wore me out," Patricia grumbled. "There were days I wanted to lay hands on you, but I was in too much agony."

"Look at you now." Gia chuckled. "You're

doing yoga, aerobics and running around here like a twenty-five-year-old."

"Sam and I are going dancing tonight."

"How fun…"

"What's on your agenda for this evening?" Patricia asked.

"I'm going to do some self-care," Gia responded. "Mani-pedi and a long soak in the tub with lavender bath salts and scented candles."

Her mother eyed her. "You know…there's a twinkle in your eyes I haven't seen in a long time. You're attracted to Trey Rothchild. Don't bother to deny it. I know you well, daughter."

Gia smiled. "I admit it. I do like him a lot."

"I have a feeling he's just as interested in you."

"You really think so?"

Patricia nodded.

"I think he's comfortable with me. He's been sharing things with me about his time in Afghanistan. He even asked me to proofread the letters he's writing to the families." Gia was touched that Trey would trust her with something so personal and emotional. She was honored to help him with the special project.

"That's very thoughtful of him to do that."

Gia agreed.

"Can you date Trey and be his physical therapist?"

"Mama, where in the world did that come from?"

"I've known you your entire life, Gia. You like Trey. *A lot.*"

"The answer to your question is no. It wouldn't be ethical."

"Then if I were you—I'd start looking for your replacement," Patricia advised.

"You're assuming Trey is interested in me that way. We're just friends."

"Uh-huh…keep telling yourself that."

Gia couldn't help but wonder if there was a grain of truth in her mother's words.

GIA PICKED UP a tissue to wipe her tear-streaked face.

"Is it that painful?" Trey asked.

"I'm sorry…it's… These letters are so honest and heartfelt. I can also feel your pain." Holding up the one she'd just read, she said, "This just broke my heart. It's obvious you have a lot of respect for Corporal Laura Hudson." Gia dabbed her face with a tissue—she didn't want her tears staining the note that would be sent to Laura's spouse.

"Hudson was tough, but she never let you forget that she was not only a marine but a wife and a mother. She wanted to build a good life for her family."

"You did a wonderful job with all of these letters," Gia stated. "I'll drop them off to the post office when I leave."

He smiled in gratitude. "Thanks."

"How are the plans going for the Praise House and museum?"

"We're meeting with an architect later this afternoon."

"I'm so excited about the venture. I especially love the idea of the museum," Gia enthused. "Every time I visit a new town, I make it a point to check out their local museum. I love strolling through the history, looking into the lives of others. It just brings the past to life for me."

"I feel the same way," Trey admitted.

She glanced over at him. "I'm really excited for you. You'll have the museum, and I'll have my clinic and the B and B."

"How's the search for a building going?" Trey asked.

"I found a couple that have some potential, but I haven't found *my spot* yet."

"You will," he responded. "We need a clinic here on the island, then you wouldn't have to transport your clients to Charleston."

Gia nodded in agreement. "That's what I was thinking, too. Keep the money on the island."

Trey handed her the last letter. "I appreciate you taking these to the post office."

She smiled and rose to her feet. "My pleasure. While I'm gone, I want you to do your stretching, then ice. You did great today with your exercises."

He groaned in response. "I can certainly feel it."

Gia left the house ten minutes later. Trey seemed to be in good spirits, but she intended to call and check on him later. She hoped writing to the families of his team members would bring him some peace.

CHAPTER FOURTEEN

"JUST RELAX AND FLOAT…"

Trey hadn't felt this relaxed in months. He closed his eyes, allowing his body to become one with the water. Regaining this small sense of movement was a defining moment for him—he felt a sense of freedom he'd thought was long gone.

"You're doing fantastic," Gia murmured.

At every encouraging word and smile from her and Gia's obvious faith in him, Trey's heart turned over in response. There was no fighting it any longer. He wanted something more than friendship from her. He'd been crushing on her at first like before, but what he felt now defied words.

However, reality sank in. What could he offer Gia?

Yet…the way she looked at him motivated him to take a chance with her. After all, she was his biggest cheerleader and she often reminded him that he could continue to improve his quality of life, including having a family.

At the end of the aquatic therapy session, Gia assisted him back into his wheelchair.

He decided to take the leap. He didn't just want to be her friend. He wanted more. He wanted Gia.

"How do you feel about mixing business with pleasure?"

She dried herself off. "I'm not sure what you mean by that."

His eyes traveled over her face, studying her expression. "Will you have dinner with me? As in a date."

Gia gave a slight nod. "I'd love it." She handed him a towel. "But I can't unless you fire me, or I quit. It's not ethical for me to date my patients."

"Then you're fired."

Grinning, she responded, "In that case, I have a replacement in mind for you."

He was surprised. "Were you planning to quit on me?"

Gia laughed. "No, I simply wanted to be prepared in case something happened to me, or if we decided to be more than friends."

"We have gotten pretty close," Trey said. "I've tried to keep it professional, but I really care for you."

"I feel the same way," Gia responded.

Her words thrilled him. Clearing his throat, he stated, "If you don't mind coming to the house later, I can order some food from the café. I really don't enjoy eating alone. I never really have."

"How about I cook something?" she suggested. "I'll have to check your refrigerator to see what I have to work with."

He chuckled. "It should be pretty well stocked. Aunt Eleanor sends groceries every week. Renee doesn't get home until late most nights and I'm not that great a cook… Leon or Misty will usually bring meals for us." He dried himself off. "For clarity, this isn't what I had in mind when I asked you out. I intend to take you on a real date."

"Trey, it's fine," she assured him. "You know I'm a simple girl. Staying in and cooking is one of my favorite things to do."

After arriving back at the house, Gia stayed for a few minutes to inspect the kitchen.

"I can make salad and shrimp scampi over linguine," she said after scouring through the refrigerator and pantry.

"That's one of my favorite meals," Trey responded. "What can I do to help?"

"Can you make a salad?"

"Can I make a salad?" he repeated with a laugh. "Honey, I'm a master at making salad."

"All right salad expert… I'll be back in an hour," Gia said.

"See you then," Trey responded. He watched her drive away before making his way to his bedroom.

He looked forward to spending the evening with Gia. And he was touched by her offer to cook dinner—he would've settled for just her company.

He had come to enjoy their PT sessions together, but he wanted more. A smile tugged at Trey's lips. He wondered what his new physical therapist was going to be like—hopefully, not as tough as Gia was on him.

Trey was a marine. He could handle just about anything… Anything but losing his entire team. He was still haunted by what had happened in Afghanistan. It bothered Trey more that he couldn't go back to help his platoon capture the people responsible.

He pushed away the troubling thoughts. Tonight, he intended to enjoy a nice dinner with the woman who'd stirred his emotions in a way he hadn't felt in a long time. Trey intended to focus all his energy on her this evening and not on the ghosts hiding in the shadows of his mind.

He showered and was dressed close to the time Gia was scheduled to return. He laid everything out in the kitchen that they would need to prepare dinner, then wheeled himself to the living room to await her arrival.

Lacking confidence when it came to women had never been a problem for him. But after losing his limbs, he felt less than a man—except whenever he was around Gia. She made him feel as if anything was possible. She made him feel whole and complete.

"Mom, you're on your own tonight for dinner," Gia announced when she came downstairs. "I'm going back to Trey's house. Oh, he fired me earlier. I guess you were right—he wants to date me." She did a little happy dance in the living room. The feelings she'd had when they were in school all those years ago still resided in her heart. During the past few weeks of their sessions, Gia found her emotions intensifying. She admired Trey for not giving up. He was a special man—one she could see spending an eternity with. "I couldn't say this aloud before, but Mom... I'm crazy about Trey. I'm falling hard."

"I saw this coming a mile away," Patricia said. "Don't worry about me. Sam and I are going to see a movie. We'll probably grab dinner after."

"Dancing, wine tastings, movie nights... You and Sam seem to be spending a lot more time together."

"Things are good between us."

"You deserve to find love and Sam seems

pretty wonderful." Grinning, Gia added, "And he has a good job with the post office. That means good benefits and a pension."

Patricia laughed. "You sound just like your grandmother."

"Nana told me that's what she told you when you weren't sure if you wanted to marry Dad."

"I wasn't sure if I was ready to be a wife at that time. I loved your father, but I was nervous about the idea of marriage."

"It's a life-changing decision."

"Yes, it is. But after I decided to get married, I never once regretted it. I've missed that man every day since he's been gone."

"Me, too," Gia responded.

She glanced at the clock on the wall. "I need to get going. I'll see you later."

"Have fun," Patricia told her.

"It's just dinner," Gia said. "Although he did ask me out on a date. We're going to dinner on Saturday."

"You should've led off with that," her mother said. "We'll definitely talk later."

COOKING DINNER WITH Trey sent waves of excitement through Gia.

She liked the way her name slid off his tongue whenever he said it. She tried to ignore the emotions that came with it, and dug into her meal instead, savoring every delicious, tasty bite. Gia was pleased with the way the scampi had turned out —perfectly seasoned.

"So, tell me about this new physical therapist," Trey said. "Is she as feisty as you? You know you would make a great drill sergeant."

"*He* is great at his job. Roger worked at Walter Reed for ten years before moving to Charleston. His wife is a doctor on staff at East Cooper Regional Medical Center."

"You found me a *male* therapist?"

"Before your ego inflates, it had nothing to do with jealousy. I chose Roger because I know his work ethic and qualifications. I don't have a problem with you working with another female. I just want someone good."

"I like that you're not the jealous type," Trey said.

"It's a waste of energy."

"So…have you dated anyone recently?"

"I broke up with the last guy I dated almost a year ago," Gia said, trying not to get lost in the way Trey looked at her. "We didn't want the same thing. I was hyper focused on starting my PT clinic. He just wasn't my priority at the time."

Trey nodded. "If you don't mind my asking, what are you looking for in a relationship?"

"I do want marriage and a family with the right man."

He met her gaze. "I want a family. I'm just not sure I can have it."

"You can," Gia murmured. "Your life isn't over. I know it looks different from the one you expected to live. What you've had to go through is life-altering, but you don't have to give up on your dreams."

"I've heard this from my family, but every time you say it…it really sounds possible."

"That's because it is." She met his gaze and couldn't look away. There was a deeper significance to the visual interchange.

Laying his napkin on the table, he said, "Tell me, Gia. How do you really see me? I know you'll tell me the truth."

"I see a man who is compassionate, a protector, a friend and companion," she responded. "You're a good person. Trustworthy, loyal, although a bit of a whiner…"

He laughed, then said, "You're a beast when it comes to your job, but I know it's because you want your patients to see results. When I look at you, I see a woman who's not just beautiful on the outside but on the inside, as well. You're still a cheerleader at heart. You're nurturing, loving and a good friend. You have no problem telling the truth unfiltered. Although I probably will regret telling you this—I love that about you."

Her heart nearly melted at his words. Gia awarded him a tender smile. "Sure...you say that now because I'm no longer your therapist."

He grinned and shook his head. "You're something else, you know that? I've never met a woman like you before." He leaned in closer to her.

Gia could feel her breath quickening. The aroma of his cologne was enticing. Before she knew it, Trey's lips brushed hers and then they were locked in the most passionate kiss she'd ever had.

Reluctantly, she pulled away.

"I couldn't help myself," Trey said quietly. "When I saw you that day I came home, the first thing I thought about was that first kiss the night of homecoming."

"So did I," Gia confessed. "We didn't know what we were doing, but I have to say I thought you were a good kisser back then."

"And now?"

"You're a really good kisser."

They eventually moved from the dining room to the patio.

She leaned against the rail, the wind blowing her hair gently as the warmth of the evening and the soothing waves sounded in the background.

"You really are a breath of fresh air," he told her. "I think you're amazing."

His smooth, deep voice sent excitement coursing through her entire body. When she felt calm enough to speak, she responded, "I can say the same about you. I haven't felt this good in a long time. I enjoy your company."

"I'm sorry for my behavior in the beginning. It wasn't fair to you."

"No looking back, Trey. Not tonight, anyway. Let's just enjoy our evening together."

"I guess this was a prelude to our real date. You haven't changed your mind, have you?"

"No," Gia said. "I'm actually very excited about what's to come."

Just occupying the same space as him sent a jolt of electricity coursing through her. Gia didn't know where her relationship with Trey would lead, but she vowed to just enjoy the journey.

CHAPTER FIFTEEN

TREY STAYED IN the doorway until Gia left. Their relationship had shifted, much to his satisfaction. He'd rather have her in his life as his girlfriend than as his physical therapist.

He appreciated her and she'd done a great job, but he didn't like the distance between them. Trey knew that Gia was trying to keep certain boundaries in place to avoid any ethical issues.

They didn't have to worry about that any longer.

"Hey, cousin," Renee greeted when she arrived home. "You have company earlier? I saw the food containers."

Trey grinned. "Gia made shrimp scampi for dinner. We left some for you."

"She cooked dinner *here*?" Renee's brows rose in surprise. "What did you do to deserve that type of treatment?"

"My plan was to get some food from the café, but Gia offered to cook."

Giving him a knowing grin, she said, "Looks

like things are going quite well between you two."

"I actually had to fire her today."

She gasped in surprise. "And she still made dinner for you?"

"I fired her so we could date."

Renee clapped her hands in glee. "I'm so happy for you. *I knew it*. I knew you were attracted to her."

"I've always liked Gia. I had a mad crush on her when I was in high school. I used to flirt with her, but she never would take me serious back then." Feeling lighter than he had in a while, Trey laughed. "Hopefully that's changed."

Renee stood up. "I'm starving, so I'm going to eat this delicious food."

"I made the salad."

"You know I love your salads."

"If you're not too tired, we can watch a movie when you're done."

"Sounds like a plan," Renee said, heading to the kitchen door. "Pick out something funny. No action-adventure movies tonight. After the day I've had… I need to laugh."

"You want to talk about it?"

She shook her head. "I'm pretty sure you don't want to hear about my customers. I'm really learning that I can't please everyone."

"You took a leap of faith when you came back to the island and opened your boutique. Don't let a couple of fickle buyers make you doubt your gift."

Renee ran back to hug him. "Thank you, cousin."

After she ate, Renee returned to find Trey had a movie primed to start.

"Gia makes a great shrimp scampi," she said, dropping down on the sofa. "That was so good. I hope you weren't expecting to have leftovers, because I finished it off."

He laughed.

"How did it feel? You two cooking dinner together."

"It felt good," Trey said. "It felt normal. Almost like we'd been doing it for a while —it was so natural. Gia's beautiful, smart…she knows her way around the kitchen, and she doesn't take my crap."

"She sounds perfect for you."

"Sometimes that's what I tell myself and then I make a list of what I have to offer her, which isn't much…" Trey shook his head sadly. "She has the B and B and is looking to open a clinic. I want to be able to help her—I don't want her trying to take care of me while she's trying to run her businesses. I'm going to do everything I can to be independent."

"It makes me smile to hear you talk like this, cousin."

"Gia just has this way about her. I feel differently about myself whenever we're together. Don't get me wrong… I still struggle when I look in the mirror or down where my legs used to be… I don't feel whole."

"Trey, you are *whole*," Renee interjected. "You still have your life and you're able to enjoy it. You're able to love and be loved. You may not have legs, but you still have your heart. I can tell that Gia really cares for you." Renee took a sip of her drink. "When are you going to start looking for a new physical therapist?"

"Gia's found me one already. He lives in Charleston. I'll meet him on Monday."

"That was quick," she stated. "Just how long have you two been together?"

He laughed. "I only asked her out earlier, but I'd been thinking about it for a little while. We're having dinner on Saturday, but I wouldn't call us a couple just yet."

"Well, I'm happy for you."

Trey broke into a grin. "Thanks for the talk. I'm actually feeling pretty good about life right now."

GIA TRIED ON three different dresses before deciding to wear the jade green strapless dress with metallic black sandals for her date with Trey.

"You look beautiful," Trey told her on the way to Charleston.

"Thank you," she murmured. "You're looking quite handsome yourself." He was dressed in a suit and his hair had been trimmed down neatly. Gia thought they made quite a good-looking couple. She was excited about what the evening had to offer. It felt really special because Trey wanted to get out of the house. When they arrived at the restaurant, they didn't have to wait long to be seated.

"This place is gorgeous," Gia murmured as they were led to their table by the maître d'. The rich decor of Manoir Bleu embodied history, art, romance and the architecture of New Orleans. Soft jazz played in the background to entertain guests while they dined.

Trey agreed. "The owner is Aubrie DuGrand-pre."

"As in DuGrandpre Law Offices?"

"Yeah. She's Jacques's daughter. Her mother, Rochelle, is the very vocal lawyer always advocating for the rights of fathers."

"I've heard of her," Gia said.

A server approached to take their drink orders. When he left, she asked, "How are things going with the Rothchild restoration project?"

"Going great, actually," Trey said. "I met with the architect to get an estimate of costs to draw up the plans for the museum. I've also been re-searching to see what I need to do from this point forward."

"Gia… I thought it was you," someone said.

The sudden appearance of Chris Latham shook Gia into gasping silence. He was the last person she'd expected to see ever again. She had to wonder if he were stalking her now. When she found her voice, she said, "Chris, what are you doing here?" She glared at him with burning, reproachful eyes while also trying to maintain her composure.

Chris seemed amused as he glanced from her to Trey. "I heard you'd left Charlotte. Are you living here now?"

Gia wiped her mouth on the napkin, then said, "Trey, this is—"

"I recognized Chris Latham the moment he walked up here," Trey said.

"I apologize for interrupting your evening," he said with what she knew was a fake smile. "Gia was my therapist when I was injured earlier this year. I owe her a world of thanks. I'll be back on the football field next season." His gaze swept over Trey. "I'm sure she's taking good care of you, as well."

Neither he nor Gia responded. Her hands were clenched into fists beneath the table. She exhaled softly as she relaxed them.

"I called you a couple of times," Chris said to her.

She swallowed hard, trying not to reveal her anger. "I've been busy." This was the last person she wanted to see, especially on her first date with Trey.

"If you have some time tomorrow—maybe we can meet for lunch."

"My calendar's full." Gia took a long sip of her red wine when the server placed their drinks on the table. She had no intention of meeting up with him anywhere.

"I'll be in Charleston for the next couple of days," Chris said.

"As I said… I'm busy," Gia said with quiet emphasis. She glimpsed the spark of frustration burning in his gaze. "Please tell your wife that I said hello."

He laughed and nodded. "It's good seeing you, Gia."

The lively twinkle in his eye only incensed her more. Chris seemed to be enjoying her discomfort.

"What was that about?" Trey asked when Chris walked away.

"Chris Latham thinks the world revolves around him and everyone is at his beck and call. He's very high-maintenance." Gia took another sip from her wineglass. "I'm glad I don't have to work with him anymore."

"I can believe that, but there seemed to be something else going on between you and him. You seemed pretty upset with the dude. Did he try something?" His tone was filled with concern.

"I just can't stand Chris," Gia blurted. "In fact, I despise him, so can we just change the subject?"

She didn't mean to sound so snappish. "I'm sorry. I didn't mean to bark at you. He just irritates me."

Their server reappeared to take their food orders.

"Hello, Trey."

Gia looked up at the woman who'd greeted him, curious as to who she was.

He broke into a smile. "Hey, Aubrie. I wasn't sure if you were here."

Trey introduced her to Gia. "Aubrie and I share cousins, so I would say she's extended family."

Shaking the woman's hand, Gia said, "It's very nice to meet you. I love the decor. It's very elegant and welcoming. I feel like I'm in NOLA."

"Thank you. Hey, do you mind if I sit for

a moment? I haven't seen this man in a long time."

"Please join us..." she responded. "I love family reunions."

"I heard you were living in New Orleans."

"I'm back here in Charleston now," Aubrie said. "I've been back for about a month. My brother told me they spent some time with y'all on the island. As soon as I hire an executive chef, I'll be able to take some much-needed time off. I also need to visit Aunt Eleanor."

"She would love to see you. That'll make her day." Trey smiled. "It was like old times with the DuGrandpre clan."

"I hate I missed it." She rose gracefully when the server brought their food to the table. "I hope you enjoy your meals. And save room for dessert. Everything is on me."

"Aubrie..." Trey began.

"This is my way of saying thank-you for your service to this country," Aubrie said. "Great meeting you, Gia," she added as she walked away.

"I like her," Gia said

"I'm surrounded by stubborn women. This isn't the way I wanted our first date to go."

"It's fine. I'm enjoying myself. Just relax and tell me exactly how you're related to the family who founded the first black-owned law firm in this city." Gia sliced off a piece of her smoked salmon and stuck it in her mouth. She was fine now that Chris was gone. She wasn't about to let him destroy their evening.

Trey picked up his fork and tasted the shrimp creole. "Oh man…this is good."

"So is the salmon." She took a sip of wine.

"Aunt Eleanor and Eleanor Louise DuGrandpre's great-grandmothers were first cousins."

"I know Aubrie just moved back from New Orleans. Are they related to the DuGrandpres there? The ones who own the cosmetics company."

Trey nodded. "You know them?"

"I went to college with Raven DuGrandpre. We were on the cheerleading squad together."

"I haven't talked to her in almost a year," he stated. "She was in the midst of a divorce the last time we talked."

"I'm sorry to hear that. She was such a sweetheart."

"Yeah, unfortunately, she was married to a jerk."

"Do they have children?"

"Three," Trey said. "Triplets. You know, I think I'm going to reach out to her this week. It's been a while since we talked."

"I think you should," Gia agreed. "Please tell her I said hello when you do."

"Speaking of family...have you heard anything from Braxton?"

Gia shook her head. "I reached out a few times last week but still no response. I can only assume he wants nothing to do with us."

"I don't understand your brother." Trey finished off his glass of water and signaled the server for another.

"He's always wanted our father to himself," Gia said. "I think that maybe it had to do with the fact that Dad married my mom right after he divorced Braxton's mom. She's put a lot of stuff in his head, but he and I always got along. I feel like he's dealing with some stuff, but I miss him, and I hope he'll eventually reach out to us. We're still his family."

"I can't imagine how it would feel to not have Leon in my life."

"It's hard. We used to talk regularly, but when Dad died... Braxton just sort of stop calling or texting. It's like I lost them both."

They were silent for a moment.

"I have a confession to make," Trey said. "As long as I've known you—we have always been friends. But I used to feel like you were more Leon's friend than mine. My feelings changed when you made the cheerleading squad. It was just something about you... I don't know. I just saw you differently."

"Maybe it's because when I made junior varsity, I felt a huge sense of accomplishment and confidence." Her confidence had soared. She'd tried out in middle school and never made it, then spent so many hours practicing and learning the routines and the cheers. "I used to go to the high school to watch and learn. It paid off when I auditioned, and I was thrilled."

"I felt the same way when I made the football team. I spent the summer before ninth grade going to those early-morning workouts. It paid off."

"Yes, it did," she agreed. "You were a very gifted athlete. You and your brother."

Trey looked at her. "Why is it I could never get you to go out with me back then?"

"Because you were a flirt."

"I guess I was trying to make you jealous," he confessed.

"I didn't think I could take you seriously."

Grinning, he asked, "So you liked me, huh?"

Gia laughed. "Of course, I liked you. You were a cutie."

"Okay, now that sounds like you thought of me simply as Leon's little brother."

"I didn't mean it like that," she responded. "I really liked you, but all the flirting you did really turned me off. I felt like you loved the attention from all the girls, and I didn't want to deal with that."

"Looking back, I know it was stupid. The only girl I really wanted was you." He gave her a tender look. "It's always been *you*, Gia."

His words put a smile on her lips and a flutter in her heart. She felt the same way about Trey. "I'm glad you're all grown up now. I have to admit that age was also part of my reluctance to go out with you back then."

"You cared what others would think about you seeing me?"

"Only how Leon and Miss Eleanor would feel about it," Gia stated. "I didn't want your aunt running me off the island about her nephew."

"She might have done that if you broke my heart," Trey said with a chuckle.

"You're in no danger of me breaking your heart."

Trey's gaze never left hers. He reached over and took her hand. "When I saw you the day I came back, you have no idea how happy I was. But there was a sense of sadness, too."

"Why?"

"I finally had the chance to reconnect with the woman of my dreams and I'm in this wheelchair with no legs."

Gia gave his hand a gentle squeeze. "Trey, I want you to stop seeing yourself as less than a man. Do not define your manhood by your physical body. It stems from the core of who you are. As far as I'm concerned, you are more man than some of them walking around with both legs intact."

"How was your date with Trey?" Patricia asked.

"It started off great...then Chris Latham showed up out of nowhere," Gia announced. "But we managed to get the evening back on track."

"What did he want?"

"I didn't give him a chance to say anything, really."

Her cell phone rang.

"I can't believe the nerve of this man," Gia sputtered, bristling with indignation. "That's him calling me now."

"Maybe he's convinced his crazy wife to back off," her mother suggested.

"I doubt that," Gia muttered. She released a long sigh before answering and saying, "I told you I want nothing to do with you."

"Hey, babe..." His tone bordered on mockery.

Rolling her eyes heavenward, she paused a heartbeat before uttering, "I'm not your *babe*, Chris. Why do you keep calling me? *What do you want?*"

"I thought I'd made myself pretty clear about

what I want, Gia. I leave for training camp next week. I want to see you before I go."

She suppressed her anger under the guise of indifference. "And I've made myself clear, as well. That's not gonna happen."

"Why don't you meet me in about an hour," he suggested. "We can talk about how to rectify this situation."

"How about you tell your wife the truth for starters? That would correct the situation," Gia countered.

"You don't want to admit it, but I know you're attracted to me."

"There's no way I'd ever be attracted to someone like you—you're a narcissist and very married. I have to go…" It frustrated her that he had the audacity to keep calling her. "You've done enough to try and destroy my reputation. But just so you know…you failed…and your wife failed. If you don't leave me alone—you're gonna wish you had." She considered telling him about the recordings and screenshots of his text messages to her, but Gia decided it wasn't time to show her hand.

"I never set out to hurt you. I know you don't believe me, but I'm crazy about you, Gia. I've never met a woman like you. I can't get you out of my mind."

He sounded sincere and vulnerable, but Gia

wasn't moved. She wasn't interested in Chris—never had been outside of being his physical therapist. "That sounds like a *you* problem. I was nothing but professional while working with you—I never once led you on. In fact, I did all I could to discourage your flirtation."

"I really need to see you." He sounded as if he were practically begging.

"Goodbye, Chris. I'm giving you a final warning. Leave me alone or you'll regret the day you ever met me."

Gia ended the call.

"That man is something else," Patricia uttered. "He doesn't know how to take no for an answer."

"He's so used to women throwing themselves at him. If he keeps bothering me, he'll soon learn that *NO* is a complete sentence."

"He just needs to leave you alone. But maybe you should make a report or something. Get the harassment documented with the authorities."

"I don't want to do that because of the publicity. Chris hasn't got any choice but to move on," Gia assured her. "I'm blocking him right now, so he won't be able to reach me again."

"Sweetie, you do what you have to do. I've got your back."

"I know you do."

Gia sat down on the sofa. She didn't want to

think any more about Chris. Changing the subject, she asked, "How would you have felt about my dating Trey when we were in high school?"

"I'm not sure," Patricia answered. "If he were just a year younger than you—I think I would've been okay with it, but with you being two years older... I just don't know, but it really doesn't matter anymore."

"You're right," Gia said. "I'm going up to bed. I'll see you bright and early in the morning."

"Yes, we're meeting with the landscaper," Patricia reminded her.

As Gia walked upstairs, her cell phone rang. She smiled when she saw Trey's name on the caller ID.

"Hey..."

"Were you busy?" he inquired.

"I can still talk while getting ready for bed."

"I wanted to apologize for earlier. I sensed that I made you a bit uncomfortable when I was asking about Chris."

"It's fine. Like I told you earlier—he thinks the world revolves around him. He gets on my nerves, but I tend to just ignore him."

"I have to confess that I was jealous."

His admission surprised Gia. "Why? Wait a minute... I thought you said you weren't the jealous type."

"I never was until now. You're gorgeous and..."

"Trey, you are more man than Chris could ever be. I mean that, so let's not spend another minute talking about him." She sat on the edge of her bed. "I had a great time with *you*."

"Same here," Trey responded. "Hey, are you sure about this?"

"About what?"

"I want you, Gia. I want to be the man in your life," his voice was filled with emotion. "I feel like we can have something great together."

Her insides jangled with excitement. "Since we're being honest with each other, I want you to know that I feel the same way. I really care about you."

"I have a birthday coming up soon. Leon wants to throw a party for me. I'd like for you to be my date. In fact, I'd like to tell the family that we're a couple now. Or am I moving too fast for you?"

"No, not at all," Gia responded. "Hey, you fired me—I should at least get a boyfriend out of the deal."

TREY REFUSED TO let his anxiety put a damper on what he considered the best evening he'd had in a while. He forced the shadows of panic and apprehension away from his mind. "I'm not in danger," he whispered over and over again.

He rocked back and forth.

Trey glanced around, searching…for what, he had no idea. He considered calling Renee via the intercom but didn't want to disturb her.

He lay back against the pillows, eyes closed, and slowed down his breathing. In his mind, he began replaying his conversation with Gia. He soon felt wrapped in an invisible warmth.

His breathing settled down to a more even beat.

He opened his eyes.

And lay in bed staring up at the ceiling, a tiny smile on his lips. This was the first time he'd ever been able to manage refocusing his mind from the memories of that day. It was a small victory, but a victory, nonetheless.

He felt something that he thought was long gone.

Hope.

CHAPTER SIXTEEN

"TREY AND I are dating," Gia announced a week later, while enjoying girl's night out with Shelley, Renee and Misty. They sat in a large circular booth inside the restaurant of the Polk Island Resort, the largest hotel on the island.

Shelley and Misty looked at her in surprise.

"I already knew," Renee said. "Trey told me."

"That's wonderful news," Misty responded. "I'd hoped you two would get together."

"How long have you two been dating?" Shelley asked.

"It just pretty much happened," Gia said. "We had our first official date last Saturday, but we've been spending almost every day together."

Shelley settled back in her seat. "What about PT?"

"I found him a new therapist."

Shelley took a sip of her drink. "Is anyone surprised by this news?"

"No," Misty and Renee said in unison.

"I guess I am." Gia picked up her glass. "I

didn't think Trey was interested in me, especially because of PT. I haven't been easy on him. But then something shifted and here we are... I'm really excited because I like him a lot."

A waiter arrived with a tray containing their entrées.

After he left, Shelley blessed their food.

"Trey's birthday is coming up in a couple of weeks," Renee said. "I've been trying to think of what to get him."

"I know what I'd love to buy," Gia stated. "Trey talks about how much he misses the ocean. Taking a wheelchair on the beach is a bit of a struggle in a regular wheelchair, so I'd like to get him an all-terrain one. That type of wheelchair is compact and practically glides over sand and rocks but get this—it even floats in water." She laid her phone on the table. "This is what it looks like." Gia wanted to give Trey the gift of getting back into the water—becoming one with the ocean. It would be perfect.

Misty leaned forward to get a closer look at the photo. "That would be so great for him."

Renee finished off her iced tea. "How much is it?"

"It's about three thousand dollars," Gia said.

"I agree with Misty and Gia," Shelley said. "Trey would be able to do so much more."

"I'm still hoping he'll agree to getting prosthetics, but until then he can resume doing some of the things he used to enjoy." Gia shifted her position in the booth. "I have the money to buy it, but should I? We just started dating and I don't want to make it awkward between us with such an expensive gift."

"What if others chip in? Like me and Leon?" Misty asked. "We're family."

"Sure," Gia said. "He'd probably accept a gift like this if it came from a group of people."

Pulling out her phone, Shelley said, "I'm gonna send you some money right now to help pay for it."

"Me, too," Renee stated.

"I have to say that I really appreciate all y'all wanting to contribute, but this is a lot of money," Gia pointed out. "This won't be a cheap gift."

Renee wiped her mouth on the edge of her napkin. "I'm telling you, Trey won't accept it if it just comes from you, Gia. He wouldn't want you spending this kind of money on him."

"She's right," Misty said. "He'll feel better knowing that it came from all of us. I know Leon and Aunt Eleanor will want to contribute, as well."

"Thank y'all for being so generous. I really think this will lift Trey's spirits and keep him on the road to recovery."

"Gia truly has a heart for veterans with disabilities," Shelley responded. "Her dad was wounded in the Gulf War."

"Like Trey, he was also a proud marine," she told Misty and Renee. "When he came home, I didn't even recognize my dad. If it hadn't been for a support group in Charleston for wounded veterans, he would've drunk himself to death or worse, I believe." She felt the tears come as she remembered her father at that time. "Seeing firsthand what he went through, I wanted to help other vets." Gia wiped away a tear. "Because of group therapy, my dad became my dad again—not the stranger that had come home to us. He passed away last year from prostate cancer. I really miss him."

Misty reached over and took her hand. "I'm so sorry for your loss. My father died eight months ago, from colon cancer. We weren't really close until a couple of years ago. Despite it being short, I'm glad I had that time with him."

Shelley ordered another round of appetizers for them to share. "Crab bites make everything better."

"I agree," Misty said.

"I'd better order this wheelchair so that we'll have it in time for Trey's birthday," Gia said. "Shelley, can you do me a favor and create a custom card for all of us to sign?"

"Sure."

Misty glanced down at her phone. "I sent a text to Leon and Rusty. They both think the wheelchair is a great idea. Leon wants you to know that the four of us are contributing two thousand dollars."

"Wow…thank you," Gia said, surprised. She hadn't expected anyone to contribute, but she was touched by their generosity—she'd intended to pay for it herself. "I can't wait to see his face. I'm so excited."

"We can tell," Shelley responded.

"It's ordered." Gia laid down her phone. "Now that that's taken care of—we can get back to enjoying our evening."

Their server arrived with a bottle of champagne.

"We didn't order that," Misty stated.

"Those guys seated at the table to your left sent it over," she said. "They also wanted me to tell you ladies that your smiles light up the room and to enjoy your evening."

"Please put their next round of drinks on my tab," Shelley responded. "You can tell them that they made four married women feel really special."

The server smiled and nodded. "Yes, ma'am."

"That was quick thinking," Misty said. "Although I'm the only one who's really married."

"As far as they're concerned, we're all married tonight," Renee responded. "It was nice of them to send over the champagne, but the next thing that would've happened is that they would've wanted to join us."

Renee agreed. "I've never been a fan of meeting men in hotel restaurants, bars or clubs."

Gia eyed her. "So where do you like to meet guys?"

"I don't have any special places." Renee shrugged. "It's just that at places like this, most men seem to think that it's easier to get a woman upstairs in one of the rooms. At least, that's always been my experience. After dinner…sometimes in the middle of the meal, I'm asked if I'd like to go upstairs."

"I've had that happen a couple of times myself," Shelley responded. "It's so irritating."

Gia nodded. "Me, too." She thought briefly of Chris Latham. "I can't stand men who won't take no for an answer. Men like that think they can buy women with their money or charm."

The others agreed.

"At least these guys know how to take a hint." Misty held up the bottle of champagne. "We might as well order dessert to go with this."

Two hours later, Gia entered her mother's house, singing softly. She heard masculine laughter coming from the family room and smiled.

She cut through the kitchen to say hello to the couple. "Hey, Sam. Mama, I just wanted to let you know that I'm home. Good night, y'all."

"Good night," they said in unison.

Gia took the back stairs to the second level.

She showered, then slipped on a pair of lightweight pajama pants and a cropped tank top and climbed into bed.

When she checked her phone, she saw that Trey had called.

Gia called him back. "Hey…were you sleeping? I'm just seeing that you called me."

"No, I wanted to see if you'd made it home. You have a nice time?"

She smiled. "I did. We just sat around talking and laughing over drinks and appetizers."

"Y'all didn't go too hard on us men, did you?"

Gia chuckled. "Not at all."

"I couldn't go to sleep without hearing your voice," he said.

"Talking to you is always a nice way to end the evening."

"If you're not busy with B and B projects or hanging with your mom, I'd love to see you."

Her heart fluttered at the thought of seeing him soon. "Let's go to the park in Charleston tomorrow," Gia suggested. "We can stroll along the waterfront, then have a picnic."

"I'd like that," Trey said. "You think your mother would be interested in joining us?"

"My mom has plans, so we're on our own. I'll see you tomorrow," she stated. He was a real sweetie for wanting to include her mother.

"Good night, beautiful."

Gia put the phone on her nightstand, a huge grin on her face. "I can't believe I'm dating Trey Rothchild…"

HE WAS A year older.

Trey studied his reflection in the full-length mirror that stood in the corner of his room.

Happy birthday to me.

He'd celebrated his last birthday in Aruba with friends. His life had changed vastly in the past year.

Trey's thoughts shifted to Gia, bringing a smile to his lips. She would be arriving soon.

He felt excitement coursing through his veins like an awakened river. There was no denying that Gia brought out the best in him. When Trey thought his life was over—she refused to let him give up. She remained on the sidelines cheering him on just as she'd done when he played football.

This was no game, he reminded himself.

Gia wanted him to make the best out of his

situation and Trey vowed to do so—not just for her, but for his family.

When she arrived, he assessed her from head to toe, saying, "You look stunning." Gia wore a black and fuchsia strapless sundress with matching heeled sandals. The full skirt danced around her legs as she walked.

Grinning, she kissed him. "Happy birthday, handsome."

"You've told me that three or four times already."

"And?"

He laughed. "Thank you, babe."

"You're ready to go?" she asked.

"I am," he responded.

Leon and Misty were hosting the party at their house. When Trey and Gia arrived, guests were already getting out of cars that were parked up and down the street. A few people sat on the porch, talking amongst themselves.

"Time to put your party face on," Gia said.

"Save me a dance," Trey said with a small chuckle.

"Always," she responded with a smile.

Leon met them at the door. He stepped aside to let them enter.

"Happy birthday, Uncle," Talei said as she greeted Trey with a hug.

"Hey, cutie. Where's Leo?"

"He's with Mommy. She had to change him. He got juice all over his clothes."

"She's so adorable," Gia said when Talei ran off to talk to her father.

"That's my girl," Trey responded. His eyes lit up when his gaze traveled to the entrance. "The DuGrandpre clan is in the house..." Taking Gia's hand, he greeted his guests when they approached him.

"Happy birthday, Trey," Jadin said, then reached over to embrace Gia. "You're looking good for an old man of thirty."

Jordin hugged them next.

More of his family arrived, including Aubrie and her parents, Jacques and Rochelle Du-Grandpre.

"The women in your family are absolutely stunning," Gia said. "The men aren't too bad, either."

He broke into a wide grin. "Good genes."

"You're a mess." She laughed.

"I can't believe so many people showed up," Trey stated.

Gia sat down at the table with him. "I don't know why you're so surprised. There are a lot of people who care about you on this island. That's one of the great things about this place. We're a close-knit community and we look out for each other."

Trey sat quietly observing everyone who'd come to celebrate his birthday. In that moment, he realized just how blessed he was to have so many supportive people in his life, and he was grateful.

"I'm finally happy to be alive, Gia. It's weird, but I feel like I've been reborn. It's because of you and them. I hope you get what I'm saying." His gaze slowly traveled the room.

"More than you know," she responded with a smile.

"Where's your mom?" Trey asked, looking around. "She's coming, right?"

"She's on her way. Mama texted me a few minutes ago. Sam worked in Savannah today and got a late start heading back. They should be here shortly."

Talei came to the table, asking, "Can I sit here with you, Uncle?"

"Sure." He patted the empty seat beside him.

"Miss Gia, do you like my uncle?" the little girl blurted without preamble.

"I do. I like him a lot."

Talei giggled. "Uncle likes you, too. I can tell."

Trey was surprised. "Oh, really…how can you tell?"

"Because you keep looking at her," Talei said. "That's what Dad does with Mommy. He's always looking at her and smiling like this." She showed them her impression of Leon.

Gia and Trey burst into laughter.

He glanced over his shoulder to where his brother stood, his gaze focused on Misty. "Cutie, you're right. He has this googly-eyed expression on his face. Do I really look like that?"

Grinning, Talei nodded as she patted the top of her curly ponytail.

They were soon joined by Eleanor and Rusty.

"The food should be out soon," Rusty announced. "Josh and Silas brought everything over from the café."

"I'm glad," Talei uttered. "I'm hungry."

"Lil' girl, I don't know a time when you not thinking 'bout food," Eleanor said.

"Mommy calls me a foodie. She says I'm like her. We love to eat."

"I'm right there with you," Gia added.

"I love birthday cake." Talei looked at Trey and rubbed her hands together. "I'm gonna eat a big piece of yours."

He laughed. "Just don't eat too much. I don't want you to end up with a tummy ache."

Shaking her head, Talei uttered, "I don't want that."

After they ate, they played a few games and gave away prizes. When it was time to open his presents, Trey eyed the large box Leon brought into the room and asked, "What in the world is in there?"

"I'll help you open it," his brother said with a grin.

When they got it unwrapped, Trey merely stared, tongue-tied. He sat there amazed, a myriad of emotions whirling within.

"It's an all-terrain wheelchair," Gia explained. "No more watching the ocean from your patio. We can walk to the beach, get in the water...do whatever you want to do."

Trey took the card that Leon handed him.

He read it, then looked around in surprise. "I can't believe y'all did something like this for me." Deeply touched by the gesture, he blinked rapidly to keep tears from falling. "I'm not sure I deserve this." He didn't feel worthy of such a gift. Maybe if he'd been able to save his team...

"Yes, you do," Renee responded.

Gia nodded in agreement. "You've worked so hard during your PT sessions, and you didn't quit. Besides, it's time to get you back in that ocean."

"Come here," he whispered.

She leaned forward.

Trey gave her a tender kiss. In that moment, he knew what he felt for Gia was real.

"Uncle kissed her." Talei giggled, prompting laughter from the rest of the guests. "Do it again," she said.

Trey gladly obliged his niece.

When Gia pulled away, she ran her fingers through her hair. "I think I'll get us something to drink."

She rose up and headed to the kitchen.

"You got the girl blushing," Rusty teased.

"Gia's a nice young lady, right there," Eleanor said. "Do right by her."

"I am, Auntie," Trey said.

One of Misty's employees brought over plates of food for them. He placed one in front of Trey and Talei. "I'll be right back with more for y'all."

"Thank you, Silas," Rusty said, rising to his feet. "I'll go get the rest. You can bring out food to the other guests."

Trey gazed at his aunt. "This is my best birthday yet."

She patted his arm. "It does my heart good to see you so happy, son."

Trey was surrounded by family and friends. He had Gia by his side. For the first time in a long while—he felt his life was perfect.

"THAT'S A REALLY nice gift y'all gave Trey," Patricia said when Gia eased into the seat beside her.

"We really wanted to get something that

would be meaningful and that he could use," she responded. "The VA will provide him something similar, but you can't use it in the water. I want to get Trey back into the ocean. It'll help him get back to his old self."

"Look at him, Gia. He looks so incredibly happy."

"Yes, he does." She glanced at Trey. He was watching her. The heartrending tenderness of his gaze sparked a tingling in the pit of her stomach.

"Go to him," her mother urged. "I'm going to find Sam. I'm missing my man."

"All right, now…"

"I'll see you later, sweetie."

Gia made her way, navigating around friends and family members, to where Trey was seated.

He took her hand. "I know that wheelchair was your idea." Trey smiled. "Thank you. It's the best gift ever."

"Just you."

The heat and fondness she saw in Trey's eyes pleased her. "I know how much you missed swimming in the ocean. Now you can and feel comfortable doing so."

"I also know something like that can't be cheap."

Gia kissed him. "All you have to do is enjoy the freedom you have to roam the beach, swim in the ocean, travel in the snow—whatever. Your family loves you. This community loves you…"

"And you?" he asked.

Gia broke into a grin. "That's a discussion for another time and place." Her mind relived the warmth of their kiss.

"Are you coming back to my place after the party? We can watch a movie or play Scrabble."

"Sure," Gia said. She was in no way ready for the evening to come to an end. She loved being around this more mature version of the guy she remembered.

CHAPTER SEVENTEEN

GIA WOKE UP momentarily confused.

It took her a minute or so to remember that she'd spent the night at Trey's house.

She'd stayed up hanging out with Trey and Renee after the party, and eventually, Trey had even given up and left the women to continue talking through the night while he'd gone to bed. Rather than go home late, Renee had offered her the guest room. Gia sat up in the bed, her back against the padded headboard, to call her mother.

"Hey, Mama. Did you see my message?"

"I got it, sweetie," Patricia said. "I hope you enjoyed yourself."

Gia grinned. "We *talked*, Mama. All night. I slept in a guest room upstairs."

"I just said that I hope you had fun."

"We're going to the beach today. I'm sure Trey can't wait to try out his new chair." She was looking forward to him trying it out for the first time. "Oh, before I forget, the plumber is scheduled to go to Nana's house at one o'clock.

He's checking the bathroom downstairs. The tub seems to hold water. It takes a long time to drain."

"I'll be on the lookout for him."

"Are we still working on the kitchen tomorrow?" Gia asked.

"Yes," Patricia responded. "I also want to take you by this space I found. I think it'll be perfect for your clinic."

When Gia finished talking to her mother, she picked up her bag and carried it to the bathroom. She always kept a change of clothing and a swimsuit in the back of her SUV, along with a fresh pair of jeans and a polo shirt for work.

Gia showered, then slipped on green shorts and a yellow tank top over a red one-piece swimsuit.

She then went downstairs.

"Thanks for letting me sleep over," she told Renee when she entered the kitchen.

"You're always welcome to do so." Renee grinned. "This is the happiest I've seen Trey in a long time and it's because of you."

"We all had a part in this," Gia responded. "But I appreciate your saying this. It means a lot." She didn't want to get emotional, but Renee's words truly meant a great deal to her. "Do you know if he's up?"

"He is," Renee said. "Remind him that breakfast is ready, please."

"Will do," she responded with a smile as she made her way to his room.

"You're doing great," Gia said as she helped Trey maneuver the new wheelchair in the ocean.

He felt as if he were in heaven. It was the only thing he could think of to compare being back in the ocean he loved so much. "Wow... I can't believe the chair becomes a floatation device. *I love it*." He lay back, soaking in the sun. "There are no words to describe how I'm feeling right now."

Smiling, Gia said, "You feel freedom."

"Yeah... I think if I could stay out here all day I would—just so I can keep feeling like this."

"You'd look like a wrinkled prune if you did," Renee teased.

"It would be worth it." He flopped around, splashing water everywhere. He felt a bit clumsy in the device, but Trey intended to master it. He felt like a kid with a new toy. Gia and Renee had to coax him to come out of the water by promising they could come back later in the afternoon.

Renee was hungry and wanted to eat something. Gia's stomach growled in agreement, so they went back to the house.

After a lunch of sandwiches and chips, they returned to the beach as promised.

Trey didn't want to waste a moment. He headed straight for the water.

Gia glanced over at Renee. "At least he's getting his exercise in."

"That's for sure."

She stayed in the water with him.

"Babe, I don't know what my life would be like if you hadn't been here," Trey said. "I'm not sure I'd be taking physical therapy—I just didn't see the point in it after everything that happened. I didn't think I'd feel this way again." And now that he did, he felt a sense of accomplishment. He found himself really excited and looking forward to the future.

"It was still very fresh. You might have changed your mind without me."

"I don't know," he stated honestly.

"Well, I'm here, so it was meant to be—I was supposed to be here so I could get you out of your own way."

"We're still working on that," Trey said with a wry smile.

After another two hours at the beach, they made their way back to the house. He was exhausted but in a good mood.

Gia left for home around seven thirty.

He missed her already. Trey thought about calling but didn't want to be a pest. They'd spent all day together—he should be satisfied with this.

"I'M GOING TO New York for Labor Day," Renee said while she and Trey were spending the day with Leon and his family. "I was able to snag plane tickets for a good price."

"How long will you be gone?" Misty asked. They had just sat down for dinner in the dining room.

"For a week." Renee reached for another yeast roll. "Trey, why don't you ask Gia to stay over while I'm gone?"

He glanced over at his cousin, scanning her expression. "You think I need a babysitter?"

"No," she responded quickly. "I just thought you might want some company, especially since you two spend so much time together anyway."

"I think it's a great idea," Leon said.

Holding up a glass of water, Misty asked, "Are you opposed to Gia spending the week at the house with you?"

Trey chuckled. "See…you're trying to start something. I'm all for it, but I just didn't want y'all thinking I couldn't handle being home alone. We'd have to see what Gia has to say about it."

"I'm pretty sure she won't mind," Renee said. "She can sleep upstairs in one of the guest rooms."

"I'll ask her." Trey was secretly delighted with the idea of having Gia stay over for a few days. They always had a great time together. He was already thinking of things they could do—cook meals together, play Scrabble… They could go down to the beach and swim in the ocean.

"Trey, are you still with us?" Leon asked.

"Huh?"

"You were thinking about Gia." His brother laughed. "You got it bad for her."

Trey grinned. "I won't deny it. I really care for her."

"It thrills me to see you so happy," Leon replied.

"I am," Trey confirmed. "I never thought I'd feel this way again. It feels good to be in this space." Trey sliced into the roast. "Misty, this meat is so tender… I won't tell Aunt Eleanor, but I think yours is now my favorite."

"Oooh…" Renee uttered, then laughed. "Actually, I have to agree. This roast is perfection."

And Gia was perfect for him. He didn't want to imagine what his life would be like if they hadn't reconnected. Gia inspired him—she cheered him onward toward a new perspective. Trey also had to give credit to his family, as well.

Despite all that had happened, he was a lucky man.

CHAPTER EIGHTEEN

"How are things going with Roger?" Gia asked when she and Trey found a spot on the beach to settle down. After her last patient, she wanted to decompress with a late afternoon swim.

"Great," Trey responded. "He's got me working on my core strength. He has me going back and forth holding onto parallel rails for hours."

She laughed. "You're exaggerating."

"It feels like hours to me."

"He's preparing you to get accustomed to using prosthetic legs and regain your sense of balance."

"It's frustrating at times, but I'm not going to give up. I'm determined to walk again, Gia." He rubbed the back of his shoulder.

"Sounds like you're emotionally ready for prosthetics."

"I'm going to be fitted at my doctor's appointment at the end of next month. I'll be twelve weeks post-surgery."

Gia grinned. "That's great. Do you want me to go with you?"

"Yeah. I'd like that." He glanced over at her. "By the way, Renee's going to New York for Labor Day week. How do you feel about spending that time at the house with me?"

"How do you feel about it?"

"I think it'll give us a chance to spend some quality time together."

"We do that all the time," Gia responded. "I don't want you getting tired of me," she teased.

"Never that," Trey stated, taking her hand in his. "I love being around you."

Gia picked up a shell. "I used to collect these all the time when I was younger. We had enough to fill four lamps. We're putting them in my grandmother's house. Actually, are you interested in a tour of the first B and B on the island?"

"Sure."

When they arrived, Trey noticed a ramp had been installed. "When did you do this?"

"A couple of weeks ago," she said. "Mama and I want everyone to be able to enjoy the place, so the bedroom on the main floor is equipped for wheelchair users."

Gia guided him around the main level of the house which featured a great room for guests to gather, a formal dining room and a kitchen. A large screened-in porch with two ceiling fans was at the back of the house. An outdoor kitchen completed the patio.

"I love it," Trey said. "I like the way you incorporated a beach theme throughout the place."

"Here are some pictures of the rooms upstairs," she said as she handed him a photo album.

"Everything looks really nice," Trey stated. "This place is going to do quite well on the island."

"We think so, too." She was extremely proud of the work she and her mother had done to make the place warm and welcoming.

"What about the PT clinic? What do you need to do to get started on that?"

Gia settled back against the cushions of her chair. "I've been doing some research and it seems that solo clinics are not as profitable as those owned by two or more people—I guess two heads are better than one."

"How do you feel about that? Are you thinking about getting a partner?"

"Initially, I was a little disillusioned, but the more I thought about it, the more I liked the idea. So yes, I am," she replied. "I was thinking about asking Roger."

"You can also talk to my cousin Ethan about a potential gym partnership," Trey said. "He's been looking into information about a gym for youth and adults with autism, which I'm sure could benefit from the expertise of a physical therapist. He's planning to test the first one in Charleston."

She was genuinely interested. "Really?" Gia had worked with patients with autism. She was intrigued by the idea.

"Yes."

"What prompted him to do this?"

"Their youngest child is autistic," Trey said. "He and Jordin have been researching and learning a lot about autism. Do you have any experience working with autistic patients?"

"I've worked mostly with adults who have autism spectrum disorder, but I've been able to help a couple of children with low muscle tone and poor balance in the past."

"If you want, I can give Ethan a call."

"That would be nice." Gia leaned over and hugged him. "Thank you."

TREY AND GIA drove to Charleston to meet with Ethan and Jordin a few days later.

"Wow," she murmured. "Look at this house. It's gorgeous."

The sprawling two-story house sat with its back to the ocean. They lived near the waterfront park that Gia loved visiting whenever she came here.

Jordin ushered them inside. "Have a seat in there. I need to check on our dinner."

Gia loved the interior design of their five-bedroom house, especially the amazing views of the ocean and the city lights. The decor looked like it was inspired by one of the Caribbean islands. From where they sat, she had a clear view of a colorful flower garden on the left, the sprawling deck and the ocean beyond.

"The deck actually leads to a patio area complete with an outdoor kitchen," Trey said.

"This house is stunning." Gia's gaze traveled from the faux-finished stucco walls to the hand-painted furniture and to the huge, overstuffed sofas and the marble flooring.

"There's also a guesthouse on the property. Ethan's mom lives there."

"That's really sweet."

When Jordin appeared, Gia said, "Your home is really beautiful."

"Thank you. I can't take credit for the decor. Ethan bought this house and had it professionally decorated before we got married."

"He has great taste."

"It's *all right*," Trey said, prompting laughter from Jordin.

Gia put a hand to her mouth and said in a loud whisper, "Sounds like he's a bit of a hater."

Ethan joined them five minutes before they

gathered at the dining room table to eat. "My apologies. I was on a business call."

While they ate, he discussed his ideas for the new gym. "I'd like to establish a program for individuals with autism and related disorders to promote learning, community involvement and disability awareness."

"It's a wonderful idea," Gia responded. "What you're proposing is more of a sensory gym. Most children with special needs may require occupational or speech therapy but a program like what you have in mind will help amplify the other therapies."

"Trey mentioned you were looking into establishing your own PT clinic?"

"That was the plan," she said. "But after doing some research on the current market trends, I've been rethinking a solo clinic. I'm looking to partner with someone."

They spent the meal chatting with each other about their work experience and found that their ideas werc for their prospective business ventures were similar.

"What would you say to a partnership between us?" Ethan asked. "We could incorporate the sensory gym into your PT facility."

Gia was speechless for a moment, then moved to tears that Ethan would offer a partnership. She'd done some research on him before this meeting and was impressed by his business acumen. She picked up her napkin, dabbed at her eyes, then said, "I'm sorry... I came here with the hope that I could rent space in one of your gyms, but this is so much better." She looked at Trey, then Jordin. "Oh, *wow...*"

Trey took her hand. "I think Ethan's waiting on an answer, sweetheart."

"She can take some time to think about it."

"Actually, I don't have to think about anything," Gia stated. "Ethan, I would love to be your partner."

He wiped his mouth on a napkin, then said, "Let's meet in my office next week and we can discuss how to merge our vision for this facility. Jordin and I would also like to discuss you working with Ethan Jr."

"I'm free Wednesday morning," Gia offered. "I have a client later in the afternoon."

"Is nine o'clock good?"

"It's perfect."

Gia was still in shock on the way back to the island. She could hardly believe what had just happened. Her dream was on the verge of becoming a reality. She couldn't wait to share the news with her mother.

"You all right, babe?" Trey asked.

"Did that really just happen?"

He laughed. "It did."

She glanced at him. "Thank you for making this connection. I can't put into words just how much it means to have you support me like this. This venture is gonna involve long hours and a lot of time. Are you okay with this?"

He reached over and took her hand in his. "You've done so much for me," Trey responded. "I'm glad I was able to help in some small way. I'm willing to make the sacrifices necessary to see your dreams come true. Besides, I'll be working on the museum, but we will be intentional when it comes to our quality time."

"Agreed," she murmured. "I don't want to get so caught up with the work that we don't take out time for us." Gia kissed his cheek. "Trey, I'm so happy right now."

"Really? I can't tell because you're always happy."

"I'm not gonna let you ruin this for me. You can tease me all night long, but I'm just gonna sit here and relish this moment."

"YOU NEED TO hurry up," Gia said. "We don't want to leave at the last minute." Trey had surprised her with tickets to a Labor Day concert. Which was huge because he didn't particularly care for crowds. She knew he was doing this for her.

"We have special seating, thanks to me." He

maneuvered his wheelchair to the dining room table—she'd made dinner so they could eat together ahead of the show.

She glanced at Trey. "That's because you went to school with the guy who is running the event."

"Actually, they give free concert tickets to all veterans, but he did give us VIP seating," Trey explained. "We are right up front and center of the stage. We'll be able to see everything unless a bunch of screaming women run up there."

"One of them might be me," Gia teased. "I love Van Banks's music."

She placed a plate of food in front of him.

Trey's stomach rumbled as he gazed down at the meat loaf with mashed potatoes and gravy.

"Before you get too excited, I have to make a confession," Gia said. "This didn't come from the café. I made it from scratch."

Trey laughed. "I'm sure it's delicious. I already know you can cook."

"I haven't made meat loaf in a while, though." Smiling, Gia sat down in the chair across from Trey. "Josh makes the best on the island."

"I'll reserve judgment until after I taste yours." He sliced off a piece and stuck it into his mouth. "Mmm…this is delicious, Gia. Josh makes a good meat loaf, but I'm loving yours. It's got a little bit of a kick to it."

"I add jalapeños in mine."

Trey took a long sip of his iced tea. "This feels nice. I've enjoyed having you here at the house."

"Don't go getting any ideas, Trey Rothchild. I'm only staying here while Renee's gone. Don't get any ideas about this becoming permanent. I want a husband—not a roommate."

"Message received," he responded with a grin. "You want to marry me."

Gia's eyebrows rose a notch. "That's not what I was saying exactly."

"Then you don't want to marry me?"

"Trey…" He was pretending to look hurt, and she knew it. Still, she said, "I would be honored to be your wife if that time ever comes."

"I'm just messing with you." He stuck a forkful of food into his mouth.

"You're terrible," Gia said with a chuckle.

"Dinner was outstanding," Trey praised when they'd finished eating.

Gia smiled. "Every time you say *outstanding*, it reminds me of my dad. I know it's a thing you marines say."

"Rah…"

"He would be so proud of you. Dad really liked you."

"I know," Trey responded. "He checked on me while I was in boot camp. After I received my PCS orders to Camp Pendleton, we lost touch. It's mostly my fault. California was my dream assignment. Near the Pacific Ocean… you know how much I love the water."

"I didn't know that about my dad, but I'm not surprised. He tried to keep in touch with all his *boys*—that's what he used to call y'all," Gia said. "I love California, too. I worked in Los Angeles for a while. But then my grandmother got sick, and I didn't want to be that far away, so I moved to Charlotte."

"You lived in Hawaii for a while, didn't you?"

Gia nodded. "That's where I was born. We lived there until I was twelve."

Trey stacked their plates. "How long will it take for you to get ready?"

"Not long."

She pushed away from the table and took their plates to the kitchen. "You go on and get ready while I clean up my mess."

"Just put them in the dishwasher," Trey suggested.

"Go get dressed," Gia said. "It's an order."

"Yes, ma'am."

An hour later, they headed to the Rhythm on the River concert. Gia enjoyed open-air music events like this. She hoped that Trey would enjoy it, as well, since they would be outside on the lawn with a sea of people all around them.

As soon as they arrived, Gia noted the area sectioned off for VIP seating. "Wow...you're right. We are really close to the stage." She was glad they hadn't needed to bring chairs, as they were provided as a perk. She didn't want to have to lug around a lawn chair and help Trey navigate.

"You won't have far to run."

Gia gave him a gentle nudge. "No, I can actually leap from my chair to the stage."

"I must admit I'd love to see that." Patting the arm of his chair, Trey said, "I'm really loving this wheelchair. It's so much easier to travel in—I can do some of the things I enjoy. I love the other one, too, because I can enjoy the ocean."

Trey had found out the VA would cover the cost of a smaller, more compact, all-terrain wheelchair. It was similar to the one Gia had ordered, but it didn't have the flotation tires.

"When you see your doctor at the end of the month, he's going to fit you with your new prosthesis," Gia said. "Training with Roger is going to be really important to learn—"

Trey kissed her to stop her from talking. "Sweetheart, you're my girlfriend. I just need you to be that for me. Trust me, Roger is on it." Grinning, he added, "You might want to do some stretches before you do your jump from here to the stage."

She burst into laughter. "You're absolutely terrible."

"Hey, you said it. I just want to see you do it."

Gia gave him a playful jab on his arm.

"Don't let me call security on you for abusing a disabled veteran," he teased.

"What am I going to do with you, Trey?"

"I can think of a few things," he responded. "For starters, you can kiss me."

She gave him a soft peck on the cheek. "Enjoy the concert."

Before he could respond, Gia said, "Don't you dare..."

Trey gave her a look of complete innocence. "What? I was just going to tell you to do the same."

"No, you weren't, and you know it."

He laughed. "You're right. I wasn't."

Gia stole a peek at Trey once the concert started. He looked like he was enjoying the music. She settled back in her chair and moved her body to the rhythmic sounds.

When the concert ended two and a half hours later, they headed back to his place.

"Do you want to watch a movie before we go to bed?" Trey asked when Gia walked out of his bathroom wearing a pink tank top and loose gray sweatpants.

"Sure. You pick one and I'll go prepare a plate of cheese and crackers for a snack."

"Gia…"

She paused in her tracks. "Yes?"

"I'm glad you're here." Trey pulled her into his lap and kissed her. "You're so beautiful. Inside and out. You're special, you know that?"

She pressed her lips gently to his. "I think you're pretty special, too. Now, find a movie while I go to the kitchen."

When Gia returned, she sat the plate down on the coffee table.

He pulled her back down into his lap.

Gia wrapped her arms around Trey, pulling him closer to her. She could feel his uneven breathing on her cheek, as he held her tightly. Her life was going exactly the way Gia wanted—her dreams were becoming reality and she'd reconnected with her first love. Despite being happy, in the back of her mind, Gia worried that she might end up being too busy for Trey. But she wanted to continue to be a source of support for him as he continued his recovery. She couldn't let Trey down.

He traced his fingertip across her lip, causing Gia's skin to tingle. He paused to kiss her, pouring into that kiss every emotion that seemed to be inside him.

She wrapped her arms around his neck, the intensity of her feelings for him threatening to engulf her.

"I can't tell you how happy I am to have you back in my life," Trey said. "The thing you have to ask yourself is if I'm everything you need."

Gia placed a hand to his cheek. "You have everything I need and some of what I want. Trey, I really want to be with you. Just hold on to that truth."

"Everything okay?"

"Yes, I was just thinking that with everything we both want to do—time is going to be precious."

He covered her mouth with his own, kissing her tenderly. "We'll work it out, sweetheart. No worries tonight. Let's just enjoy this time we have right now."

"You're right," she said. Handing him the remote, she added, "This movie isn't going to watch itself."

"I'm crazy about you," he told her. "Sometimes it's hard to believe that this is real. It feels like a really nice dream."

"It's a beautiful one," Gia whispered.

After the movie ended, she went upstairs. She

slept in Renee's room so she could be near the intercom in case Trey needed her.

She woke up with a start at the sound of a loud crash.

Gia pressed the button on the intercom, "Trey, are you okay?"

"I knocked my chair over. I was trying to get up…"

He sounded confused, even fearful.

Gia was motivated to action. "I'm coming down."

She rushed barefoot out of the room and down the stairs.

She burst through the door, asking, "What were you doing? Was it another nightmare?"

"Yeah," he muttered. "I hate dealing with this stuff." Panting, Trey glanced at her. "I know what you're thinking, so please don't say it."

Gia hugged him. "Everything is gonna be okay. You had a bad dream. You're home, babe. Just breathe in slowly…think about something that makes you happy. Breathe out…think about how it felt to get back into the water. Now imagine yourself in the water and relax your body."

Gia picked up the wheelchair, setting it upright. "Inhale…exhale…you're doing great."

"Don't leave," he said.

His body was trembling. He was still shaken.

She stroked his perspiration damp forehead. "I'm not going anywhere, Trey."

She climbed into bed beside him. "I'm gonna lie here with you until you fall asleep."

"You feel good," he uttered.

She placed an arm over him and whispered, "Go back to sleep."

When Trey finally drifted off, Gia eased out of the bed and padded barefoot across the hardwoods to the sofa. She suddenly felt cold and alone without the warmth of his body.

Gia covered herself with the throw that was on the sofa and lay her head on one of the pillows. She was hesitant to go back upstairs for fear that he'd have another nightmare. She didn't want Trey to wake up and find himself alone.

CHAPTER NINETEEN

THE NEXT MORNING, Gia was in the kitchen making breakfast when Trey ventured out of his bedroom. The last thing he remembered of the night before was feeling as if he couldn't breathe. His fight-or-flight response had kicked in and before he knew it, he'd somehow knocked over his wheelchair.

"Why didn't you wake me up?" he asked.

"It took you a while to fall back to sleep. I felt you needed your rest."

Gia took their plates to the table.

"I guess it was a good thing you were here. I've never knocked over my wheelchair before. This time it seemed so real. The fear… I…"

"How often do you have these nightmares?" Gia asked.

Trey wiped his mouth on his napkin. "Maybe once or twice a week, but it's never been that bad. They used to happen every night. Drinking would help."

She reached over and took his hand in her

own. "Why won't you consider a therapist or support group?"

"I really don't think it'll do me any good. I'm not comfortable opening up to a stranger or a bunch of strangers. Aunt Eleanor took us to see a therapist when we lost our parents. Neither Leon nor I had anything to say to her. We just sat down for an hour saying nothing. I didn't want to share something so personal with someone I didn't know. It was hard enough living with the pain we were in—we didn't want to give voice to it."

"Talk to your doctor at least," she suggested. "Maybe he can give you something to help."

"I don't like taking pills, but I might do that," he said. "I can't keep living this way."

He was silent for most of the drive to Charleston for his session with Roger. He wasn't trying to be rude. He was embarrassed over what had transpired the night before. Trey never wanted Gia to see him like that—so vulnerable and needy. It made him appear weak.

After his PT session, Trey was exhausted, so Gia dropped him back at the house to rest.

"I'm meeting my mom for lunch and then I have to see a patient. Call me if you need me," she told him.

"I'll be fine," he assured her.

Despite the nightmares, Trey was perfectly

capable of taking care of himself. He didn't want Gia feeling sorry for him or staying with him out of pity. He could manage.

I can get through an afternoon without her help.

THE OPEN BUFFET at the Polk Island Hotel was spectacular. The delectable aroma of chicken, prime rib and other tasty entrées really got Gia's senses going.

"I love this place," Patricia said.

"It's pretty nice," Gia agreed. "It's not cheap to eat here but the food is always delicious. I really love their pineapple lemonade."

"It's my favorite, too," Patricia agreed.

After they got their food, Gia said, "I meet with Ethan tomorrow. Mama, I'm so excited. We'll be able to accomplish so much more as a team. I'll finally have my clinic."

"I'm thrilled for you," her mother said. "Who knows, you may end up having a chain of PT clinics all over the country."

"Whoa… I don't want to think about that right now. I just want to see the *one* come to fruition. That's all I can handle at the moment."

"Your father and I have always taught you to dream big. I doubt if your partner will stop at one facility."

"I hear you," Gia responded.

"How did your night go with Trey?"

She wiped her mouth, then said, "He had a nightmare and it really left him shaken. I felt so helpless. I really wish he'd consider seeing a psychologist or getting some support through group therapy."

"It reminds me of what I went through with your father," Patricia said. "They think it makes them appear weak."

"It just makes them human," Gia stated. "I don't understand why some men are so afraid of displaying their feelings—we all have them. I always remind Trey that what he's dealing with happens to a lot of people. He's not alone, but still, he isn't comfortable talking with strangers."

"I know, but there are people who feel the same way he does."

"Trey will open up to me, but whatever he may be feeling deep down…he keeps to himself and just shuts down. It's so frustrating, Mama."

"Sweetie, you're just going to have to let Trey be. That's what I had to do with your father."

"Did he have nightmares?"

"He did," Patricia responded. "Whenever he would have one—I'd just tell him that he was at home with his family, that he was safe, and then I'd tell him to go back to sleep."

"Did you ever feel helpless?"

"Yes, of course. At one point, I felt like I was failing my husband because I couldn't really help him the way he needed, but then I realized that only Eugene could help himself. He had to want to receive help."

"Trey isn't comfortable talking to a therapist."

"Like I said, sweetie. Trey has to *want* the help. Until then, all you can do is be there for him while also giving him space to process his emotions."

She embraced Patricia. "Thanks, Mama. I appreciate being able to talk to you about this. It helps to have your perspective."

"Trey's gonna be fine. You just continue to be there for him."

"I am," Gia responded.

Two hours later, she returned to the house. Gia used the key Trey gave her to let herself inside.

He was sleeping, so she ventured to the patio and sat outside enjoying the weather.

"I didn't think you were back," Trey said when she went back into the house thirty minutes later.

"You looked so peaceful when you were sleeping. I didn't want to wake you."

"How's Miss Patricia doing?" Trey asked.

"She's fine. Mama told me to tell you hello."

Gia picked up the Scrabble box. "You ready for another round?"

"I stay ready."

"Try not to cheat this time around," she said, picking up his cell phone. "I'm going to keep this near me."

Trey burst out into a round of laughter. "Just accept that you're the queen of the three- and four-letter words…"

AFTER HER MEETING with Ethan Holbrooke, Gia drove to Trey's house. She'd already called her mother and asked Patricia to meet her there. She wanted to share her news with both of them at the same time.

Patricia was already at the house by the time she arrived, and Gia found them in the living room engaged in conversation.

"How did the meeting go?" Trey asked.

"Great," she responded.

Gia sat down on the sofa beside her mother. "Ethan and I are officially partners. I asked him to consider opening the clinic on the island versus Charleston, especially since we have the sensory school. We don't really have a local gym, either."

"You're right," Patricia said. "We have the yoga place and that aerobics room, but that's about it."

"Even if it's best to open it in Charleston—I'll be okay with it, but I'd really like to open something here, as well. We have another meeting in a couple of weeks," she stated with enthusiasm.

"That's great," Trey said. "Are you going to work with Ethan Jr?"

"Yes, I am. He is such a sweetie."

Trey agreed.

"Is there any apple cider? We should have a toast," Patricia said.

"We can toast with water as far as I'm concerned." Gia chuckled. "I'm just really happy with the way things are turning out. I have a wonderful man in my life. I have my mom. We have the bed-and-breakfast, and coming soon, a PT clinic with a sensory gym."

She took Trey's hand in her left and her mother's hand in her right. "It just doesn't get any better than this."

CHAPTER TWENTY

"I TOOK ON a new client today," Gia announced Thursday afternoon as she replaced wilting flowers in a vase with fresh ones on the counter. "She's an elderly stroke patient."

"That's great, sweetheart," Trey responded. "That's six for you now."

"You've been keeping up with them." She kissed his cheek. "I love that you're so sweet and thoughtful. That's why you'll always be my favorite ex-patient."

"I'm really happy for you. In fact, why don't you let me cook dinner for you tonight? To celebrate." He removed a roasting pan from a drawer near the stainless-steel oven.

Gia's eyebrows rose. "*You.* You're gonna cook for me? You make a great salad, Trey, but can you really cook?"

"Yeah. Don't sound so surprised. I worked at the café as a cook's apprentice in high school and before I left for the Marines. Roger's been helping me with navigating my kitchen like a pro."

Gia fought back tears, hearing the pride in Trey's voice.

"I even ordered that lap desk he recommended to help me when I'm taking food out of the oven or when I have to chop up stuff. I find it more comfortable than the counter. I've watched a couple of cooking classes online conducted by instructors in wheelchairs."

"This is quite an achievement. Trey, I'm so proud of you."

More and more, he seemed like himself, the guy Gia knew back in high school, although he was now a mature version of the younger Trey.

"To be honest, I've actually developed a fondness for cooking. I find it calming."

"That's wonderful."

"I'm thinking of making roasted chicken breasts, wild rice and mixed vegetables."

"Sounds yummy. Is there anything I can do to help?"

"You can chop the veggies," Trey said, pointing to a knife set.

They laughed and chatted as they prepared dinner together.

"I've been toying around with the idea of putting in some hours at the café," Trey said. "I'll have to talk to Misty about it, of course."

"I don't think it'll be a problem," Gia stated.

"Getting out of the house regularly will do you a world of good."

"I thought so, too," he responded. "It will give me something more to do besides think until we can move forward with our plans for the museum. I'm realizing that I don't do well when I have nothing to do. I need to stay busy. I understand why my aunt still helps out at the café."

Trey thoroughly washed the pieces of chicken out of the package as he spoke.

Gia eyed him for a moment. "I'm pretty sure that chicken is clean by now."

"Hey, I don't play around with poultry."

She chuckled. "*I see you.* You trying to act like you know what you're doing."

He laughed. "I know a little something." Trey placed the meat in a baking pan, then into the oven.

When dinner was ready, they sat down at the table to eat.

After Trey blessed the food, Gia tasted the chicken. "This is perfect. Very tasty." She took another bite. "Oh, this is delicious."

"It was a joint effort," he responded with a smile.

"I'M HOME," RENEE CALLED out as she entered the house on Friday evening.

"Welcome back," Trey and Gia said in unison. They were sitting in the living room talking.

"Did you miss me?" she asked, kicking off her shoes and dropping her tote in a nearby chair. She then sat her suitcase near the stairs.

"I've been enjoying the company of this beautiful woman right here," Trey commented.

"We made spaghetti for dinner," Gia announced. "You're welcome to join us."

"*We* as in you and Trey?" Renee's eyebrow rose in surprise. "My cousin actually lifted a finger to cook?"

"He made dinner last night and Trey made the sauce tonight. I only cooked the noodles."

Renee sat down and began playing with the fringe of a colorful throw pillow. "I'm so proud of you, cousin."

He laughed. "I know it's taken me a while, but I'm getting there."

"Well, I'm starving, so I'm looking forward to this meal," she stated. "I'm going to take my stuff upstairs and freshen up. See y'all in a few." Rising to her feet, Renee took her tote and suitcase to her room.

When Renee returned, they navigated to the table.

"How was New York?" Trey asked. "Family good?"

"Daddy and my brother are both doing great,"

Renee said. "It was nice being back there, but this is my home. As much as I enjoyed my time there, I couldn't wait to get back here." She reached for a piece of garlic bread. "I noticed the Scrabble game was out."

"Your cousin cheats," Gia quipped.

"Gia happens to be a sore loser." Trey grinned.

"Wow…this spaghetti is delicious," Renee stated, quickly changing the subject.

Gia laughed, then took a sip of her iced tea.

"Oh, by the way, while I was in New York, I did run into my former friend who couldn't wait to tell me that she and Kevin are engaged," Renee said.

"How do you feel about it?" Gia asked.

"I was hurt, but I didn't let her know it," said Renee. "I was also a little petty," she added with a grin.

"How so?" Trey wanted to know.

"I told her to enjoy her distinction of being Kevin's *first* wife. Then I told her she wouldn't be the last."

Trey and Gia exchanged a look of amusement before the three of them burst into a round of laughter.

After dinner, Gia helped Trey clean the kitchen. Once they finished, she said, "Now that Renee's back, I need to get back to my place."

"You don't have to leave, sweetheart."

"I told you I was only staying until today. Spend some time with your cousin," she responded. "Renee may need to vent. Besides, your friend arrives tomorrow morning and you need to prepare for this visit."

"I'm going to miss our late-night talks."

Grinning, Gia said, "You mean our cuddling."

"That, too."

She kissed him. "You can always call me. We can talk until we fall asleep."

"It's not the same," Trey uttered.

She leaned forward, kissing him again. "I'm going to miss you, too. I got used to being around you every day."

Rising up, she said, "I need to go upstairs to get the rest of my stuff."

Trey really hated seeing Gia leave. He'd enjoyed this week with her. It had given him a chance to experience what his life could be like if he had a wife.

The thought stopped him in his tracks.

Wife.

Gia.

The image of him marrying Gia formed in his mind. He could really see himself married to her—spending the rest of their lives together. Only in his vision, he wasn't in a wheelchair. He had his legs.

The image bought a smile to his lips.

"Trey…"

He looked up to see Gia, who said, "I'm about to leave. I'll give you a call later. Spend some time with your cousin."

"Text me when you get home."

She smiled. "I don't live that far from here, but I'll do it just because you asked me so nicely." Gia kissed him, then made her way to the door.

"How did things go while I was away?" Renee asked Trey after Gia left.

"Great," he responded.

"And…"

Trey broke into a grin. "Gia and I had a great time together. We went to a concert, we had dinner with Jordin and Ethan—everything was nice." Things between him and Gia were really good. He hadn't verbalized it yet, but Trey knew he loved her. He loved her beyond what he thought he could possibly feel for anyone.

She was the only woman for him.

Renee glanced at the television, then back at Trey. "I'm glad to hear you two had a good week."

"Oh, my friend Greg is coming for a visit. He'll be here for a week. I hope that's not a problem." Greg had picked the best time to visit him—he was in a good space. For the first time in months, he felt good.

"It's your house—more yours than mine," Renee said. "It's not an issue at all. He can stay in one of the guest rooms upstairs. We have plenty of room."

"Greg is a good guy. I think you'll like him." He picked up the throw Gia had used earlier, folded it and placed it back across the arm of the sofa.

"I'm just glad you're finally reconnecting with some of your friends," she said. "I thought you were on the way to becoming a recluse."

Trey looked forward to his best friend's visit. He'd already planned a tentative itinerary for them. "I met Greg when we were in boot camp. I don't know if I'd have made it through without him— he says the same of me." Trey gave a short laugh. "I guess we leaned on each other."

"I'm looking forward to meeting him," Renee said. "Do you want me to cook something for dinner tomorrow night?"

"No," Trey responded. "I think we'll go to the café. I've bragged about it so much I figure Greg should experience it for himself. Hey, why don't you join us?"

"Really?"

He nodded. "Yeah. It'll be fun, plus Gia will be there, too."

"Okay. I'll come over after I close the boutique. Your old bedroom has clean linens on the bed. You can have Greg stay in there."

"Are my posters still on the wall? The ones of my favorite ball players."

"No. We took them down when I moved in. Aunt Eleanor had all the bedrooms upstairs painted."

"Soon I'll be able to walk up there," Trey said. "Gia's made me believe that just about anything is possible. Her belief in me... It's given me hope. Walking again has become my goal and my love for Gia is part of my motivation."

"I know," she responded. "I'm so excited for you."

RENEE MADE A cup of coffee. "You want some?" she asked, pointing to the Keurig when Trey entered the kitchen.

"I'm good," he responded as he grabbed an apple from a wire fruit basket in rose gold color.

"What's on your agenda for today?"

Trey bit into an apple. "I have a session with Roger. Greg should be here in time to drive me. Gia can't do it because she has a patient scheduled at the same time."

He glanced up to find Renee staring at him, a smile on her lips.

"What?"

"Seeing you like this makes me happy. When you first came home, you were like a person walking around and waiting to die."

"That's exactly how I felt. When I first came home, I didn't want to live, Renee. I didn't feel worthy of being alive. If it wasn't for all of you and Gia… I honestly don't know where I'd be right now."

"I understand," she responded. "I've had to fight those same feelings."

"I used to think a person should be able to control his or her thoughts but now I've realized I was wrong. Trauma is real and things like depression, anxiety, PTSD—all real."

"Yes, it is."

"Gia's been after me to get out of the house more. She thinks it'll keep me from just sitting around thinking. I'm going to talk to Misty about a part-time job until we get moving on the museum plans."

"That's so great," Renee said. "I have to leave, but I will see you tonight at the café. That's still the plan, right?"

"Yeah," Trey responded.

She picked up her tote and coffee tumbler. Trey wasn't sure Renee could function without coffee in the mornings and herbal teas at night. He'd never noticed her going without either. "Have a great day, cousin." She headed out.

Greg arrived shortly after 9:30 a.m.

"Hey, brother," Trey greeted. "Glad you finally made it to paradise."

"This island is beautiful," he said. "When I came across the bridge… I felt like I'd stepped into a piece of history," his friend said.

"I'm glad you're here."

"Me, too," Greg said. "I needed a vacation."

Trey laughed. "From what? Chasing women?"

"No," he responded. "I'm not dating anyone right now. I'm not in the mood for drama."

Trey nodded in agreement. "That's one of the things I love about Gia. She's not the jealous type and she's not moody. She doesn't switch up on you. She's a genuinely happy person."

"Is this the same girl you told me about back when we were in boot camp?"

"Yeah."

"So, she moved back here?" Greg asked.

Trey nodded. "When I first arrived, seems like the whole town came to welcome me home. The only person who grabbed my attention was Gia."

"I'm looking forward to meeting her."

"She'll be here later this afternoon," Trey announced. "You'll meet my cousin Renee tonight when we go to the café."

Greg grinned. "The famous Polk Island Bakery & Café. I can hardly wait."

"I'm actually working on plans to restore the Praise House and the family has decided we're opening a museum."

"That's wonderful," Greg said. "I'm assuming the Praise House is a church."

"Yeah. I don't know if I told you, but Polk Rothchild was a preacher."

"I think you did mention it once." Settling back in his chair, he asked, "What's on the agenda after your session?"

"I was thinking we'd go to the beach. I have this cool wheelchair with flotation tires."

"Sounds like a plan."

CHAPTER TWENTY-ONE

"How long will you be in town?" Gia asked as she hung her purse on the back of her chair.

"A week unless Trey gets tired of me before then."

"You don't have to worry about that," Trey responded. "I haven't seen you in a while. We have a lot of catching up to do." He enjoyed the sound of cutlery clinking on tables and scratching on plates amid the sea of people talking and enjoying their meals.

The door to the café opened, catching Greg's attention. "Wow," he uttered. "Who is that?"

"That's my cousin." Trey and Gia exchanged a look of amusement. "She's also my roommate."

"Really? *She's Renee?*"

"Yeah." Trey noted how Greg couldn't seem to keep his eyes off his cousin. He'd never seen his friend react like this over a woman ever.

"Hey, y'all," Renee greeted when she approached the table. "Sorry, I'm late."

"No, you're just in time," Trey said. "Renee, this is my friend Greg Bowman."

She extended her hand. "It's very nice to meet you."

"Same here, ma'am." Greg pulled out a chair for her at the table.

"So, what do you think of our little island?" Renee asked as she sat.

"It's beautiful, from what I've seen so far." Greg gazed directly at her.

Trey glanced at Gia and smiled. He couldn't believe what he was seeing. Renee seemed to be just as mesmerized by Greg as he was with her. He played with a bottle of hot sauce as he continued to observe their interaction.

Silas had one of the servers bring drinks to the table.

"Trey told me about the restoration project," Greg said. "The Rothchild family has an incredible history. One that shouldn't be forgotten."

"That's our mission," Renee said.

"I'm looking forward to coming back to visit the museum when it opens." Greg picked up the menu. "I hear that everything in this place is delicious."

"It is," Gia and Renee said in unison.

Greg looked at Renee. "What's your favorite?"

"It just depends on whatever I'm in the mood

for," she responded. "You can't go wrong with any of the choices here."

Greg glanced at Trey. "That's good to know."

Trey looked over at the table next to them. He could smell the spicy barbecue sauce on the wings and the tangy vinegar wafting off fresh coleslaw.

His stomach rumbled.

Gia reached over, covering his hand with her own. "I feel like it's been hours since I ate lunch," she said.

"Greg and I ate early," he responded. "I took a nap after my PT and then we went to the beach."

In the kitchen, Josh could be heard calling out orders in diner slang. Trey slid a look at Renee and Greg again, who appeared to be in deep conversation.

"Are you seeing this?" he asked Gia in a low voice.

She nodded in response.

Trey cleared his throat noisily and said, "So, is everybody ready to order?"

LIKE TREY, GIA watched the interaction between Renee and Greg in amusement. It was like they were being drawn together by an invisible thread.

"What are you getting?" Trey asked, pulling her attention to him.

"I think I'm going to have the Swiss mushroom burger," Gia answered.

"Hmm…that's what I think I'll have," Renee said.

"I'll have that, too," Greg said.

Trey placed his napkin on his lap. "I'm not going to be the odd man out, so I'll have the same."

When the server appeared, he placed the order for four Swiss mushroom platters.

"This meal is on me," Trey announced after the man walked away. "Brother, your money's no good here," he said to Greg.

"Thank you, but I'ma give you fair warning," Greg stated. "I'm taking all of you to dinner tomorrow night."

"You don't have to do that," Renee said. "I'm making dinner. I've already bought the food. I'm making chicken marsala."

"You're beautiful and you can cook…" Leaning back in his chair, Greg uttered, "I'm in heaven."

"You might want to reserve that thought until you actually taste my cooking."

"She's a good cook," Trey interjected. "She just doesn't do it a lot."

"Really, cousin…"

"Well, you don't. I don't expect you to do it

for me, so it's not a big deal, but you are a fantastic cook."

"Let me just put it out here. I'm not cooking every night, so don't be expecting that," Renee stated.

"She's blunt, too." Greg grinned.

Gia eyed him. "Are you keeping some type of list?"

"More like checking things off," he responded.

"What list would this be?" Renee inquired. "If you don't mind my asking."

"The qualities I want in a woman. The type of woman I'd want to marry."

Gia glanced at Renee, who appeared stunned into silence.

Trey chuckled. "I think you're the only man who's ever effectively stopped my cousin from talking."

Renee reached over and gave Trey a sharp jab in his arm.

Their food arrived.

Greg bit into his burger, and Gia stuck a fry into her mouth, chewing thoughtfully. When she swallowed, she asked, "What do you think, Greg?"

"No lie…this is one of the best burgers I've ever tasted."

"Better than what you can find on the West

Coast?" Renee asked. "They have some great burgers out there."

"They do," Greg admitted, "but I'm really liking this one."

After dinner, they decided to take in a movie. The foursome walked the short distance from the café to the theater.

"I hope y'all left some room for popcorn," Gia said.

A large marquee with black letters listed the movies playing. Stepping inside, Gia eyed the posters in the lobby displaying upcoming movies. She could smell the popcorn, and it tickled her senses. Gia couldn't wait to get some.

She strolled to the glass counter displaying rows of candy, chips and cookies. "I'd like a box of popcorn with extra butter."

She glanced over her shoulder, asking, "Anybody else want some?"

"I'll take a box," Renee said. "Lightly salted and no butter."

"I'm good," Trey told her.

"Maybe Renee will share some of hers with me," Greg stated. He gave her a flirtatious grin.

"Sure," she said. Renee stole a peek at Gia and winked.

"Babe, do you want anything to drink?" Gia asked Trey.

"Water," Trey responded.

Popcorn and two bottles of water in hand, Gia led the way to the first theater on their left.

GREG STEPPED OUT of the bathroom just as Renee opened her bedroom door. She averted her gaze away from the bath sheet around his waist. She tried to fight the image of the man in front of her.

"I'm sorry. I thought you'd already gone to bed. I forgot to pack my robe. I plan to buy one tomorrow."

"No problem," she said, looking away from Greg.

"Are you okay?" he asked.

"Uh-huh… I was on my way downstairs to make some herbal tea because it helps me sleep." Renee could sense the self-confidence that made him so appealing, but there wasn't a hint of arrogance.

"If you give me about five minutes to jump into some clothes, I'll join you."

No no no no no…

"Sure," Renee responded, ignoring her internal voice. It was going to be a long few days while Greg was in the house. She hadn't been on a single date since her engagement ended. That was intentional on her part, because she needed time for her heart to fully heal. Renee didn't want to bring old baggage into a new relationship.

Greg walked out of the bedroom five minutes later wearing a pair of gray sweatpants and a black T-shirt.

"Trey looks good," he said when they were in the kitchen. "I was worried about him when things first happened."

"It was really hard on him at first, but he's getting better with each passing day," she responded. "I don't know if he told you, but Trey's thinking about getting a part-time job at the café."

"Wow, that's great."

Renee made two cups of tea. She gave one to Greg before sitting down across from him. "Gia's had a positive influence on him."

Greg smiled. "I can tell. He told me about her when we were in boot camp. He described her back then as the one who got away. I'm glad they were able to reconnect."

Renee took a sip of her tea. "They're very happy together."

"A stunning woman like you has to have a man."

"Nope. I'm free and single," she responded, ignoring a tingle in her belly. "What about you?"

"I'm single, as well," he stated.

He was tall, muscular and handsome. Renee

loved his almond-shaped eyes. They were a bright and warm brown color. She could easily allow her attraction to him to take control, but she couldn't afford to let that happen. "Greg, you seem like a really nice man, but I have to be honest with you. I don't date military men."

"May I ask why?"

"I don't want the stress of worrying about the man I love fighting or even patrolling other countries. I'm a person who worries to the point that it can trigger panic attacks. I know this about myself, so I see no point in putting myself or anyone else though it."

"I want you to know that your words have wounded me." He feigned hurt, then his face split into a grin. "I'm truly heartbroken."

Renee chuckled. "Yeah, right."

"But seriously, life in the military isn't really all that different from civilian life."

"Maybe not to a certain extent," she stated. "But it does change whenever you're ordered to deploy. You have no say in that matter. I was worried about Trey when he was gone. I won't ever forget when we found out he was injured. It was so upsetting that I had several panic attacks. My medication had to be adjusted just so I could cope with what happened to him." She'd practically had to see her therapist daily just to help her refocus her thinking and to help eliminate the triggers. "I've never told him this…"

"I won't say a word to Trey," Greg promised. "I really appreciate your honesty. It's refreshing."

"The reason I shared all this is because my panic disorder was a problem for my ex…but also, you're just very easy to talk to, Greg."

He smiled before finishing off his tea. "Tell me this…if I weren't in the marines, would you go out with me?"

"I guess we'll never know," Renee replied.

"Do you think we can at least be friends?"

She searched his gaze. "I don't see why not."

CHAPTER TWENTY-TWO

TREY HAD AN early PT appointment, so he had Gia come to the house at 7:00 a.m.

"While you're taking PT, I'm going to take a walk along the beach," Greg announced the next morning while Trey and Gia were eating breakfast.

"I'll see you in a couple of hours, then."

"You might run into Renee out there," Gia said. "She usually goes running around this time."

Greg broke into a smile. "Great. Maybe she'll be interested in having a partner." He headed to the door. "Enjoy PT."

Gia leaned against the counter in the kitchen. "How do you feel about Greg's attraction to Renee?"

"He's a good guy," Trey said. "I know he'll treat her well."

It didn't bother him that Greg was into Renee. She deserved to be loved by a good man. His friend was loyal, and he desired a woman who would be a devoted wife and mother.

"Do you think she's interested in him?" Gia

scooped up a forkful of scrambled eggs and stuck it in her mouth.

"I know they were up late last night talking, but Renee's always been against dating guys in the military."

"Maybe you should warn him," she suggested as she buttered a piece of toast. "No point in Greg wasting his energy."

"I figure I'll stay out of it. My cousin will let him know if it comes to that."

"You're right." Gia sat down at the table. "We should focus on us."

"Speaking of *us*…" he said. "Can we have brunch tomorrow? I'd like to take Greg to Manoir Bleu."

"Sure, babe. I love that place." She checked her watch. "We need to get going in about thirty minutes."

"Okay," Trey said. "I'm already dressed. I can clean up the kitchen when I get back."

She pushed away from the table. "Are you finished?"

Trey nodded.

Gia took the plates to the kitchen. "I'll help you. We should be able to get it done before we leave."

"I'm a very lucky man."

"And it's great that you know it." She winked.

"Your family's very nice," Greg said. "I've really enjoyed getting to know your brother and sister-in-law. They're great people."

"Yes, they are," Trey agreed. They'd all attended a cookout at Leon and Misty's place the night before.

"I'm glad I had a chance to come visit Polk Island. I wanted to come here to check on you earlier."

Trey gave a slight nod. "I know, but I just wasn't ready to see anybody."

"I understand."

"You know, I've always wanted to have a family," Trey said. "I always dreamed of having a son I could play ball with or a little girl I could spoil rotten."

"Looks like you'll have that soon enough. I've been observing you with Gia. She's the one for you, Trey."

"I feel the same way." Trey grinned. "When I was in the hospital, I'd given up all hope. When they started talking about prosthetics, I told them I wasn't interested. I couldn't see beyond my own grief and pain." And despite that, in a few weeks' time he'd be going to an appointment to be fitted with his prosthesis. He smiled at the thought. "I've been watching you with Renee." He gave Greg a knowing grin. "What's up?"

"We're just hanging out as friends."

"Are you really okay with that?" Trey asked, eyeing his friend. He knew that Greg was looking for more than friendship.

Greg nodded. "I don't have much of a choice. She just wants us to be friends."

"Right now, she needs a good friend."

"That's me," he responded. "A good friend."

Trey nodded in approval. Rubbing his stomach, he muttered, "I'm full. I brought home some dessert, but I'm too stuffed to eat any."

"I know the feeling." Greg got up and stretched. "Your brother can throw down on some ribs. And that mac and cheese…man, that was some good eats."

Trey chuckled. "I'm surprised I don't weigh three hundred pounds, surrounded by great cooks." He stifled a yawn. "All I want to do right now is take a nap."

"Is Gia coming over?" Greg asked.

"Naw. She's got an early morning meeting in Charleston." Trey was happy she'd found a great partner in Ethan. She'd told him the other night they worked well together and shared common goals. Trey was trying to be supportive. And yet… He picked up a throw pillow. "I'm missing my woman."

"Oh man…you really got it bad," Greg teased.

"I guess that makes two of us, huh?"

CHAPTER TWENTY-THREE

RENEE ONLY HAD to hear Greg's voice and her heart fluttered madly. Just being in his presence brought her senses back to life. She tingled whenever Greg said her name.

Girl, you vowed to stay away from men in the military, so what's up?

Greg was handsome and they had a lot in common. But she took issue with the path he'd chosen for a career. Renee wanted a man who'd be home at night—not deploying all over the country.

As a fashion designer, she could pretty much work anywhere, but her boutique wasn't mobile. Besides, she loved being back on Polk Island.

She heard a soft knock on her door.

"Come in," Renee said. She sat cross-legged in the middle of her bed.

Greg walked inside her bedroom. "Did I catch you in your creative zone?"

Her pulse quickened on seeing him. "No, I was just about to chill and watch a movie. Care to join me?"

"Sure. Trey just fell asleep. Roger wore him out today."

"I can't wait for him to get his prosthesis," Renee said. "He's working hard on those parallel bars."

He gestured toward the door. "Would you be more comfortable if we watched the movie in the living room?"

"No, I'm good with you being in here," Renee said. She patted the empty spot on the bed beside her. "You can sit here."

Renee found it a struggle to focus on the movie with Greg so close to her. His nearness was a bit overwhelming.

"Renee…"

"You're supposed to be watching this movie."

"Yes, ma'am," Greg said with a grin.

GIA AND RENEE sat in the reception area, drinking mimosas while awaiting Shelley's arrival for their spa appointment. Comfortable chairs and sofas in warm earth tones were arranged around the room. A table nearby contained pitchers of complimentary coffee and water with cucumber slices floating in it. The lavender scent wafting in the air tickled Gia's nostrils.

"So, what do you think of Greg Bowman?" Gia asked. "I saw the way he was flirting with you yesterday."

"He's handsome," Renee answered, "but I don't date military men." She put the glass to her lips and took a sip.

"Why not?"

"I don't want to be with a man under the beck and call of someone else. I don't want him going off to fight wars I don't believe in or condone. Look what it's done to my cousin. Trey came home a mere shadow of himself. He's getting better, but look at the price he paid fighting a war we shouldn't have been in."

Gia understood Renee's perspective, although she felt differently. She admired and had great respect for service members and veterans. "He was deployed as part of a peacekeeping mission, Renee. We're not at war. Trey will recover. It'll take some time, but he will get there."

Shelley rushed through the double doors of the hotel spa.

"It's about time," Gia said.

"There's a good reason why I was late." Holding up her left hand, Shelley broke into a grin. "I'm getting married!"

"Congratulations, Shelley!" Renee exclaimed.

Shelley smiled at her. "I want to look at your wedding dresses."

"If you want, we can go to the boutique when we leave here," Renee suggested. "I have a brand-new collection. You're getting an exclusive look."

"Great!" Shelley turned to Gia. "I want you to be my maid of honor. We can look at some gowns for my bridesmaids."

Embracing her, Gia responded, "I'd be happy to be in your wedding."

"I don't know about you but I'm having a hot stone massage and facial," Shelley said. "I went to the nail salon on Saturday, so I'm good there."

Gia eyed the services listed. "I'll do the same."

Renee stayed long enough to get a facial, manicure and pedicure but then had to get back to the store. They met up with her three hours later to view the couture wedding dresses at the boutique.

Gia was in awe of the collection. Renee was incredibly talented, and her gowns were all—without exception—beautiful. Although she liked all of them, her favorite was the flowing, beaded, silk chiffon strapless gown. It was the perfect choice—if she were the one getting married.

Shelley pointed to the model wearing it and said, "I love that one. It's perfect. We've decided to have the wedding and reception at the Polk Island Resort and Spa. I checked and they're available on October twenty-fourth."

"So, you've already booked it?" Gia asked. "You're not wasting any time."

"I waited for a long time for John to propose." Shelley grinned. "I'm not waiting a year to marry him."

"I can make any changes or adjustments to the gowns, if you'd like," Renee said.

"I like the strapless one, but I'd like to change the colors of the ribbon around the waist to a deep orange color. We're planning a fall-themed wedding."

"I can do that," Renee assured her.

"Can you remove that huge bow off the back?" Shelley asked.

"I'll need to attach the ribbon to the dress, then."

Shelley smiled and nodded. "That's fine."

With her dress selected, Shelley then turned her attention to shoes.

Renee and Gia followed her.

"This one just came in yesterday," Renee said, holding it up. "What do you think?"

"It's totally gorgeous," Shelley murmured. She sat down and tried it on, but it was too small. "I could use a half size larger."

Gia loved the design of the pump. A few small beads set amongst the rich embroidery caught the light and sparkled.

Shelley pointed to a high-heeled sandal in a silver color.

Gia sighed. "Now, that's both beautiful and sexy."

"Try them on," Renee encouraged. "Walk around the shop…"

"This is pretty," Gia said as she fingered a bridesmaid gown in a vivid tangerine color.

"I'm thinking of something more like a spice orange," Shelley stated.

They continued shopping for dresses and shoes, before leaving the boutique an hour later. "You're actually getting married in a few weeks," Gia said. She scanned her friend from head to toe. "You're not pregnant, are you?"

Shelley broke into a smile. "Not yet, but we are trying."

"Wow, that's really exciting."

"To be honest, I never thought the day would come when I'd be planning a wedding," Shelley said. "John and I have been together for six years. I didn't think he would ever get to this point where he'd propose."

"Well, now he has…so you've got to get busy planning. October twenty-fourth is just around the corner."

ON HIS LAST NIGHT, Greg insisted on making dinner for Renee and Trey as a way to show his appreciation for their hospitality. He offered Renee the pan and she dipped a fork into the potatoes, stuck one in her mouth and moaned with pleasure. "Butter, garlic...delicious."

"Wait until you taste my grilled salmon," Greg responded, apparently amused at her enjoyment.

"I'd better warn you that I'm starving."

"Don't worry. There's plenty." He eyed her, then said, "I love a woman with a good appetite."

A smile tugged at her lips. "I actually think I'm going to miss you around here."

"I know I'll definitely miss you."

They stood there staring at one another until Renee broke the gaze. "I'd better set the table for dinner."

She walked out of the kitchen, her heart beating frantically.

Renee put the plates on the table while Trey fetched three glasses and a bottle of chardonnay.

He looked up and caught her eye. "I'm just going to have a little."

Smiling, she said, "You may want to grab another glass. I invited Gia to join us."

"Oh, that's why she told me she was busy," Trey responded. "I invited her, as well."

"Act surprised," Renee said. "She wanted to surprise you."

He laughed. "No problem."

Dinner was ready by the time Gia arrived.

When they finished eating, Renee and Greg went for a walk along the beach in the moonlight.

"Dinner was delicious," she told him.

"Thank you," he responded. "My mom taught me to cook when I was twelve." Greg inched nearer to her and took her hand in his. "I really hate that I have to leave tomorrow." He sighed. "But I will say that you never know what will happen." He gazed at her. "I think our story has yet to be written, Renee."

His words sent a chill down her spine.

Later, when they returned to the house, he said, "I guess I need to make sure I've packed everything. I'll be leaving early in the morning."

"I'll be up," Renee said.

When she entered her bedroom, she could still feel his nearness—the tingle in her fingers as if he was still holding her hand.

CHAPTER TWENTY-FOUR

"RUSTY…HEY…" GIA GREETED. She could tell by his expression when she answered the front door that something was wrong. "Are you okay?"

"Is Eleanor here with Trey?"

"She's not here right now, but I don't know about earlier. Trey's taking a shower. He should be out shortly."

"Where is she?" Rusty muttered as he paced the length of the living room.

"I thought I heard your voice, Rusty," Trey said, wheeling himself out of his bedroom.

"I'm looking for your aunt."

Looking bewildered, he asked, "What do you mean that you're looking for her? She's not at the café?"

Rusty shook his head. "I've looked there and went over to Leon's place. She's not at Renee's shop, either… I thought she might be here."

"We need to go out and find her," Trey stated.

"I'll drive," Gia responded, feeling a flash of concern. "We can ride together."

"We'd better call Leon," Trey said as he navigated to the front door.

Rusty nodded in agreement.

Inside the SUV, Trey asked, "Has she ever disappeared like this before?"

"No. I did catch her trying to leave the house one day last week. She was confused at the time. She thought she was still living in your place. Her condition is getting worse," Rusty said.

"I think it's time I closed up the hardware store. I need to be home with Eleanor."

"There are resources available," Gia said. "You can have someone come to the house to stay with her."

"I know, but I don't think Eleanor will like that. She'd be more comfortable with me."

"Rusty's right," Trey said. "She can be a bit territorial at times."

Gia eyed Trey. He seemed worried but also frustrated that he wasn't able to just get up and go looking for Eleanor. She could tell he felt completely helpless. "Babe, think of places your aunt would go," she suggested.

They met up with Leon, who asked, "Have y'all heard anything?"

Trey shook his head. "Not yet. We're going to drive around to look for her. We're going to check out the cemetery and a few other places she used to visit."

"I've looked everywhere. I thought she would be over by the Praise House, but she wasn't there."

"Leon, we're going to find her," Rusty vowed.

"Let's head to the bakery," Trey stated. "Leon's already covered the other places."

Gia drove to the bakery, but no one there had seen Eleanor. She then stopped by her house, as well, just in case Patricia had talked to her, but she hadn't. She prayed in earnest that Eleanor was fine and would remain safe.

"WE'VE DRIVEN ALL over this island twice," Trey said when they got back to the house. He didn't want to consider that Eleanor had ventured out to the beach and into the ocean. The thought sent waves of apprehension through him.

"Misty's walking the beach with Renee now, looking for her," Leon announced.

Gia reached over and took Trey's hand in her own. "She's fine, babe, and we're going to find her."

"Where can she be?" Trey asked. "She didn't drive anywhere."

Gia pulled out her phone. "I'll call the taxi station to see if anyone there picked her up. If not, then I'll call the police. She doesn't know how to use any of the other car services, right?"

"No, she doesn't," Rusty said. "I don't know

how to use them, either. Let's just call the police and file a report."

Trey's phone rang.

"Hello."

"Trey, it's Eleanor Louise. I'm calling to let you know that Aunt Eleanor is here in Charleston. I have her at the house with me."

Trey released a long sigh of relief. "She's fine," he told the others. "She's with Eleanor Louise."

He put the phone on speaker. "How did she get there?" Trey asked his cousin.

"From what I understand, a woman visiting the island found her walking toward the bridge. She seemed very confused, but when she saw a billboard advertising our law firm, she pointed to it, so the woman drove her there. I happened to be there, so I brought her home with me."

Rusty shook his head. "If anything had happened..."

"It wasn't your fault," Trey assured him. "And she's fine. She's with family. Thanks so much for calling us, Eleanor Louise."

"She's resting right now," she stated. "Etienne's having his doctor come by the house to check her out just as a precaution."

"Thank you," Rusty said. "I'm leaving right now."

Leon sank down on the sofa, his hands over his face.

"She's fine," Trey told him. "Aunt Eleanor is safe."

Gia called to give her mother an update. When she was done, she saw that Trey had retreated into his bedroom.

She knocked on the open door.

He was over by the window, looking out.

"Are you okay?" Gia asked.

"My aunt was out there all alone and there wasn't anything I could do," Trey stated. "I'm tired of not being able to protect the people I love." The fear of what could've happened to his aunt Eleanor had him in a viselike grip. In her confusion, she could've been attacked or much worse. He shook his head to shake the turbulent thoughts. Trey reminded himself that Eleanor was safe and would be home soon.

She placed her hands on his shoulders. "Babe, it's not your job to try and protect everyone. This is an impossible burden that you're placing on yourself."

"I can't stand feeling so helpless." He was even more determined to do whatever he had to do to be more self-sufficient.

GIA DROVE TREY to the café. "Are you excited about your first day at work?"

He laughed. "I'm just glad to get out of the house. After everything with Aunt Eleanor… I really need to keep my mind busy."

"I hope you have a great day," she told him. "I'll see you when you get off."

Trey kissed her gently on the lips. "Thank you, Gia. For everything."

"I didn't do anything," she said.

Placing a hand to her cheek, he said, "You gave me the push I needed."

Misty was inside, waiting for him. She was seated in a booth working on payroll. "Hey, you…" she greeted.

"I'm ready to work," Trey said. "What do you want me to do?"

"Can you handle the burgers and fries? You'll also make sandwiches."

He smiled. "That's what I used to do back in the day," Trey stated.

She gave him a tour of the kitchen, which had been updated since he'd seen it last. "We've switched some things around here. Let me know if you need anything special."

Trey spent most of his day in the kitchen with Josh, who'd been working there for almost fifteen years. There was enough space to accommodate his wheelchair.

He did most of the prepping for lunch that morning, then Josh had him assist Silas on the grill for a couple of hours. During the lunch rush, Trey made sandwiches since it was his first day. Josh wanted to see how quickly he could complete his tasks.

Trey caught on quickly, having worked at the café in the past, but after the kitchen had caught on fire a few years ago—and with updated appliances—it was more like a new experience for him.

A few people who knew him waved and, to his amazement, left tips stipulated just for Trey. He knew they meant it as a way of encouragement, but Trey couldn't help but wonder whether they would have left the money if he'd been able to walk around.

When he tried to split the tips with Silas and Josh, they refused.

"Use the money for the museum," Josh suggested. "Don't take getting a tip as a form of pity. Use it for the greater good. Polk Island should be in the history books. Just like the other islands. Even Sapelo Island down there in Georgia is finally getting the attention it deserves. Your family's museum is gonna help with that, but it won't run itself without the help of others."

Trey considered his words. "Thank you, Josh. I hadn't looked at it in that way."

When Gia returned to pick him up, he gave her a recap of his day.

"That's a great suggestion by Josh," she said.

"His family has been on this island from the beginning. When Polk left the island to find a wife—some of her relatives came along. Josh's many great-grandparents came back with him. His great-grandmother and Polk's wife were close friends."

"They saw an opportunity to live their lives as they desired," Gia said. "The only other Black municipality in South Carolina during that time was Mitchelville, which is now known as Hilton Head."

Trey nodded. "The only difference is that the island was basically nothing. It was unoccupied and unowned land—people must have assumed it was uninhabitable," Trey said. "After the Civil War, Congress passed laws restoring lands to the former landowners. That's part of what happened on Hilton Head," he explained.

"Have you all talked about who's going to run the museum?" Gia asked.

"Leon and Renee think I should do it."

"As do I," Gia responded. "You've been working so hard on this. I really believe you should be the executive director."

"You have so much faith in me." Gia had always been in his corner. Her support meant the world to Trey. It made him love her even more.

"Of course, I do," she said. "I know how much you love this island. You've absorbed the history like a sponge. Look at how much you've gotten accomplished with the restoration project. You've set up the nonprofit foundation…"

"I was thinking of having a fundraising gala," he told her. "I'm going to ask Eleanor Louise to help me. She's an expert when it comes to these types of things."

Trey smiled in satisfaction. He'd found another purpose for his life and along with it—a project he was passionate about: restoring his family's history and preserving their legacy for future generations.

CHAPTER TWENTY-FIVE

"YOU'LL NEED TO make several visits for adjustments as your residual limb changes and continues to heal…" the prosthetist explained. "Make sure to let me know if the prosthesis is uncomfortable."

"I will," Trey said. "I've had enough pain to last me a lifetime. My question is how long will my prosthesis last?"

"It can last an average of three years. However, you may experience some changes due to the residual limbs shrinking. Keep in mind that this is a preparatory prosthesis, so while it doesn't look like a natural leg, it's a positive alternative to the wheelchair. You'll wear this for three months, and once you achieve alignment, I'll prescribe a definitive prosthesis."

Trey glanced over at Gia and grinned. "I never thought this day would come." He had barely slept a wink the night before because he was so excited about this very moment.

Freedom.

The word entered Trey's brain the moment the prosthesis was fitted to his limb.

"You'll be able to walk out of here," Gia murmured, taking his hand into her own.

"You'll need to use an assistive device," his doctor said.

"I already have one," Trey said. "I brought my cane with me. I'm ready."

"Did you bring a pair of shoes?"

"I did," Trey confirmed, grinning.

"Now, let's see you walk."

Taking those first steps felt like an enormous milestone. There were no words to define the amount of joy he felt deep down.

Trey took his time walking between the parallel bars.

His doctor made a few adjustments, then had him walk a second time.

Gia smiled. "You're walking, babe."

"I'm walking…" Tears running down his face, Trey burst into laughter. "I can walk again."

On the way home, Gia said, "I like your doctor. He's very thorough."

Trey agreed. They'd even left the office with a supply of prosthetic socks.

At the house, she said, "Remember what he told you. Just wear it no more than three hours today."

"I remember," he responded. "I have to increase my wear time by an hour each day."

He pulled her into his arms. "It feels good to hold you in my arms like this, Gia. I feel like my life is whole again." Trey kissed her thoroughly.

"I love seeing you so happy," she said.

"I want to take walks on the beach, be able to dance with you... I'll have to figure out if I can even do that and not look foolish. I want..." Trey stopped short.

"What's wrong?"

"It's just that we take so much for granted in life. Walking... I feel like a new man, Gia." Trey knew he still had a long way to go, but he felt an unmeasurable amount of excitement about the future. About their life together.

"MAMA, WHAT'S THIS?" Gia asked, looking at the certificate her mother held up.

"I took an online course for bed-and-breakfast owners. I feel more comfortable now. I feel like I know what to do."

"Congratulations!"

"Sam also finished the website. When you get a minute, please look at it."

"I will." Gia checked her schedule. "I have a guy coming to add the additional parking spaces. Two of them should be marked accessible and the other four will be regular parking."

Gia had hated having to tear down Nana's sewing room, but they'd need the space so guests wouldn't be parking on the street. They didn't need any zoning issues.

"This is really happening, isn't it?" Patricia said.

Smiling, Gia nodded. "Yes, it is."

"I've already had a couple people ask me about jobs. I told them we'll start to look for staff soon." Patricia grinned. "We could hire Trey to cook."

"Yes, we could, but I think he's going to be busy soon enough with the museum. They're looking into funding and grants. The DuGrandpre family have promised a donation. Trey has been working so hard on this project." She was so proud of him. Sharing the moment he was fitted with his prosthesis was special. He'd worked hard to get to the point and his efforts had paid off.

"Good for him. After everything he's been through—he deserves something good to happen. Although he's already won the prize. He has you."

Gia hugged her mother. "I love you, Mama."

"I know. And from the expression on your face, Trey's appointment went well?"

"It did," she confirmed. "He left the office walking. He has to use a cane, but yes… Trey is walking, and I wish you could've seen him. He's so happy."

"I can understand," Patricia said. "I'd be hollering all over the island, 'I can walk!'"

Laughing, Gia shook her head. "I had to keep him from shouting out the car window on the drive home."

"How do you feel about it?"

"I love Trey no matter what. I'm just so relieved that he's finally excited about living his life. If this is what it takes for him to feel whole again—I'm happy for him."

THE FOLLOWING SATURDAY, Leon, Trey and other members of the community came together to restore the Praise House.

Gia pointed at a black-and-white photograph of the old church as they compared it to a painting that hung inside the foyer. "We can use this as a guide to keeping the renovations as accurate as possible."

Trey followed her gaze. "Yeah. That's a good one." He wanted to keep the Praise House as close as possible to the way it had looked originally. All the work inside was finished, and they'd been able to keep the original stained glass windows. Now they needed to restore the exterior.

Leon arrived with the painting supplies. "We

can get started, and the volunteers should be here soon."

"I have some free time," Gia said. "I can help out with the painting."

"The more the merrier," Trey responded. "Some of the guys from the firehouse are coming over. They should be arriving soon."

"My supervisor pretty much made it an order," Leon said with a chuckle. "He's giving time-off hours in exchange for a certain amount of volunteer hours."

"The hospital does that, too," Gia announced. She picked up one of the paintbrushes.

Trey held his up, too. "You ready?"

Gia nodded. "Let's do this."

While they painted the exterior, he said, "Have you and Ethan decided where you're going to open the clinic?"

"He's leaning toward Polk Island," she responded. "We'll make a final decision by the end of next week. We've found two great locations. One's here and the other is in Charleston. The one on the island is very close to the sensory school."

"That sounds like it would be the perfect location."

"I think so, too." Gia glanced at Trey. "You're gonna be busy with the museum and I'll have the clinic—do you still think we'll have time for each other?"

He was silent a moment. "What about the B and B?"

"Mama will pretty much run that."

"To answer your question, babe, I would say yes. We're going to make it work."

"How is the prosthesis feeling?"

"Each day it feels more like a part of me," Trey responded. "I haven't had any pain or anything."

"That's good."

"Roger's really working with me on my gait."

Gia nodded in approval. "I know you, so don't try to rush this. Take your time through this process."

He smiled as he walked over to get more paint. Trey once again felt the same confidence he had when he was younger. He was ready to face whatever the world threw his way.

CHAPTER TWENTY-SIX

"HEY, BIG BROTHER," Trey said after opening the front door to find Leon on the porch. "I didn't expect to see you today."

"I was on my way home from the firehouse when I received a call from the mayor."

"What did he want?"

"Mayor Floyd wants to honor you as a hometown hero along with other veterans. The event is scheduled for Veterans Day."

"He doesn't have to do that," Trey stated, taking a seat in a nearby chair. Tugging at the neck of his shirt, he said, "Tell him I appreciate it, but I don't want to be a part of any type of celebration." He didn't want any public acknowledgments or anything in his honor. He was fine with the way things were going in his life.

Leon seemed perplexed. "Why not?"

"I just *don't*," Trey snapped. "Why can't people just respect my wishes and leave me alone?"

"He's already planned the celebration. The high school band is coming. There will be a parade. He wanted it to be a surprise. You and the other veterans on the island will be honored. You're all heroes to the community. I thought you'd be okay with this after all the strides you've made. I didn't think you'd be upset by this."

"I'm not a hero. People died on my watch."

"That wasn't your fault."

"It *was* my fault," Trey argued. "They were my team. I was responsible for keeping them safe. They looked to me to have their backs." He paused a moment. The fact that his team died on his watch would forever be in the shadows of his mind. "Leon, I didn't know what I wanted to do when I graduated high school. I went to college, but after two years I knew it just wasn't for me. One day while I was at the café working, Mr. Harris came in. He was wearing his dress blues. He asked me what I wanted to do in life. I couldn't answer, but I kept staring at his uniform. I could tell from his stature he loved being a marine."

"He looked good in it," Leon agreed.

Trey nodded. "We sat down, and I asked him what it was like. The first thing he told me was that it wasn't for everyone, but if I joined, the men and women I'd meet would be the best friends I'd ever meet and want to die for. He was right. The Marine Corps is built on motivation and discipline—it was life-changing for me."

"I know," he responded. "I watched you grow from a boy who just wanted to hang out at the beach flirting, to a well-rounded man. I'm so proud of you, Trey."

He didn't respond.

"I know you feel I don't understand since I didn't go into the military," Leon said. "But I don't have to go through the same experiences to relate to the pain you feel. When I lost my first wife and daughter, I blamed myself, but there was nothing I could've done to save them." Trey knew Leon had gone through indescribable pain when he'd lost Vee and Selena. "When we lost Lloyd Abrams, a year ago fighting a fire in California, I felt responsible because I was the one who asked him to go in my place. I chose to stay home with Misty and the kids because they weren't feeling well."

"I didn't know that," Trey said.

"Talking to a therapist helped me," Leon stated. "I know how private you are, so I need you to tell me what you need or how I can help, little brother."

Trey was shocked to hear that his brother had seen a therapist of any kind. Trey knew Leon well enough to know if he'd done that—he had been experiencing some deep anguish. Leon was just as private when it came to his emotions. Trey wasn't ready to talk to a therapist, but he decided to open up to his brother.

Rising to his feet, he paced in front of the fireplace. "Laura Hudson…she planned to retire. She wanted to be home with her children. I can't get her out of my head because right before the explosion, she told me that she felt something wasn't right. I could see the fear on Hudson's face—she was fearless, but not this time…"

"I'm listening," Leon said. "Just talk. You don't have to go into a blow-by-blow account of what happened that day unless you want to do so."

"That's just it. I see it so vividly in my mind. Hudson sitting beside me looking scared…it's etched in my memory. If I'd just listened to her. I just keep thinking they'd be alive if we'd just turned around and headed back to base."

Leon hugged his brother.

"Trey, it wasn't your fault. If I have to tell you this every day, I will. What happened out there is that you and your team were ambushed. You were badly injured. If you weren't—I have no doubt in my mind you would've gone down with them fighting.,"

"I love you, big brother. I hope you know that."

"I do, and the feeling's mutual. What the mayor is doing—it's a good thing, Trey."

Trey thought about his brother's words long after Leon left. When he heard a knock on the front door, he peeked out the window.

It was his neighbor.

He opened the door. "Hey, Jay…"

"How are you doing?"

"I'm good," Trey responded.

"I'm about to make a store run. I wanted to see if you needed anything."

"Do you mind if I ride with you?" he asked.

"No, c'mon…it's sho' nice to see you up and about again, Trey."

"Thank you. I appreciate you always checking in and willing to run errands for me."

"I have to go to the store anyway. It's no problem."

I just need a little drink to calm my nerves.

GIA GREW WORRIED when Trey didn't come to the door after the second time she knocked. Renee's car was gone, so he was home alone. He could be sleeping… But Gia's gut signaled that something just wasn't right.

She knocked a third time, then called out. "Trey…"

Gia heard a noise inside before the door opened.

She stepped inside. "I was worried about you.

Were you sleeping?" Gia quickly noted there was something off about him. "Are you okay?"

Trey grinned. "I'm fine, baby." Reaching for her, he said, "C'mere."

He pulled Gia close and whispered, "I need you."

She smelled the alcohol on his breath. "You've been drinking."

Retreating a step backward, she asked, "Did something happen?"

"It was one drink."

"I don't believe you. Where's the bottle?" Gia wondered what could've happened to trigger his drinking. She was concerned.

"None of your business. I'm a grown man and this is my house. If I want to drink—I can."

"What made you pick up a bottle of rum after all this time? You've been doing so well."

He didn't respond.

"Does it have to do with the Veterans Day celebration?" Gia asked. "I know stuff like this makes you feel undeserving because of what happened, but this is a good thing. Don't you see that you're a hero to this community? To me? The celebration is to honor all who fought for this country. Who fought for us."

"People like you don't get it," Trey sneered. "I didn't fight for you or anybody else on this island." His face full of conviction, he continued, "I fought for the marine to my left and my right. The thing is that every person who has served this country pays a price…mentally, physically or with their lives. I don't want to be celebrated… I just want to be left alone."

Her eyes filling with tears, Gia said, "I saw what it did to my dad, but at least he had the courage to acknowledge he needed help, Trey." She released a short sigh. "I've done everything I can to help you, but it's obvious I'm wasting my time. You have to want it more than I do."

"Then why are you still here?" Trey demanded. "Leave… I don't care. I knew you'd abandon me sooner or later."

"You really shouldn't drink." Her voice broke miserably. "It makes you a real jerk!" She grabbed her purse and rushed out. She'd done nothing but support him—how could he accuse her of abandoning him now?

Wounded by what had just happened, Gia didn't release her tears until she was inside her car.

She drove back to her house.

"I didn't expect you home until later," Patricia said when she walked through the front door. "I thought you and Trey had plans to see a movie."

"We had a change of plans."

Patricia eyed her. "What happened?"

"He's not ready to live life beyond his injuries. *I'm over it.*" Gia's sorrow was a huge, painful knot inside.

"Trey's been through a lot, Gia."

"Mama, I know that. We went through all this with Dad. But at some point, he *wanted* to change. Trey doesn't."

"What about your relationship?" Patricia inquired.

"I don't know," Gia shrugged. "I have a lot to think about because I'm not one to live my life in the past. I deal with it and move on. I do realize that Trey has real trauma, but he's refusing to get the help he needs." She was frustrated, seeing him revert back to the drinking.

Her phone began to vibrate.

It was Trey.

She decided not to answer.

She wasn't really to have any type of conversation with him. She was hurt and disappointed in Trey. He'd come so far.

He'd made great strides in moving forward with his life—at least that was what she thought. But maybe she was wrong.

GIA ADMIRED HER reflection in the full-length mirror near the dressing rooms at Renee's boutique. "It's really beautiful, Renee."

Shelley had chosen a simple, strapless A-line shift dress for her bridesmaids. It was a rich orange color, appliquéd up to the knees with silver embroidery and beading. Renee had designed a matching loose thigh-length coat on which the appliqué was repeated around the edge and on wide fold-back cuffs. Embroidery trailed over the silk and tiny beads caught the light as Gia moved.

"I love the jacket."

Renee smiled. "It was Shelley's idea. She didn't want y'all catching a chill in the evening. And it's a dress you can wear again—not just another bridesmaid gown hanging in your closet."

"I wasn't sure about the whole navy and orange theme for the wedding, but the way she's pulling the colors together—it's perfect for fall."

"I heard you and Trey had a bit of a disagreement," Renee said after Gia changed out of the dress.

"Did he also tell you that he's drinking again?"

"He did and I asked him why. He told me about the Veterans Day celebration. He said he needed something to calm his nerves. Trey also told me he was rude to you and that he's tried to apologize but you're not taking his calls."

"I can't talk to him right now. I know Trey blames himself for what happened to his team… It's not his fault, but he refuses to see it for the truth. The people who ambushed them are the ones responsible."

"I agree with you. I really think my cousin should see someone, but you know how stubborn he can be—he doesn't want to talk to a therapist."

Gia shook her head in dismay. "I love him so much, but I went through this with my dad. I'm not sure I have the mental capacity to deal with it all over again. I need some time to process everything. I'll call Trey when I'm ready to talk."

"I hope you won't give up on him. He needs you. Most of all, he really loves you. I can see it every time he looks at you."

"He told me that he wasn't fighting for me in Afghanistan—he was fighting for the person on his left and his right. Well, this time, I need him to fight for *me*."

The two women embraced.

"I completely understand," Renee said. "Just don't give up on him yet."

Gia gave a slight nod.

"I'll call you later," Renee said.

She walked out of the boutique and headed to her grandmother's house.

"It must be fate."

Recognizing Chris's voice, Gia froze in her steps and turned around. "What are you doing here? Shouldn't you be on a football field somewhere?"

"This is our bye week. I'm just here for the day."

Her day was just getting worse. The last thing she needed in this moment was coming face-to-face with Chris yet again. She was not in the mood for his foolishness.

"It's just pure luck that you walked out of that dress shop when you did. I was heading to the bakery to grab a salad before looking for you. I would've given you a heads-up but you've blocked me."

"How did you even know I lived here?"

"There was a nice little article about your new bed-and-breakfast. I thought you wanted your own PT clinic. You know I can make that happen for you."

"I can make it happen for myself," Gia responded. "Chris, I want you to leave me alone. Your wife caused enough problems for me in Charlotte. I won't let her do it here."

"You don't have to worry about Cindy ever again. We're separated. Our marriage is over."

"That's really too bad," Gia uttered. "You two deserve each other."

"She got pregnant, so I stepped up and did the right thing. But I feel like you're more my equal. I know you don't believe me, but I have strong feelings for you."

Gia was astounded by the lengths Chris was prepared to go with his attempts to seduce her.

She never once felt an ounce of attraction for him. "You're right—I don't believe you."

"Why would I come here looking for you?"

"Chris, what you want is never gonna happen, so go home to your wife."

"My marriage is over," he repeated.

"You were my patient, Chris. That's all."

"I don't believe you," he responded. "And I know you lied when you said you don't date your patients. I'm not stupid. You were on a date with that wheelchair dude."

"His name is Trey Rothchild and he's not my patient." She wasn't surprised by this tactic of a veiled threat. It only validated what she already believed about Chris. He was nothing more than a snake. Trey had always been and still was a real gentleman. He wasn't one to cross boundaries—a quality she respected greatly.

"Oh, I'm sure he was at one time," Chris retorted. "Is that what happened? You stopped working with him so you could date him?"

"It's none of your business."

Chris eyed her. "I know when a woman is attracted to me." He looked at his reflection in a nearby store window with approval. Dark, wavy hair, deep brown eyes, mocha-tinted complexion, the fitted shirt over his toned body… Chris smiled at himself.

He turned that wide smile on Gia. "Look at the women walking by us. They're practically falling all over themselves trying to get my attention, but I only have eyes for you."

She let out a short laugh. "You're so full of yourself."

"Look me in my face and tell me that you're not attracted to me."

Gia met his gaze. "I am not attracted to you, nor have I *ever* been."

"I'm in love with you."

She knew Chris would lie and say anything just to her into bed, like the others he'd seduced, but she remained silent.

"You don't have anything to say?" Chris demanded. "I'm standing here pouring my heart out to you and I get nothing."

"Go home."

Gia tried to step around him, but Chris blocked her path. "I don't want to," he countered.

"Then find your next wife, girlfriend, mistress… Just stay away from me."

"I can't just walk away from you like that."

She gave him a sharp stare. "You don't have any other choice." Gia was not going to let him sabotage her projects. She never wanted to use the information she had in her possession, but this time she would fight back.

"You're being this way because of Cindy. Honey, you don't have to worry. She can't do anything to you."

"You had the chance to stop her by telling the truth, but you didn't," Gia reminded him.

"I was wrong for that," Chris said. "I can't change the past, but I promise it won't happen again."

"Gia, are you all right?"

She was stunned by Trey's sudden appearance. "I'm fine," she said as calmly as she could manage. She didn't want to draw unwanted attention to them on the streets.

"Miss Harris and I were in the middle of a personal conversation," Chris interjected. "We weren't finished."

"Yes, we were," Gia brushed past him. "Goodbye, Chris."

"Wait until the physical therapy board hears about your exploits. I have photos to go with my claims. You really should reconsider."

Furious, Gia kept walking.

Trey followed her. "Wait…"

Irked, she stopped and turned around to face him. "What is it?"

"What just happened back there between you and Chris Latham?"

Gia glared at him. "Nothing."

"It didn't look like nothing," Trey stated. "It

looked like you two were in the middle of a lovers' quarrel."

She folded her arms across her chest. "Let me make sure I have this straight. You're accusing me of having an affair with Chris. Did I get that right?"

Frowning, Trey stared at her. "I overheard him telling you that you don't have to worry about his wife—that his marriage is over. Just now it sounded like he intends to tell the board about your relationship."

"Wow…" Gia shook her head and released a long sigh. "I don't have time for this drama. Just don't say another word to me, Trey. You have enough going on with yourself—focus on that."

Not sparing him another glance, she continued on toward her grandmother's house.

When she arrived, Gia wiped her fingers over her eyebrows, as if it might help to relieve the tension that was building up in her head.

CHAPTER TWENTY-SEVEN

TREY CALLED GIA but she still wouldn't answer his calls. He hadn't really expected her to pick up, but he'd hoped she would—he desperately wanted to talk to her. Motivated by jealousy, he'd said some offensive things to her. Even if she'd been involved with Chris Latham, he had no right to judge her.

Leon walked out of the café. "Hey, I thought we were grabbing some lunch."

"I'm sorry," he said. "That guy Gia was talking to—"

"Chris Latham. I recognized him. He plays for the Charlotte Patriots." Leon held the door open for Trey to enter the café.

Renee arrived shortly after they sat down.

"You missed Gia. She just left the boutique," Renee said as she joined them at a table in the middle of the room.

Trey placed his napkin in his lap. "I saw her, and I think I made things worse." He shook his head sadly.

"What in the world did you do now?" Renee asked.

Confused, Leon asked, "What is going on?"

"She and Chris Latham were just outside your shop talking. I overheard him telling her that his marriage was over, and Gia didn't have to worry about his wife anymore. She didn't look happy, so I interrupted their conversation to see if she was okay." He'd thought she was being harassed and intervened. Now he regretted his actions.

"Chris also said that he was going to the PT board to inform them about their exploits. He said he could back up his claims with photographs. Gia walked away and I followed her. I basically told her that I'd figured out she'd had an affair with him, and his wife found out." He glanced out the window. "I guess that's the real reason she came back to the island."

Groaning, Renee covered her face with her hands. "No, you didn't…"

"Look, I know something happened between them, cousin," Trey said. "Why would he be trying to blackmail her?"

"I don't believe any of that about Gia," Leon said. "Guys like Chris aren't her type. They never were."

"Trey, you have no idea how wrong you are about this whole situation."

"What are you talking about, Renee?" He was

truly puzzled by her words. "What do you know about this?"

"When Chris was Gia's patient, he tried to seduce her. His wife caught him trying to get her into bed during a session and confronted them. He blamed Gia, which is why Cindy set out to ruin her business reputation in Charlotte."

"Is this what she told you?" Trey asked, feeling smaller by the minute. No wonder Gia had gotten so upset with him.

"I know she's telling the truth because Cindy is one of my clients and Chris has made a number of passes at me, too," Renee said. "He's nothing but a womanizer."

Trey suddenly felt sick to his stomach. Was he wrong about everything? "Then what exploits is he talking about?"

Renee shrugged. "I don't know. Only Gia can answer that for you."

"She's not talking to me right now."

"Trey, you told me that you and Gia ran into him when you took her to Manoir Bleu," Leon said.

"Yeah, it was our first date."

"That was right after you fired her—you told me that was the only way Gia would go out with you. Maybe this is what Chris is talking about. He could've taken photos of you and Gia—and I'm sure to anyone looking at them, you look more like a couple than patient and physical therapist."

Trey was quiet for a moment, then said, "I'm such an *idiot*."

"Your words, not ours," Renee responded. "I think Leon's right. Chris would naturally assume that you're Gia's patient. He wouldn't know that she stopped being your therapist. She could lose her certification and license."

"I don't know if I'll ever be able to fix this." The thought that he'd lost Gia forever hurt worse than losing his legs. It was like there was a permanent hole where his heart used to be, and his heartbreak was his own doing.

"It may take some time, but you will. I know that Gia loves you," Leon assured him.

"I love her, too. I just don't know if we're meant to be together."

"Trey, what are you saying?" Renee asked.

"I'm so messed up," he told his cousin. "The last thing I need right now is to be in a relationship." He wanted nothing more than to be with Gia, but he wasn't in the headspace to love her the way she deserved. There were things he still needed to sort out for himself. It was a painful revelation.

Leon shook his head. "I can't believe what I'm hearing."

"Gia deserves better than what I can give her," he told them.

Renee picked up her glass of water. "You're going to regret this, Trey Rothchild."

"Trust me. I already do."

"CHRIS, WHAT ARE you doing here? Did you just follow me home? This is crossing major boundaries." Gia stood in the doorway of her mother's home blocking his entrance. *How dare he just show up unannounced like this!* She was glad her mother was in Savannah with Sam, or things would've quickly escalated.

"I have enough money to get the information I need," he said.

Arms folded across her chest, she uttered, "I thought I'd made myself clear earlier. Leave me alone." She stepped outside on the porch. "Don't make me call the police on you, Chris." Gia held up her phone for emphasis. He was beginning to creep her out with this sudden appearance on her doorstep, but she hid her true feelings behind a wall of calm. She'd taken her Taser out of her purse and placed it in her pocket when she'd seen him pull up and get out of his car.

"Please," Chris pleaded. "I just want to talk."

"We have nothing to talk about."

"I love you. Why can't you see that?"

A wave of frustration rose up in her. "Will

you quit with this? You're not in love with me, so please stop with this game of yours. I'm not interested."

"This isn't a game, Gia."

She was both shocked and relieved when Trey pulled up and parked behind the rental car. He'd started driving again a couple of weeks after his fitting for prosthetics.

"Why is this dude always showing up?" Chris demanded. "If you're here for PT, you gon' need to reschedule. If you're here for something else—that's not about to happen, either."

"I'm pretty sure you're the one who isn't welcome in this house," Trey stated.

Visibly bristling, Chris uttered, "You better be glad you nothing more than a legless man."

He stepped to Trey, who calmly responded, "Don't let that stop you."

"Just because you got new legs don't mean nothing to me…"

Gia moved swiftly, getting between the two men.

"Stop it, Chris." Her voice rose an octave. "This is *my* house, and you will not disrespect anyone in here. You need to remember that you weren't invited here in the first place."

"I came here to finish our conversation." He glanced at Trey, then turned back to her. "You and I belong together. I can give you everything you need and want."

Gia released a long sigh, then turned to face Trey. "I'm actually glad you're here. Maybe you can help Mr. Latham understand what I'm saying to him. We don't appear to be speaking the same language."

"I'm more than happy to translate."

Chris glared at Trey, then said, "Gia, I don't need this dude to interpret anything for me."

"It's pretty clear to me that she doesn't want to be alone with you. She also said you're not welcome here," Trey stated. "Why don't you just leave?"

"You're her protector?" Chris released a harsh laugh. "That's real funny. What can *you* do without some *real* legs, dude?"

"I told you a few minutes ago that I won't allow you to disrespect this man in my presence." Gia scrolled through her phone. "I should've done this a long time ago."

Chris laughed. "What, you're going to take a photo of me? I got some nice photos of the two of you all cozy on your date, holding hands and all."

"I'm not her patient," Trey responded. "Not that it's any of your business."

"Chris, you should listen to these." Gia played

several recordings of him coming on to her during their sessions.

She played another and another until he uttered, "Stop…you didn't have permission to record me."

"Actually, I did. You signed a release allowing me to record some of our sessions if necessary. However, you didn't have my permission to harass me the way you have," she stated. Gia hadn't wanted to take things this far, but it was past time to put Chris Latham in his place. It gave her a degree of pleasure in doing so.

"I could've played these for your wife and exposed you back when everything happened, but I didn't. When Cindy spread all those lies about me—I could've made this public, but I didn't want to hurt your children." She tilted her chin up in defiance. "I'm telling you for the final time to *leave me alone*. If you ever try to contact me again in any form—I'm going to file a lawsuit against you and your wife. I mean it, Chris."

"Give me the recordings," he demanded. "If you don't, I'll file a complaint against you with the PT board. You'll lose everything."

"With the money I get from suing you—I won't need to worry about working," Gia countered. "As long as you stay away from me—these recordings will never come to light."

Chris looked defeated. "How do I know that you'll keep your word?"

"I guess you're gonna have to trust me, huh?" Gia said.

"I don't need this… I can buy five fine women like you." He glanced at Trey. "I'm a real man."

"Real men don't stalk women who clearly want nothing to do with them," Trey responded. "By the way, congratulations on the new baby. Your wife confirmed her pregnancy this morning on the Entertainment Channel."

The color drained from Chris's face.

Gia broke into a grin. "That's wonderful news. I'm thrilled for you. I saw it, as well. According to Cindy, the rumors of a divorce were just that—rumors. You two have never been happier."

Chris walked briskly to the car, opened the door, and got inside. He drove away without preamble.

Relieved, Gia turned to Trey. "Thank you for being here."

"I came because I owe you an apology for accusing you of being involved with that narcissist. Renee told me what really happened."

"I accept your apology," she said. "Is this the only reason why you came?"

"Partly," he responded. "I've had some time to really reflect over my life and I realize that you're right. I'm not capable of giving you what you deserve. As much as I love you, Gia… I have no choice but to let you go." His eyes filled, but he continued. "I want you to find a man worthy of you."

"I suppose it doesn't matter what I want," she stated, looking taken aback by his words. "You've made your decision, so I have no choice but to respect it." Maybe he was right…maybe it was for the best.

"Gia…"

She shook her head. "Please don't say anything more." She swiped at her eyes so he wouldn't see the tears that filled them. "I want to be alone."

"I'm so sorry."

Brokenhearted, Gia turned away from him.

"This isn't easy for me. I want you to know that," he said.

She didn't respond.

Trey made his way to the door, and she resigned herself to the fact that she'd lost him forever.

CHAPTER TWENTY-EIGHT

GIA TRIED TO hide her broken heart and enjoy the pre-wedding dinner held at Shelley's house two days before the wedding. She wanted to be with Trey more than anything, but it simply wasn't meant to be. She didn't know why, but she struggled with accepting that as truth.

"You look so miserable, Gia," Shelley said.

"I'm sorry," she told her friend. "I don't mean to be a downer. You're getting married the day after tomorrow—we should be having a great time right now."

"Have you spoken to Trey since the day he showed up at your place?"

"No, there's no point. He refuses to see himself the way the rest of the world sees him. He doesn't feel like he's the man for me." Her heart broke all over again at the thought. "Shelley, there's nothing I can do to change his mind. He has to *want* to fight for our relationship."

"It sounds like you've given up on him, too."

"I haven't. I love Trey, but I've done all I can. The ball is in his court now."

"Do you know if he's still coming to the wedding?"

Gia gave a slight shrug. "I have no idea. All I know is that he won't be coming with me."

Shelley headed to the bar. "Let's have a glass of wine and forget the stressors of the day."

"That works for me," she responded.

Handing her a glass, Shelley sat down beside Gia. "Trey loves you and I have a feeling that he's going to come around. Trust the love that the two of you share."

"I don't know that I can." Running a hand through her hair, she said, "Let's not talk about this anymore. I want to have a good time."

Gia was determined to take her own advice about moving forward. No point lingering in the past. She'd initially held on to the hope that once Trey was up and walking around on his prosthesis, things would be better. He'd be happy and they would live happily ever after.

I forgot all about the invisible wounds. They were still there, festering. As much as she wanted to help him through this—Trey had to take the lead.

She managed to get through dinner without bursting into tears. Gia left Shelley's house shortly after ten o' clock.

After a nice long, hot shower, she climbed into bed but didn't fall asleep until around one in the morning. She'd stayed up late, alternating between watching a romantic comedy and crying. She was grateful that her mother had gone to bed earlier, because Gia wasn't in the mood to talk about Trey. She wasn't ready to give voice to her emotions a second time after purging all to Shelley earlier.

All cried out and mentally exhausted, Gia found a comfortable position in her bed and closed her eyes. However, sleep dodged her. The shadows cast in the moonlight became her companions for the night.

TREY TOSSED AND turned all night long, unable to erase Gia from his mind. He'd hurt her and found himself wanting to take her pain away. He realized he had two people to prove something to: himself and Gia.

He had to find a way to move forward, away from the past. He had to find a way to forgive himself for the deaths of his team and for not dying along with them. Trey was tired of being sad and angry. He was weary of the nightmares and the fear that had become his constant companion. Until he could rid himself of his demons, he wasn't any good for Gia or anyone else.

Forsaking all attempts to sleep, he turned on the light on the nightstand and propped himself up in bed. Trey was restless but didn't know what to do with the nervous energy he felt rolling around his stomach.

He put a hand to his head as a wave of dizziness washed over him.

"Nooo," he uttered, struggling against the attack. Trey hated feeling disoriented and like he was spiraling out of control. He felt the familiar stirrings of defeat and didn't know how to make it go away.

Rubbing his chest, Trey prayed for the panic sensation to fade away.

When it did, he was left trembling.

It was times like this when he needed Gia. Trey considered calling her, but it was late. More than that, it wasn't fair to her when he'd been the one to put distance between them.

GROGGY FROM LACK of sleep, Trey eased out of bed and made his way to the bathroom. He could smell the delicious aroma of bacon and turkey sausage cooking when he opened his bedroom door.

"Morning," he grunted.

"Somebody's not in a very good mood," Renee quipped as she tossed an egg into the frying pan on top of the stove.

"I didn't sleep well," he responded.

"Can't say I'm surprised." Renee handed him a cup of coffee. "You were up really late."

"Thanks." He inhaled the French vanilla scent before taking a sip. "I had a hard time falling asleep."

"Are you still going to Shelley's wedding?" Renee asked as she sank down in the chair facing him.

Trey shook his head.

"I can't believe you," Renee uttered.

"Excuse me?"

"Trey, you're wrong. Gia deserves so much better than the way you're treating her right now."

"I ended things because I thought it was for the best."

"But you're both so miserable," Renee stated. "How can this be right when you're both so unhappy?"

"I think it's just part of the grieving process."

She stared at him. "Do you really believe that?"

Trey sighed, weary of the argument. "Yeah, I do," he confessed. "I lost her for good."

"I don't think so," she countered. "I know that Gia's in love with you, too. She wants to be with you, Trey."

"Then why didn't she put up a fight?" he demanded. "If she felt that way, why just let me walk away?"

"Gia figured it was what you wanted, Trey."

"So, what do you think I should do?"

"Make sure you really want her back in your life. If you don't, then just leave her alone."

"I don't have to think about it. Gia is the only woman for me," Trey stated. "I'm just too messed up right now. I'm not worthy of her like this."

"I hope you know what you're doing, because I'm not sure Gia will wait for you. Get it together, marine, or be prepared to lose her forever."

CHAPTER TWENTY-NINE

GIA WOKE UP EARLY.

She rushed out of the house into her car an hour later. She'd promised Shelley that she'd meet her at the hotel no later than 9:00 a.m.

The ceremony was scheduled to begin at noon.

Minutes after she arrived, Gia and Shelley took a stroll to check out the room where the ceremony would take place.

"I just need to see for myself that everything is perfect," Shelley told her.

"It's your wedding day, so I understand."

The Polk Island Resort and Spa had everything in place for the wedding. The banquet room had floor-to-ceiling windows that overlooked the beautiful ocean. The elegant architectural lines of the room provided the perfect backdrop for the ceremony. The rows of seating were garnished with lavish displays of multicolored flowers arranged with silver bows and baby's breath.

"Everything is breathtaking and perfect. We

should head back so you can get ready," Gia said. "You don't want to be late for your own wedding."

They walked briskly out of the room and took the elevator to the fourth floor, where they would get dressed.

Back in the suite, Gia said, "It's time for you to start getting ready."

"I'm nervous. What if I've forgotten something?"

"Everything is good," Gia assured Shelley.

And an hour later, romantic music wafted out of speakers as the guests began to arrive.

Shelley released a soft sigh. "Sounds like things are starting on time."

"You look exquisite," Gia said. "You are the most beautiful bride I've ever seen. I'm just not saying this because you're my friend. I mean it."

Shelley embraced her. "I love you, girl."

"Don't ruin your makeup," Gia said. "We'll cry after the ceremony."

Shelley gave a slight nod as her father entered the room. "It's time," he announced.

Gia grabbed her bouquet and followed the other four bridesmaids out of the room and to the elevator.

Trey was supposed to be here with me.

She forced the thought away from her mind.

Today, she just wanted to celebrate Shelley's nuptials.

When it was time for her to walk down the aisle, Gia was surprised to see Trey among the guests. She truly hadn't expected him to attend the ceremony after they'd broken up. When their gazes met and held, she gave him a polite smile before looking away. Polk Island wasn't that big—they would often run into each other, so Gia hoped they could find a way to get away from the awkwardness.

"Trey isn't coming to the reception," Renee told Gia. "He asked me drop him off at home."

Reaching for a glass of wine from a passing waiter, Gia responded, "I'm not gonna let that stop me from enjoying myself." However, her spirits sank even lower.

"How is he doing?" Gia asked after a moment.

"He's sad," Renee responded.

"Is he still drinking?"

"I don't think so. He gave me the bottle that he had in his nightstand."

Gia heaved a sigh of relief. "That's good to hear."

She made her way to the table with the other members of the bridal party and sat down. Gia pasted on a smile, hiding her true emotions.

The round tables were covered with silver tablecloths and colorful floral centerpieces. In one corner was a bar staffed with a female bartender. On the other end of the room was a small table containing the wedding cake. A photographer roamed around, taking candid pictures. Waitstaff moved through the crowd with trays of appetizers and drinks.

Gia had a waiter bring her another glass of red wine.

Her gaze landed on Shelley, and they exchanged a knowing grin.

She was truly happy to see her friend looking so radiant and happy. Gia's eyes continued to travel the room.

Guests were laughing and chatting with each other as a three-man ensemble played music softly in the background. A DJ was set to play music after everyone finished eating. They dined on chicken breasts stuffed with mushrooms, wild rice and mixed vegetables.

Gia allowed herself to drink more than she normally did.

I'm no better than Trey. I'm using alcohol to numb my pain.

At the moment, she didn't care.

"I'm driving you home," Patricia said, taking the wineglass out of her hand.

"F-Fine by me… I'm not gonna drink anymore," Gia responded in a singsong voice. "I wanna dance."

She swayed to the music as she made her way to the dance floor, where she was joined by Shelley and the other bridesmaids.

Gia forced her thoughts away from Trey. Instead, she enjoyed her time with her friends.

CHAPTER THIRTY

TWO AND A half weeks later, Gia ran into Renee outside of the café.

"Hey, were you looking for Trey? He's working this afternoon."

"Actually, I'm hoping not to run into him," Gia responded. "Things are just too awkward between us. I'm actually glad I ran into you," she said. "Can you do me a favor and give this to Trey, please?"

Renee sighed in resignation. "Sure. No problem."

"Thanks, Renee."

She hugged the woman. "I'll talk to you later," Gia said, her eyes wet from unshed tears.

She drove to the cemetery and parked her car.

Opening her door, she could smell the freshly cut grass and the eclectic scents from the flowers placed on and around graves. Gia made her way to one in particular.

She sat down on the bench at the foot of the grave.

"Hey, Daddy... I guess you know what day

it is. I bought a piece of your favorite cake. I'll eat it for you. You know I've never been one to pass on dessert." She smiled. "I got Trey a piece, too. He's back home, but he's not the boy you used to know. He went through something horrible, Daddy."

Her eyes filled with tears. "He lost his legs, but it's those scars that you can't see that seem to affect him the most. I know you can relate to what he's going through. I really wish you were here. You could talk to him…"

Gia wiped her eyes. "I love him so much. I think that I pushed him away by wanting him to just move on. Daddy, I've lost him for good."

"You haven't lost me."

She turned around to find Braxton standing nearby, flowers in his hand. Gia jumped up and fell into his arms, sobbing. She was overcome with emotion to see her big brother. She needed the support of his strong shoulders in this very moment.

"It's gonna be all right, sis," he told her. "Calm down and tell me what's going on."

Gia pulled herself together long enough to ask, "What are you doing here?" She glanced at her father's grave, then said, "I guess that's a really stupid question."

"I stopped by here to put some flowers on

Dad's grave and then I saw you. I came to the island to see you and Patricia. It's been a while."

"I didn't think you ever wanted to see us again."

He touched her cheek, wiping away her tears. "No, I'm sorry I didn't keep in touch. I was going through a lot of stuff, and I just shut down. Losing Dad was harder on me than I thought."

"It was hard on all of us," Gia responded. "I'm so glad to see you, Braxton. I really am. I've been worried about you."

"Who were you talking about when I walked up?"

"Trey Rothchild."

"What happened to him? Wait…are you with him?"

"We're not together anymore," she responded. "Trey is a marine… He was wounded badly in Afghanistan. He lost both legs in June."

Braxton embraced her. "I heard you say something about pushing him too hard."

"I wanted him to keep moving forward. I guess I should've been more understanding. I know with Dad—he came to the decision to get help on his own. It just seemed like Trey wasn't interested, but maybe he just wasn't ready." She felt guilty for wanting him to move at her pace. Gia regretted pushing Trey so hard.

"I can talk to him," Braxton offered.

Gia shook her head. "No, don't do that."

He pointed to the cake. "Care to share?"

Smiling, she said, "There's another piece in the box."

Gia was happy to see her brother. She wanted to use this visit to build a closer relationship with him. "Mama's gonna be so happy to see you."

He chuckled. "Think she'll make me some fried chicken? I was thinking about it all the way here."

"You know she will."

TREY STRODE OUT of the kitchen to join Leon in the dining area.

"Looks like you're getting used to moving around pretty well," Leon observed.

"I'm getting my permanent prosthesis in January," Trey announced. "It feels good to drive again and just walk. I feel like a new man." Things were going well for him but there was one important part of his life missing. Gia.

"How do you like being back at the café? I used to hate working here in the summer."

"I enjoy it. Today was pretty busy, so I didn't have time to think about anything other than work. That's always a good thing for me."

"Have you spoken to Gia?"

"No."

"What is wrong with you, man?" Leon asked. "You know that Gia is the one woman for you. Why are you acting this way?"

"Leon, I'm not the man for her," Trey said. "It's time I accepted it. I'm dealing with a lot, and I can't just get over it—not the way Gia expects me to. It's taking me a while to process everything."

"Did she tell you that?"

He shook his head. "I just figured she'd know this already."

"You love Gia. Don't you think she's worth fighting for?"

Trey didn't respond.

"You know I'm right."

"Looks like you two are in a deep discussion," Renee stated when she walked over to the table. "Am I interrupting?"

"No," Leon responded, "I'm just trying to get my brother to see the error of his ways. He's got a good thing with Gia and he's about to blow it."

"I told him the same thing," she responded.

Renee sat down in the chair opposite Leon.

"Look, I don't need the two of you ganging up on me," Trey said. "We need to stay focused on finishing up the work at the Praise House." Eleanor Louise had sent over the date for the museum fundraiser she was planning there. The family was holding one locally and another in Charleston.

"We're not ganging up on you. We just want you to be happy. I know Gia loves you. She asked me to give you this."

Trey looked at Renee. "What is it?"

"I don't know. I'm just following instructions."

He opened the box. Inside was a piece of birthday cake.

Renee looked at Leon, who shrugged in confusion.

"Is it her birthday?" Leon asked.

"No, it's the Marine Corps birthday," he said.

"That's proof that this woman still loves you, Trey," his brother said.

"It may not be enough," he uttered. "I promised I'd never hurt Gia. It's a promise I didn't keep. It also doesn't change the fact that I'm messed up inside."

"I think you're being way too hard on yourself," Renee said. "We all have issues, Trey."

Leon agreed. "You *are* being too hard on yourself in every area of your life. There's help out there for you, but you keep rejecting it."

"You sound like Gia."

"Have you ever considered that maybe she's right?" Leon inquired. "Put away your pride, little brother. Our high school team was the

Charleston Warriors. Do you remember what our coach used to say whenever we lost a game?"

"Yeah," Trey responded. "A true warrior knows that when he loses a battle, he is improving the skill to fight harder the next time."

"Trey, I know you feel like you lost a fight you didn't see coming. One of my favorite quotes by Carl von Clausewitz is this—'Courage above all things is the first quality of a warrior.' The same can be said of not only the Marines, but all branches of the military."

"Awww…you lost me with that part after the Marines," Trey teased. "Seriously, though, I hear you, Leon."

His brother's words stayed with him through the night.

"You don't look like you slept well at all," Patricia said when Gia came downstairs for breakfast.

"I didn't," Gia admitted. "I couldn't stop thinking about Trey. Mama, I love him so much." She pulled out a chair from the table and sat down.

"Then why don't you go talk to him?"

"I don't think it would do any good. I need to give him the space he needs. I've pushed him enough." Gia picked up a plate. "Is Braxton still sleeping?"

"I think he's up. I heard him talking to someone earlier." Patricia lowered her voice. "Sounds like he's in love."

Amused, Gia asked, "Were you listening to his conversation?"

"No, of course not."

She gave her mother a sidelong glance. "Uh-huh…"

Patricia picked up two pieces of bacon with tongs and put them on her plate. "Now, you know I wouldn't do a thing like that. I'm just saying that from his tone, it sounds like he's in love."

They heard footsteps on the stairs and quickly changed the subject.

"Are you still going to the Veterans Day celebration?" Patricia asked. "Sam and I are going."

"I'm going," Braxton interjected. "We can all go together. I don't mind driving."

Gia poured orange juice into a glass. "Yeah, I'm still planning to attend. Trey and I might not be together, but I wouldn't miss this event. It's not just about him but all who serve, like Braxton here."

"And Dad," her brother added.

"One thing's for sure," Patricia said. "Y'all loved your daddy and he loved y'all like crazy. He was a hero, a good husband and father… I miss him so much."

"He would've wanted you to move on," Braxton said.

"She has Sam, and he adores her." Gia reached for more bacon. *Me... I'm left with the memories of what could've been.*

TREY WAS LIKE a zombie through most of the Veterans Day celebration. He was glad when the parade ended. Now they were seated on stage with the mayor. When it was time for him to speak, Trey stood up and walked to the podium, cane in hand.

"Hello, everybody..." he began. "I keep hearing the word *hero* and it takes me a minute to process that it's me people are talking about. The thing is...y'all got it all wrong. I'm nobody's hero. The real heroes are not here today. They can't be here because they sacrificed their lives for this country. My team... Corporal Laura Hudson, Lance Corporal Erik Jenkins, Private First-Class Lamar Mitchell...they're the heroes. I was just doing my job." He shook his head. "Two more brothers in my battalion died over there a few months later.

"A hero isn't about just an accomplishment. It's the influence that the individual's achievement has on us and what we can learn from the adversity they've overcome or endured." Trey's gaze traveled to where Gia was seated. "Master

Gunnery Sergeant Eugene Harris is someone I consider a hero. He always made time for all the kids on this island. He's the reason I enlisted. All these men seated behind me are heroes." He eyed one of the local vets in particular. "Master Sergeant Bremen still has a bullet in his head, but he doesn't let it stop him from being an outspoken advocate for education…"

Trey was relieved when he stepped away from the microphone and returned to his seat.

As soon as the event ended, Trey left the stage to try to catch up with Gia. He wanted to talk to her.

"Excuse me."

Trey turned to find a man standing a few feet away, with two small children.

"Yes, sir," he responded.

"My name is Asher Hudson. Laura was my wife."

Trey felt as if he were about to lose his balance. He gripped the cane and tried to steady himself. "Mr. Hudson…"

"Call me Asher. I wanted to come and personally thank you for your letter. I found out about this event through your friend Greg."

He felt his eyes go wet. "It was the least I could do. I'm so sorry for your loss. Hudson… Laura was an outstanding marine. It was an honor to have her on my team."

"She thought a lot of you, as well," Asher responded. "I listened to you talk up there and I have to say you're wrong. You are also a hero. I know that you feel you were at fault for what happened, but you're not. They told me when the medevac arrived, you were in and out of consciousness, yet you shouted for them to take care of Laura first. They said you wanted them to make sure your team was okay in spite of your own injuries."

Trey didn't remember any of this. "They didn't get there in time."

Asher offered a tiny smile. "Laura was alive when they took her to the medevac. She died on the way to the hospital. You gave her a fighting chance—it was just her time to leave us."

Trey was stunned. "I didn't know that."

A lone tear traveled down his cheek as Asher pointed to one of the ribbons on Trey's uniform, for his actions on the day of the bombing. The tiny V in the center stood for valor. "You should always wear it with pride.

"They told me about the bombing," Asher continued, "and there was absolutely nothing you could do but fight to survive. As far as I'm concerned—that alone takes a lot of courage. If you truly want to honor your team...*live*. Just merely existing would do them a great disservice."

Trey considered Asher's words. He was basically saying the same thing Gia, Leon and everyone else had been trying to tell him. However, he'd always felt something was missing—that was why it didn't click for him until now. Hudson's spouse had provided the missing piece. He'd tried to save his team when help arrived, even though they felt he was the most critically wounded. He'd demanded that they do what they could for his team first. This part had escaped his memory.

"Asher, thank you for your kind words," Trey said. "How are you and the kids?"

"We're taking it one day at a time."

Trey saw a shimmer of sadness in Asher's eyes. Offering his hand, he said, "I hope you'll keep in touch."

Accepting the handshake, Asher responded, "I'd like that. At some point I'd like to hear more about Laura's time in Afghanistan. Right now, it's still too soon."

"If you need anything," Trey said, "please do not hesitate to let me know."

CHAPTER THIRTY-ONE

THE DINING AREA of the café was beautifully decorated in red, white and blue.

Trey smelled the apple pie as soon as he opened the door.

Misty placed a plate of fried chicken, potato salad, beans, cornbread and macaroni and cheese in front of him. On the smaller plate, she included a slice of warm apple pie. Trey didn't realize how hungry he was. He ate all of it except for the pie.

Eleanor sat down across from him in the booth. "I'm so proud of you, son."

He smiled. "Thank you, Auntie."

"You've grown into a fine young man, Trey. I don't know where the years went. Seems like yesterday you were just a wee boy."

"How are you doing?" he inquired.

"I'm a bit forgetful, but I'm gwine be fine," Eleanor stated. "Rusty takes good care of me. I don't know why, but he won't let me out of his sight."

"That's because he loves you so much, Auntie. Remember, you kept that man waiting for years."

Eleanor glanced around. "Where's Gia?"

"I don't think she's coming, Auntie."

"Why not?"

"Gia and I broke up," Trey said. He'd told her this when they were at the park earlier. Her short-term memory was fading more and more each day it seemed, and the thought filled him with sadness.

Trey was glad to see Gia at the park earlier. Despite their breakup, he knew she'd come not just to honor her late father, but also to support him.

His conversation with Asher had opened his eyes to the fact that he'd falsely believed he was responsible for the deaths of Jenkins, Mitchell and Hudson. The only persons responsible were the insurgents who'd detonated the bomb and launched the rocket.

"HELLO, TREY. MAY I join you?"

He looked up to find Gia standing there and smiled. "I wasn't sure I'd get a chance to talk to you."

"Would it have mattered?" she asked.

"Yes." He responded. "I'm glad you're here because I'd really like to have a conversation with you." He wasn't sure she'd ever give him a second, chance but Trey had to try.

"About what?"

"About us."

"Are you sure you want to have this discussion? I warn you that you may not like what I have to say." Her gaze met his. "You're the one who pushed me away, but then it made me realize that I was being a bit unfair to you."

He frowned in confusion. "In what way?"

"I guess I had some timeline in my head of how long you were supposed to stay in your struggle. It seemed to me like it didn't take long for my dad to realize he needed help, but in talking to my mom—I found out that it wasn't that easy for him, either."

"Gia, this is all on me," Trey said. "Growing up, I heard over and over how strong I was. I guess I perceived strength as the opposite of weak, which to me translated to crying, complaining, losing—all these were signs of a weak man. I was strong. I was a warrior. I'm a marine. Nothing bothers me. I don't fall apart or get scared…"

Gia took his hand into her own. "It's okay to ask for help sometimes, Trey. Sometimes we need that. Even marines."

"I realize that now." His voice broke. "I have been trying to just make it to the next day, but I want more than that, Gia. I really want to live…"

She brushed away an escaping tear rolling down Trey's cheek. "I love you. I want you to know that I will be by your side until I breathe my last breath. You own my heart, and you always have."

His body relaxed and Trey felt hopeful that he hadn't lost her. "I've thought about everything you've said to me, Gia. You're right. I need help and I'm finally ready to admit this. I'm ready to get help. I acknowledge that I can't do this on my own. I'm going to call the VA and see if I can join one of the support groups. I want to start there before I try one-on-one counseling."

"Okay," Gia said. He knew she wasn't going to take the lead in this. Trey had to make a decision that he would be able to live with, as this was his journey to wholeness. "What can I do to help?"

"Marry me," Trey said. "I know that I have a lot of issues I need to resolve within myself, but I can't do this alone. I'm asking you to be by my side through the rest of this process."

Her eyebrows rose a fraction. "Did you just ask me to marry you?"

"Yes," he said. "I would've liked to have purchased a ring first and done it the traditional way, but I'm not sure how that would've turned out."

She laughed.

"I love you, Trey Rothchild. And yes… I'll marry you."

"Did I just hear…" Eleanor said as she approached their table.

"There's nothing wrong with my aunt's hearing," Trey said, lowering his voice.

"I can still hear you, son. Now, back to my question. Did you just propose marriage to Gia?"

"Yes, ma'am."

"And you did say yes?" she asked Gia.

"Yes, ma'am."

Eleanor clapped her hands loudly to get the attention of everyone in the café. "'Scuse me, y'all. I'm happy to announce that Trey and Gia are engaged. He just popped the question."

The applause overshadowed the music playing in the background.

"I knew I should've done this when we were alone," Trey said.

Gia laughed.

Ten Months Later

GIA STOOD OUTSIDE the church, made of old stone and stained glass, her hand on the arm of her brother.

"I bet Dad's looking down on us right now and smiling," Braxton said.

"I hope so." She stared down at the photo of him that was attached to her bouquet. "He's definitely with us today."

"Do I go in now?" Talei asked. She was dressed in a long-sleeved royal blue tea-length taffeta dress with a red bow around the waist. Soft ringlets framed her face.

Misty opened the door and said, "C'mon, sweetie. It's time for you to walk down the aisle with Emery."

"We're up next," Braxton said. "Nervous?"

"No, I'm not. I'm so looking forward to being a wife to Trey and the mother of his children. We're going to wait at least a year before having kids, though."

"That's probably a good idea. You two have a lot going on right now."

Misty opened the door.

Dressed in a simple long-sleeved white gown made of floral lace, Gia floated down the aisle on her brother's arm. Baby's breath was sprinkled throughout her short curly hair in lieu of a veil.

Her eyes watered at the sight of Trey standing in his dress uniform. Greg and Leon stood behind him. He stood there handsome and so proud. It was an image she never wanted to forget.

They stood facing each other as they said their vows.

Gia could hardly contain her excitement as she waited to hear the words that would seal their union.

"I now pronounce you man and wife…"

Trey pulled her into his arms, drawing her close and under his protection. He pressed his lips to hers in a chaste but meaningful kiss.

"You look so beautiful, wife."

"And you look very handsome, husband."

She held up her left hand and eyed her wide, platinum wedding band. "I've never been so happy, Trey."

"You're sure you don't want a set?"

She looked at him. "I told you—I'm a simple girl. This band tells me everything I need to know." He'd had it inscribed to say: *I'll Love You Forever.* Trey had written those very same words in her senior yearbook.

"I meant them then and I mean it now, Gia. I'll love you forever."

EPILOGUE

Christmas Day

THE RESIDENTS OF Polk Island decided to take up donations to help Trey fulfill his desire to give stockings to the patients in the VA Hospital.

He and Gia spent the morning going from room to room, handing out stockings. Trey ventured into a room where the patient was a double amputee like him. He saw the Marine insignia on one of his greeting cards and said, "Semper Fi, brother."

"Oorah," the young man responded. He shifted his position, so he was sitting up.

"Merry Christmas," Trey said, handing him a stocking.

"Thanks." Pointing to his cane, he asked, "If you don't mind me asking, what happened to you? You were in Afghanistan, right? I saw you one day going to group."

Trey nodded. "Ambushed by insurgents. They had a car bomb on the side of the road, then used a rocket launcher. I lost my whole team and both my legs, as well." It was becoming easier for him to share with other veterans now that he no longer blamed himself for what happened.

"Brother, that's rough…"

"Indeed," Trey said.

"Like you, I was first team leader. We'd got a tip that some guys were using a car to move a mortar tube around, so we set up a vehicle checkpoint. This car comes barreling down toward us. One of our guys opened up on him, but he kept coming. My guys—they dived out the way. It happened fast but in slow motion. He just barreled into me. Seems like it took forever for them to come pick me up. Things did not look promising when they got there, but here I am. I'm thankful to be above ground. That's for sure."

"You hang in there," Trey said.

The marine looked toward the door than back at Trey. "I'm trying… Say, do you ever have flashbacks or nightmares?"

"I do," he replied.

"Does it ever end? That feeling of not being in control?"

"Not for me, it hasn't. Through group, I'm learning how to cope. Don't be afraid or too proud to ask for help. If you ever need to talk, you can give me a call."

Gia was in the hallway when he walked out.

She kissed him on the cheek, then said, "I'm so proud of you, Trey."

"Proud enough to put on that cheer outfit?"

"We really need to talk to someone about this cheer thing you got going on," Gia said.

He burst into laughter.

* * * * *

If you enjoyed Her Hometown Hero, *then be sure to check out*
A Family for the Firefighter, *the first book in Jacquelin Thomas's Polk Island series!*

Available now from Harlequin Heartwarming.

Get 4 FREE REWARDS!

We'll send you 2 FREE Books plus 2 FREE Mystery Gifts.

Love Inspired books feature uplifting stories where faith helps guide you through life's challenges and discover the promise of a new beginning.

FREE Value Over **$20**

YES! Please send me 2 FREE Love Inspired Romance novels and my 2 FREE mystery gifts (gifts are worth about $10 retail). After receiving them, if I don't wish to receive any more books, I can return the shipping statement marked "cancel." If I don't cancel, I will receive 6 brand-new novels every month and be billed just $5.24 each for the regular-print edition or $5.99 each for the larger-print edition in the U.S., or $5.74 each for the regular-print edition or $6.24 each for the larger-print edition in Canada. That's a savings of at least 13% off the cover price. It's quite a bargain! Shipping and handling is just 50¢ per book in the U.S. and $1.25 per book in Canada.* I understand that accepting the 2 free books and gifts places me under no obligation to buy anything. I can always return a shipment and cancel at any time. The free books and gifts are mine to keep no matter what I decide.

Choose one: ☐ **Love Inspired Romance Regular-Print** (105/305 IDN GNWC) ☐ **Love Inspired Romance Larger-Print** (122/322 IDN GNWC)

Name (please print)

Address   Apt. #

City   State/Province   Zip/Postal Code

Email: Please check this box ☐ if you would like to receive newsletters and promotional emails from Harlequin Enterprises ULC and its affiliates. You can unsubscribe anytime.

Mail to the Harlequin Reader Service:
IN U.S.A.: P.O. Box 1341, Buffalo, NY 14240-8531
IN CANADA: P.O. Box 603, Fort Erie, Ontario L2A 5X3

Want to try 2 free books from another series? Call 1-800-873-8635 or visit www.ReaderService.com.

#411 A DEPUTY IN AMISH COUNTRY
Amish Country Haven • by Patricia Johns

Deputy Conrad Westhouse has one job—protect Annabelle Richards until she can testify. The best place to keep her safe is his ranch in Amish country, but getting to know the beautiful witness means risking his heart...

#412 THE COWBOY MEETS HIS MATCH
The Mountain Monroes • by Melinda Curtis

Cowboy Rhett Diaz is starting an outdoor adventure company—with needed help from Olivia Monroe's family. He just has to get her across the country first... Can the road trip of a lifetime lead to lifelong love?

#413 TO TRUST A COWBOY
The Cowboys of Garrison, Texas
by Sasha Summers

Hattie Carmichael's brother is marrying her childhood bully. Participating in the hasty wedding is one thing—doing it alone is another. Thankfully, Forrest Briscoe plays along with her fake relationship ruse...until neither can tell what's real from pretend.

#414 SECOND CHANCE LOVE
Veterans' Road • by Cheryl Harper

Marcus Bryant returns home to Miami—and to old friend Cassie Brooks. Their friendship never survived his joining the air force after graduation. Planning their high school reunion together might help them unravel the past...and find a future.
